OF WORDS & MUSIC

OF WORDS & MUSIC

LYNDA FITZGERALD

FIVE STAR
A part of Gale, Cengage Learning

Detroit • New York • San Francisco • New Haven, Conn • Waterville, Maine • London

FIC
FIT

GALE
CENGAGE Learning

Copyright © 2009 by Lynda Fitzgerald.
Five Star Publishing, a part of Gale, Cengage Learning.

ALL RIGHTS RESERVED
This novel is a work of fiction. Names, characters, places and incidents are either the product of the author's imagination, or, if real, used fictitiously.

No part of this work covered by the copyright herein may be reproduced, transmitted, stored, or used in any form or by any means graphic, electronic, or mechanical, including but not limited to photocopying, recording, scanning, digitizing, taping, Web distribution, information networks, or information storage and retrieval systems, except as permitted under Section 107 or 108 of the 1976 United States Copyright Act, without the prior written permission of the publisher.

The publisher bears no responsibility for the quality of information provided through author or third-party Web sites and does not have any control over, nor assume any responsibility for, information contained in these sites. Providing these sites should not be construed as an endorsement or approval by the publisher of these organizations or of the positions they may take on various issues.

Set in 11 pt. Plantin.
Printed on permanent paper.

LIBRARY OF CONGRESS CATALOGING-IN-PUBLICATION DATA

Fitzgerald, Lynda.
   Of words & music / by Lynda Fitzgerald. — 1st ed.
      p. cm.
   ISBN-13: 978-1-59414-776-0 (hardcover : alk. paper)
   ISBN-10: 1-59414-776-0 (hardcover : alk. paper)
   1. Domestic fiction. I. Title. II. Title: Of words and music.
PS3606.I883803 2009
813'.6—dc22   2008049400

First Edition. First Printing: March 2009.
Published in 2009 in conjunction with Tekno Books.

Printed in the United States of America
1 2 3 4 5 6 7 13 12 11 10 09

OF WORDS & MUSIC

Chapter 1

The only sound in the room was the monotonous ticking of the huge grandfather clock in the corner. There were no traffic noises, no honking horns or screeching brakes this far back off Riverside Drive. Usually, Lilah Kimball found the silence comforting. With social worker Felicity Greenlea sitting in a nearby chair, the quiet hung in the air like a toxic red mist.

Lilah relaxed her tightly clasped hands. "The girl means nothing to me. Surely you can understand that."

The young social worker flushed under Lilah's regard and swallowed hard. "I understand that you don't really know Bethany, but—"

"I've never laid eyes on the girl." Nor heard of her, Lilah thought. Another oversight, no doubt, like not being informed of her daughter's death until three months after the fact. Still, if they thought they could compound their behavior by attempting to foist a strange girl off on her, they could think again.

"You are her grandmother, Mrs. Kimball."

"By blood only."

"By blood and legality," the young woman said with more force, "and that is relevant, since both of Bethany's parents are deceased and you are her closest living relative. You and your son."

The silence hummed as Lilah waited for the woman's next sally. Finally, she could bear it no longer. "Didn't her father have any people?"

"None that we're aware of and none that Bethany knows about. He was an only child, and his parents died years ago. There may be a distant cousin somewhere. We're still investigating. Bethany knew about you, of course."

"Why do you say of course?" Lilah asked, her voice sharp.

"Were you never in your daughter's home?" When Lilah shook her head, Felicity Greenlea said, "There were several framed pictures of you there. Bethany knew who you were and where you lived."

"It's been almost three months since the accident. Where was the girl until now?"

"She's been staying with a neighbor who only recently told us about you."

Lilah raised an eyebrow.

Felicity looked away, then back. "Until last week, we saw no paperwork on Bethany. We had no idea of your existence—or hers." She shifted in her chair. "Once we were aware of the situation, we immediately took steps to contact you."

"I still don't understand why it took so long."

The young woman flushed. "The neighbor Bethany was staying with is one of our case workers in Athens. Apparently she and Bethany had some kind of arrangement. Barbara, the case worker, put the paperwork on hold."

"Was that so bad?"

"*Yes*," Felicity blurted. Then she seemed to compose herself. "What Barbara did was certainly unethical and possibly illegal. Whatever her motivation, we do have rules in our profession and also a moral obligation to the people we work with. There will be an investigation, and she will probably be reprimanded or even suspended."

Lilah waved her hand in dismissal. "This girl—she was their only child?"

"Yes."

"Was there nothing in Elizabeth's will about godparents or anything of that sort?"

"There was no will."

A deep sigh escaped before Lilah could contain it. She turned and stared across the room.

"Mrs. Kimball, I'm only asking you to consider taking Bethany temporarily. As a trial. If the two of you find the situation intolerable, we'll make other arrangements. We will continue to investigate her father's family. There may be relatives somewhere. On your side, of course, there's your son. We could approach him if you wish. He and his wife might be more receptive."

"Don't bother," Lilah said. "I can tell you right now that his answer will be a resounding no. He and his sister were never close."

"Perhaps I could understand that kind of reaction if his sister was asking him for a loan," Felicity said, frustration clear in her voice, "but she's dead."

Lilah's breath caught in her throat, but she kept her face impassive.

"We're talking about a human being here, Mrs. Kimball. A child."

"A twelve-year-old young woman."

"Who is still very much a child and very much alone. Can you imagine the emotional upheaval she's been through in the last several years? According to our records, her father died of adult leukemia after battling the disease for years. Then for Bethany to lose her mother this suddenly? She's been through more than anyone her age should have to experience."

Lilah rose and walked to the fireplace, swept clean now in June. She had learned more about her daughter's life in the last hour than in the previous fourteen years. She hadn't realized Elizabeth lived in Athens, Georgia. So close? Elizabeth and the child—was her name Bethany?—had stayed on in the house after her husband's death, but the social worker had made it plain that they had struggled to make ends meet. Lilah couldn't imagine what Elizabeth's life had been like, but it couldn't have been pleasant. Bitterness surged through her as she looked around the room. It needn't have been that way. Elizabeth had been born into wealth and privilege, but had chosen to turn her back on both it and her family.

The room was silent except for the rhythmic tick-tick-tick of the grandfather clock. No sounds from the outside grounds penetrated the room, no movement sounded in the other parts of the house. The air seemed to quiver, then go still.

"Mrs. Kimball?"

Lilah started. She turned to Felicity. "Aren't there other arrangements you can make?"

"As I said, we'll continue to try to locate other relatives, although I'm afraid it may be a long shot." She hesitated, her face going through several contortions. Then she said, "We can also look for a permanent arrangement for Bethany if that's what you want."

"You mean adoption?"

The social worker winced. "Adoption is certainly an option, although that might take some time."

"Is there nowhere she can stay in the meantime?"

A flush spread up Felicity's neck and across her face. "Like a foster home?"

"If the issue is money, I could have my attorney make arrangements."

Felicity jumped to her feet, startling Lilah. The flush on her cheeks had gone fuchsia. "I'll be glad to look into the foster home option and keep you informed," she said stiffly. "I had hoped that Bethany could be placed with a family member. At least temporarily. The girl has been through hell. She is alone in the world and feels it acutely, and I am afraid that getting shifted around like unclaimed baggage will do her irreparable harm. But never mind." She hoisted her handbag to her shoulder and started for the door. "I'm sorry I bothered you, Mrs. Kimball. As I said, I'll let you know. As Bethany's grandmother, you're legally entitled to that information."

"Miss Greenlea."

Felicity stopped at the door and turned. "Yes?"

"May I have another moment of your time?" Lilah gestured at the sofa. "Please. Sit down."

Felicity looked wary, but she walked back and sat on the edge of the cushion, keeping her purse clutched in her lap.

Lilah sat at the other end of the sofa, crossing her ankles and folding her hands in her lap. "Miss Greenlea—" Lilah paused and then went on. "My daughter and I were estranged. She has not been a part of my life, nor I hers, for over fourteen years. I don't feel any emotional attachment to her child. I'm a widow, as I told you. My husband died just over two years ago. Elizabeth, my daughter, didn't even see fit to attend his funeral."

"Did she know about—"

A look from Lilah silenced her.

"So you see, there is—or was—very little family feeling between us. Elizabeth made her own life, as did we. It was perhaps not the best situation, but it was one we all lived with for quite a long time. And now this." She looked away. "I never expected to be put in this position. It's quite a shock to me, as I'm certain you can imagine. I want to do what is right, of course—for all concerned," she added with a glance in the social worker's direction, "but I'm not at all certain what that is. I will have to think it through and discuss it with my son. May I call you later in the week with my decision?"

It clearly wasn't what the social worker wanted to hear. Lilah watched the young woman battle her emotions. "All right, Mrs.

Kimball. Please let me know as soon as you come to a decision. I'd like to have arrangements made for Bethany by the end of the week. She is still staying with the neighbor at this point. Despite what happened, it seemed that it would create the least disruption in Bethany's life, and that is my top priority at the moment. But we need to get her settled as soon as possible."

"Does the girl know you've come to see me?"

"No, she doesn't," Felicity said, rising. "I didn't want to tell her until I had spoken with you. Bethany is very confused right now. I didn't want to make things any worse for her."

Lilah nodded. "That was probably best under the circumstances." Standing, she took the business card Felicity held out without glancing at it. "I'll be in touch before the end of the week."

Felicity made her own way out of the room. Lilah heard voices in the hallway, and a moment later, the front door opened and closed. Lilah watched from the window until long after the social worker had driven away in her ancient Honda. Why did these people always drive such shabby cars? Was their pay really that bad?

She didn't turn when her housekeeper entered the room, or when she put the tray down on the coffee table. "You'd best get over here before I drink it all," Marabet said.

Lilah looked over her shoulder and shook her head.

Marabet was Lilah's housekeeper, but they had been friends since childhood. After high school, they'd lost touch and didn't meet again until they were both married, Lilah to Gerome Kimball, and Marabet to some loser who robbed her blind and abandoned her. Lilah had finally convinced Marabet to come live with her, but Marabet had insisted it be as a maid. She had said—rightfully—that Gerome Kimball would never tolerate her living there as a friend or border. While Gerome was alive, Lilah had kept their earlier friendship under wraps. Gerome made

Marabet feel badly enough. God forbid what he might have done and said if he had known her history. Marabet had managed to get her little digs in as the years passed, but for the most part she stayed out of Gerome Kimball's way.

Lilah walked over to the sofa and picked up the coffee Marabet had poured for her. "I suppose you listened," she said, sitting down beside her.

"To every word." Marabet lounged against the sofa back, stirring her coffee. Her loose silver curls formed a deceptive halo around her face, and her blue-bird eyes sparkled with humor. She put her feet up on the coffee table and balanced cup and saucer on her ample stomach.

"And?"

"And what?"

"And what's your long-winded opinion, which I know I'm going to hear eventually, whether I like it or not?"

Marabet sipped her coffee. "Not this time, Lilah. I know you'd like someone else to make the decision so you could blame them if it doesn't work out, but I'm not the fool who's going to do it. Ask Charles. He's a big enough fool to get in the middle."

"I wish you wouldn't talk about my son that way."

"If he weren't such an arrogant ass, I wouldn't talk that way."

"Marabet."

"Oh, all right. He's your arrogant ass, so I'll hold my tongue. You were right about one thing, though. He wouldn't consider taking the child. No one's ever accused him of too much Christian charity."

"Marabet, please." Lilah stood and moved across the room. "I can't imagine what these people are thinking, suggesting that I take the girl."

"They're probably thinking you're her grandmother." Marabet put down her cup and walked over to Lilah. "No matter how much you want it to, this situation isn't going to go away. You lost your daughter, and now it looks like you may have a chance to know her child."

Lilah looked at her with raised eyebrows. "You think I should take the girl?"

"Don't put this on me," Marabet said, holding up her hands. "This doesn't affect me at all, except that it will double or triple my workload. But don't give that a thought."

Lilah rested her elbows on the mantel, dropping her forehead in her hands. "I just don't know what to do."

"You'll figure it out, and I'm sure you'll do the right thing." Marabet gave her shoulder an affectionate pat. "Since you told the lady you'd be talking to your son, I imagine you'll be inviting him to dinner?" When Lilah nodded, she picked up the tray of coffee things. "What do you want me to serve?"

"Pork loin?"

"I kind of had a yen for stuffed chicken breasts."

"Then let's have chicken breasts, by all means," Lilah said, frowning at the woman's back, but the twitch at the corner of her mouth ruined the effect.

Charles Kimball poked at the chicken with his fork, dislodging some of the spinach and mushroom stuffing. "You're actually thinking of letting this child come to live with you?" he asked, peering at his mother over his glasses.

Charles wore forty awkwardly. Sparse brown hair. Cheeks rapidly turning to jowls that quivered as he chewed. He swallowed the bite and washed it down with a gulp of wine and a look of distaste. An accountant by trade, Charles tended to be strong-willed and critical even at the best of times. Lilah had expected his reaction. Still, it rankled. "I'm considering it. After all, she is our flesh and blood."

"Hardly a sound argument." Charles took a bite of chicken

and made a face. "Why don't you hire someone who can cook, Mother?"

"I like Marabet's cooking," Lilah said, glancing toward the kitchen door where she was sure the housekeeper was lurking.

"If you got out more, went to some of the finer restaurants, you wouldn't be so easily pleased." He took another bite, made another face. "Anyway, it's absurd to think of you raising this child. You're much too old."

Even though the same thought had crossed Lilah's mind, she felt a flush spread across her face. "I'm barely sixty, Charles."

"A bit too old for PTA and baking cookies," Charles said, sipping his wine. "Although you certainly have the time on your hands—and the room," he added, looking around the dining room.

"If you think I'm too old, why don't you and Lesa take her?" Lilah said, mainly to get a reaction.

Lilah was surprised by the fleeting look of pain that crossed her daughter-in-law's face. Charles's wife Lesa had sat throughout the meal looking from one of them to the other like a spectator at a tennis match. The woman was a mouse, nondescript to the point of vanishing into the chair's upholstery. Lilah had wondered over the years why Charles and Lesa had no children, but had assumed it was their choice. The idea of asking never crossed her mind. She and Lesa weren't close. Lilah had felt unequal to making an effort to get to know her daughter-in-law six years ago when Charles married her. Over time, she had grown to see her only as an ineffective appendage, like a second index finger.

Charles finished his glass of wine and reached for the carafe. "Oh, no, you don't. We're not taking Elizabeth's cast-off," he said without a glance in Lesa's direction. "Why don't you just tell them no? They can't force you to take her."

Lilah put down her fork and gave up the pretense of eating.

She really did think the chicken was delicious, but her stomach disagreed. "Because—I suppose it wouldn't look—right, if she were put in a foster home or an institution. The social worker tells me they're searching for a permanent situation for her. A legal adoption. This would only be a temporary arrangement."

Charles peered at her over the rim of his glass. "Right." He pushed back his chair and dropped his napkin on the table. "They tell you that to get her in the door. Then they stall and drag their feet until you give up and keep her."

Lilah's face remained impassive despite the sudden flash of anger that shot through her. She quashed it, saying, "You sound like you have quite a lot of experience with social workers, Charles. Do you see a lot of this sort of thing at your accounting firm?"

He stood. "I read. I hear. We'll have coffee in the living room," he said as Marabet entered the dining room.

"Yes, please, Marabet," Lilah said when the housekeeper rolled her eyes behind his back. "And dessert, if you don't mind. Dinner was delicious," she added with a glance at her son.

"Yes. Delicious," Lesa mumbled as she followed her husband out of the room.

Later, when the front door closed behind them, Marabet came into the living room and dropped onto the sofa. She propped her stockinged feet on the coffee table, grabbing a cookie from the tray. "Kitchen's all done. How do you stand those two?"

Lilah shook her head and sank back against the chair. "He is rather opinionated."

Marabet snorted. "Rather opinionated, my foot. He's just like his father was, an opinion on everything whether he knows anything about it or not."

"Marabet."

"I know. I know." She took a bite of the cookie and smiled.

"Mmmm. Good. And that mouse he's married to—"

"Lesa is a nice woman."

"She'd be more interesting if she grew a spine, which is going to happen someday, you mark my words. I hope to God I'm there to see it."

Lilah rubbed her forehead. "Marabet, go to bed."

"I'm going." She rose and picked up the tray. Stopping at the door, she asked. "Have you made a decision about the child?"

"I don't think I have a choice, do you?"

"Whatever you say."

"There's nothing for a child to do in this house."

"Something will turn up."

"I suppose school will help."

"It's summer. No school in summer."

"Oh, Lord." Lilah dropped her head into her hands. "I'm probably making a terrible mistake."

"When do you think she'll come?"

"I have no idea. Why?"

"Just trying to plan my grocery shopping."

"I'll call Ms. Greenlea tomorrow and then let you know."

"You do that." Marabet turned and headed out of the room, but not before Lilah saw tears in her eyes—or the smile on her face.

Chapter 2

"How can you make me go live with that *witch?*" Bethany flung a handful of clothes in the general direction of her suitcase. She saw Felicity exchange a look with Barbara.

They were in Bethany's bedroom at the house where she'd lived with her parents. The house was tiny and disorderly, but there was a coziness there, a warmth that seemed to wrap itself around you when you entered the front door. The living room looked like it was for that purpose—for living in—with its overstuffed sofa and chair, the nearly threadbare rug covering scratched and worn wood floors. The feeling was continued in Bethany's room. Books lined makeshift bookshelves, and stuffed animals covered almost every inch of her bed. Yellow gingham curtains fluttered in the breeze at the room's lone window. Bethany had been living mostly at Barbara's house across the street since the accident, but she'd left things here so she could come home sometimes and pretend just for a few minutes that things were like they used to be.

"You've never even met her," Felicity pointed out. "You don't know that she's a witch."

Bethany threw more clothes onto the growing pile, spinning to face Felicity. "Oh, I *know!* I know how she treated my mother and father. She acted like they didn't exist."

"Is that what your parents told you?"

"They told me *nothing*. They were so democratic it was barfy. They said she had her life to live and we had ours. What a lot of—bunk." She spun back to the closet and grabbed a handful of dresses, hangers and all, and stuffed them into the suitcase. "She never called her or wrote. I hate her. She broke Mama's heart—" Her voice choked off and she hugged herself, bending forward at the waist.

When Barbara reached for her, Bethany pushed her hand away, glaring through tears. "*Don't.* Don't pretend you care." She twisted away and faced the closet.

After a minute, she heard the bedroom door open and close. When she looked up, Barbara was gone, but the social worker was still there. Bethany felt trapped. Mad as she was at Barbara, at least she knew her. This Felicity person—that's what she'd told Bethany to call her, like they were best friends or something—she was a stranger. She had showed up at Barbara's house a couple of weeks ago, and then Bethany heard a lot of yelling. She took Jason and Missy, Barbara's kids, out back so they wouldn't be afraid. When she heard a car start and drive away, she brought them back in. Barbara said everything was okay, but her eyes were red. Bethany hadn't known just how not okay things were until the social worker came back.

Felicity moved a stuffed alligator and sat down on the bed. "Bethany? Come sit down here for a minute." When Bethany didn't move, she said, "Please?"

Bethany wiped her face with her sleeve. Avoiding Felicity's eyes, she walked to the bed and perched as far away from the woman as possible, picking up a giant ladybug and hugging it to her chest.

"Bethany, I know this is all very difficult for you." Bethany rolled her eyes, but Felicity went on. "I want you to know that however wrong Barbara's actions were, she really does care about you."

"Sure she does. That's why she's shipping me off."

"She's not shipping you off. I am, because I have no choice.

Barbara has put herself in a very bad position by keeping you as long as she did. I can't condone her actions, even though I know she did it with the best of intentions."

Bethany pulled at the ladybug's feelers. "Why can't I stay with her?"

"It isn't that simple. You just can't move in with a neighbor and become hers."

"People used to. My father told me about how back in the old days neighbors cared for children left as orphans. They just took them in and raised them like their own. He knew about things like that. He was a history professor."

"I know he was," Felicity said. Bethany could tell she was trying not to smile. "And what he said is true. That's the way it used to be, but the law now says you have to go live with a relative if that's possible."

Stupid law. "What about what I want?"

"This is to help you find out what you really do want."

"I don't want to go live with that—that *woman*. I hate her."

"You can't hate her, Bethany. You don't even know her." A note of impatience had crept into her voice.

"I know enough to hate her," Bethany said, her lower lip poking out as she picked at the dots on the ladybug's back.

"You may know something about her, but you don't know *her*. There's a big difference." When Felicity reached over and touched Bethany's arm, Bethany flinched. "This will give you time to get to know her. It doesn't have to be permanent, but you have to give it a chance."

Bethany said nothing. What was there to say? They didn't care what she thought. No one cared about her. All they cared about was the law, and if the law said she had to go live with that evil witch, that's where they were going to send her.

She heard cars on the street below, neighbors coming home from work, children shrieking as they raced their bikes and

skateboards up and down the sidewalk. A baby cried. A television blared in the house next door. All familiar sounds. Home. The breeze had gone still as evening neared. She knew Felicity was watching her. "How much of a chance?"

"What do you mean?"

Bethany cut her eyes back over to Felicity. "How long do I have to give it?"

"Well, hopefully things will work out and you'll want to stay."

"What if I don't? How long do I have to stay?"

"I can't give you an exact date, Bethany."

Bethany could hear the frustration in Felicity's voice. She felt her lower lip poke out again. Her mother always hated it when she did that. Used to hate it. Her breath hitched. "For the summer?"

"That's less than three months. That's not much of a trial."

Bethany petted the ladybug's head. She looked over at Felicity through eyelashes still spiked with tears. "We wouldn't want to wait until I started school and then move me."

She watched as the social worker bit her lip. It looked like she was about to smile. "All right," Felicity said. "We'll start with the summer and see how it works out, but only if you promise to really try to make it work."

"What if it doesn't? Can I come back here?"

"You mean to this house to live? Absolutely not. You're a minor."

"Not alone. With Barbara." She smiled as the plans she'd made late last night spilled out. "She could move in with me. Our—my house is bigger. There's plenty of room for Missy and Jason."

"I don't think there's any way the courts would allow that, Bethany. Barbara is divorced with two young children, and she showed very poor judgment in deceiving us about your status. Please don't get your heart set on that outcome, because it just isn't going to happen."

Bethany's shoulders grew rigid. "So I have no choice," she said, tossing the ladybug on the bed.

"You will have choices, but that won't be one of them." Felicity reached out and clutched Bethany's hands. "Please, Bethany, give this a chance. If you hate it, I promise we'll make other arrangements, but please, please try."

Without speaking, Bethany pulled her hands free and went back to packing, adding things one by one to her suitcase: underwear, her toothbrush and toothpaste. She snapped the suitcase closed, leaving half the clothes she'd pulled out of the closet strewn on the floor. There was no one left to care.

She followed Felicity down the stairs and into the living room, where Barbara waited at the front door. Bethany reached out and lovingly touched her mother's old wooden rocking chair. She stopped at the battered desk. It was her father's desk, where he used to grade his students' papers. Now the desk was clean. Empty. Almost against her will, she was drawn to the old upright piano in the corner. She rested her fingers on the yellowed keys, making no sound. She looked around the room. After a minute, she turned and walked out the door.

"We can come back and get more of your things later, when you've had a chance to decide what you need," Felicity said behind her.

"That's okay," Bethany said without turning. "I probably won't be there long enough to need them."

Traffic on the way to Atlanta was awful, but Bethany didn't mind. She didn't care if they never got there. Felicity tried to make conversation when they first started out, but Bethany ignored her. They could make her go live with her grandmother, but they couldn't make her talk about it.

At one point, Felicity's cell phone rang. She put it close to her mouth and mumbled into it. When she hung up, Bethany could tell she was upset.

"Was that *her?*"

Felicity looked over in surprise. "Your grandmother? No. It was a friend."

"A boyfriend?"

She could tell Felicity didn't want to tell her, but after a minute, she nodded.

"Is he mad at you?"

"He's just a little upset."

"Because you're late?"

Felicity looked over in surprise. "You heard that?"

Bethany shrugged. "A little bit. You were supposed to be at some recital."

"More than a little bit," Felicity muttered. "Yes, I was supposed to be at a recital, but they will do fine without me."

"What does he play?"

"Who?"

"Your boyfriend."

Felicity shook her head, smiling the way people do when they don't want to tell you any more but know you won't shut-up unless they do. "He plays piano, but he's not playing in the recital. He's the teacher."

"Oh."

It was almost seven-thirty when they arrived. Bethany's eyes darted back and forth to either side of the road as the houses grew larger and farther back from the street. There was a strange tightness in her chest, and she felt herself shrink into the seat when Felicity signaled and turned into the long, tree-lined drive. The house they drove up to was huge. Bethany didn't get out of the car until Felicity retrieved her suitcase from the trunk and started for the door, and then she only did it because Felicity came back and made her.

Felicity rang the bell, and the door opened. "Hi," she heard

Felicity say. "I'm sorry we're so late. Traffic was a nightmare."

"It's no problem at all. Come on in. Both of you. Welcome."

Bethany slowly raised her eyes, then her chin. The little old lady she saw was nothing like she expected. Her face was creased with a smile and her eyes sparkled. She had a warm look about her, like she was someone who hugged a lot.

"I'm Marabet," the woman said, reaching out to take Bethany's suitcase. "Your grandmother's housekeeper."

Bethany felt the air whoosh out of her. Housekeeper.

Felicity said, "This is Bethany, and she's probably about to drop."

Bethany followed the two women into the house, tuning out their voices. She tried to appear unimpressed, but it took all her concentration to keep her mouth from hanging open. The entrance had a two-story ceiling and twin curved staircases with shining wooden banisters leading upstairs like something out of *Gone with the Wind*. The floor was a shiny, slippery tile that looked like glass, and to her left she saw a living room that was almost as big as her whole house in Athens. She stood awkwardly beside Felicity, feeling small and out of place. She didn't know what to do with her hands, so she stuffed them in her jeans pockets as the housekeeper led them across a wide hallway. They walked past a formal dining room and into a bright kitchen. Bethany stopped just inside the door. The room was three times the size of her kitchen in Athens. She saw two refrigerators and an island surrounded by tall stools. The smell of pizza filled the room, making her dizzy. She wasn't sure if she was hungry or sick.

"I thought you'd rather eat in here," the housekeeper was saying. "It's cozier. Lilah ate earlier and is upstairs now. I thought we'd have a bite and then I can show you your room."

Both women were staring at her. "I'm—uh—not hungry," Bethany managed.

The older woman nodded, unfazed, taking down three plates and napkins. "No wonder, with all the goings on today, but maybe you could just keep us company while we eat. I'm starved, and I'll bet Ms. Greenlea is too. Looks like she could put on a pound or two, don't you think?"

The older woman put pizza on their plates and climbed onto one of the stools. Felicity sat next to her. Bethany felt silly standing all by herself, so she sat next to Felicity.

The two women kept up a running conversation about the house and traffic and the weather, but Bethany didn't register what they were saying. Everything felt wrong. The house was big and strange and empty. She didn't want to be there. She wanted to be back in Athens with Barbara and Missy and Jason. No, what she really wanted was to be at home with her mother and father.

She felt tears prick the back of her eyes, but quickly blinked them away and picked up the slice of pizza to cover her embarrassment. She took a tiny bite, not even certain if she could swallow. Then another. It was delicious, the best pizza she'd ever tasted in her life. Before she'd taken the last bite, another piece magically appeared on her plate. She ate that one and one more before she realized what she'd done. She drank the milk the housekeeper poured for her.

She could hear a buzzing in her ears, like ocean waves coming in and going out, and she heard, "Why, she's half asleep on her feet. Come on, honey. I'll show you your room."

First the old lady took them to the back of the kitchen. She opened a door, gesturing inside. "This is my room. If you need anything at all later, you just come on down here and let me know. Just tap on the door. I wake real easy." She pulled the door closed and crossed back to the hallway, picking up Bethany's suitcase and leading the way up one of the curving staircases. At the top, she turned left, stopping at the second door. She swung the door open. "Here you are."

They stepped inside and Bethany looked around. A loveseat and chair faced a small fireplace. An entertainment center filled one wall, and on the other, ceiling to floor bookshelves. Tucked into an alcove was a desk and chair. "There's no bed," Bethany said faintly.

The housekeeper crossed the room to another door. "It's in here." She held the door open for them to enter.

Bethany stopped just inside the door and stared. The room was enormous, bigger than her living room and dining room combined at home, with a whole wall of windows. Outside, on a high tree branch, she could see a squirrel perched his haunches looking at her, his tail twitching at the intrusion. Across the room was a huge four-poster bed, covered with a thick down quilt and puffy pillows. A deep pile rug covered most of the floor. Prints of ballerinas and painted clowns were scattered on the walls. Across from the bed was a dressing table with hair brushes and dusting powder and all kinds of pretty glass bottles. The housekeeper crossed the room, putting the suitcase on a stand near the foot of the bed. Then she opened another door. "This is your bathroom. I think it has everything you'll need, but you just let me know if anything's missing."

Bethany managed a mumbled, "Thank you."

Felicity put an arm around her shoulders. "Do you want me to stay for a while?"

"No," Bethany said, blinking back tears of confused exhaustion. She just wanted everyone to go away.

"Then I'll call you tomorrow. I'll come by in the next few days to see how you're getting along. Okay?"

Bethany nodded. As the housekeeper and Felicity started from the room, Bethany took a step forward. "There is one thing I need."

They both turned back to her. "What's that, dear?" the

housekeeper asked.

"A calendar. Could I have a calendar?"

Lilah heard the water running in the bathroom across the hall. Good. Marabet had gotten the girl settled then. One day down. Lilah heard Marabet's footsteps in the hallway. Then the soft tap on her door. She grabbed the book from the loveseat beside her and mumbled, "Come in," hoping to heaven that Marabet was alone. Lilah was wearing a long robe that covered her from her neck to her slipper-clad feet, but she still felt exposed.

Marabet stuck her head in the door. "Coast is clear. You can quit hiding now."

"I am not hiding."

"Of course you are."

Lilah reached up to remove her reading glasses, only to realize she wasn't wearing them. She covered the gesture by brushing at her hair. "Well?"

"Well what?"

"Oh, Marabet, stop playing with me. This is very difficult."

"It'd be a lot less difficult if you'd face it."

"I am facing it. In my own way." She dropped the book beside her and tucked her feet up under her. "Well? How did it go?"

Marabet walked in and leaned against the arm of the loveseat. "I've always hated this room. It's beige and bloodless. It reminds me of him."

Lilah squelched a flash of irritation. "Is that why you came in? To critique my décor?"

Marabet grinned. "I put her in Elizabeth's rooms."

"That's fine. A little bare, though, aren't they."

"I put some stuff in there."

"What kind of *stuff*?"

"You know. Books and pictures from the attic. Doodads."

Lilah nodded. "Good. We want her to be comfortable while

she's here."

Marabet made a disgusted sound in her throat. "You make her sound like a houseguest."

"She is, more or less."

"She's your granddaughter."

"Don't lecture me, Marabet. I know who she is. I agreed to let her stay here for now, but I did not commit to keep her here permanently."

"At least you could give it a try."

"I will give it a try, but I don't have any great expectation that it will work."

"It won't if you have that kind of attitude."

Lilah gritted her teeth. "You have to stop this, Marabet. We simply cannot fight the whole time the girl is here. I'll provide her with a place to stay. That's all I agreed to. I don't want you getting attached to her. You know how it broke your heart when Elizabeth left."

Marabet snorted. "Like yours wasn't broken."

"It hurt me," Lilah admitted, "but it's just the way things were."

"They didn't have to be. If the Germ—"

"I've asked you not to call him that."

"If your husband hadn't been such a hard case—"

"All right." Lilah cut her off, getting to her feet. "I can see where this is going, and I don't care to go there." She walked to the door and opened it. "Good night, Marabet."

Marabet regarded her steadily. "Some day you're going to have to face the facts and—"

"*Good night*, Marabet." As Marabet started out the door, Lilah said, "Thank you for getting her settled. We'll deal with the rest of it in the morning. Did the social worker say when she'd be back?"

"She said in a couple of days."

"That's fine, then. Good night."

Lilah closed the door softly behind Marabet. She crossed to the loveseat and sank into the cushions. She tried not to think about the girl across the hall, but was finding it hard. She tried not to think about Elizabeth. That should have been easier—God knew she'd had a great deal of practice over the years—but it had become more difficult lately.

Lilah shook off the depression that settled over her like a gray blanket. She picked up her book and put it down again, thinking about Marabet's words. Marabet was her best friend, but there were some things she could not discuss with her. Charles. Elizabeth. Gerome Kimball. Maybe more than some. She took a shaky breath. Face facts, Marabet said, but Lilah was tired of facts. Hard, painful things that crept up on her and cut into her like dull, rusty knives. She closed her eyes, unable to bear any more facts that night.

Chapter 3

Morning crept into Bethany's consciousness. First she registered a dim light behind her eyelids. She shifted in bed, feeling not right somehow. Something was wrong. Horribly wrong. Some—something—just at the edge of her consciousness. Then she remembered and had to suck in her breath against the pain of it. They were gone. They were both gone and never coming back.

Grief dragged her down. Squeezing her eyes shut against the reality, she bit her knuckle so she wouldn't cry out.

When her father died, she thought she would die from the pain. Through all those hospital stays, through all the treatments and transfusions, she had watched him fade away a little more every time. He had been so sick, so sick that you could tell that staying alive was just too much work for him, but she'd wanted him to keep trying, to keep living. Bethany knew it was selfish, but she didn't care. She needed him. Her mother needed him. How could they bear to lose him?

At the funeral home the night of the viewing—that awful viewing—she heard one of the professors, an old, gray-haired woman with a hairy face and ugly, lace-up shoes, say, "Well, it's a blessing he's gone. The poor thing suffered so much." Bethany had wanted to kill her, wanted to take a knife and stab her. She wanted to scream at her that she was wrong, that there was no blessing in his dying, but of course she hadn't. She just turned away and pretended she didn't hear.

Bethany watched as Marabet's back disappeared down the stairs like her grandmother's had seconds before. Grandmother. The word left Bethany's mouth feeling empty, but the handshake, the handshake had left her even emptier. The woman was pretty, especially for someone so old, but her face looked hard. Not hard. She looked—cold and, not mean exactly, but stern. She looked stern. And disapproving, like a teacher when she caught you talking in class after she'd already told you not to.

Marabet called up the stairs. "Bethany?"

Bethany sucked in a breath and followed the voice.

The kitchen looked like something out of a magazine, huge and shiny and clean, with pale wooden countertops and lots of glass-fronted cabinets. She remembered the big eating island from the night before. She saw another eating area off to one side in a small alcove surrounded by windows. It had a padded bench and three chairs surrounding an oval wood table. She couldn't see any other houses out the back. It sure wasn't like her house in Athens, with its little yard and neighbors within eavesdropping distance, where she could look right into the neighbor's bedroom from her own bedroom window and could hear everything that went on inside the house. Not that anything interesting ever went on there.

Marabet's voice brought her back to Atlanta. "Why don't you make the toast while I whip us up some eggs and bacon?"

"All right." Bethany looked around. The counters were immaculate—and bare. "Where's the toaster?"

Marabet reached over and slid open a panel on the counter. Recessed into the wall were all the appliances that had been missing: toaster, mixer, blender, and a few Bethany didn't recognize.

"They hide 'em in these houses," Marabet said, stretching up over the cooking island for a skillet, "like they're too fancy to cook or something, but I'll tell you what." She reached into the refrigerator and pulled out the butter. "Even fancy people gotta eat. Now I'm not fancy, but I like to eat, too. A lot," she said with a chuckle, patting her stomach. "Not that it helped me grow any. Not up, anyway. Why, I'll bet you're taller than I am. How tall are you, honey?"

"Uh—I'm not sure. About five-three, I guess. My parents are—were—tall," she added, her voice breaking on the last word. She turned away.

A moment later, she felt Marabet close behind her. "Bethany, I know you're grieving. You don't have to be embarrassed or try to hide it from me unless you want to. It's natural to feel that way. I only just met your papa, but if your mama loved him, that's good enough for me. And I can tell you, child, I'm grieving for your mama."

Bethany couldn't speak, and she couldn't look at the woman. She blinked back the tears that were burning her eyes and nodded—what? I understand? Thank you?

Marabet gave her arm a pat. "There," the woman said, putting the butter on the counter beside the bread. "I knew you were taller than me." She walked over to the stove and started laying bacon strips in the skillet. "I'm such a shrimp. Five-two at my last physical. Used to be five-three back in the old days. Either the doctor's measurer's gone wacky, or I'm the incredible shrinking woman," she added, poking at the bacon with a spatula. "But they say you shrink when you get old, and I've been doing a lot of that lately. Getting old, that is."

Bethany listened as the voice went on while she mechanically made the toast. It was soothing. Some people talked and talked and drove you crazy, like Gina in the sixth grade, but this lady—Marabet—had a voice Bethany could listen to all day. It was comforting, like a TV on in the background. It soothed her all through breakfast and while they were loading the dishwasher and doing the pots and pans. Then Marabet folded the dish-

She never told her mother about what happened at the funeral home and that, too, was hard. She had always told her everything, but her mother was suffering as much as she was, even if she didn't show it. All through those terrible days, her mother managed everything, but Bethany could see her eyes were red and her smile wobbled a bit after a minute. So Bethany pretended to be strong when all she wanted to do was curl into a ball and hide her face and be held like a baby.

They had made it through because they had each other, but just when they were starting to laugh again and mean it, the police had come. When they told Bethany about her mother's accident, the policemen and Barbara, Bethany couldn't make sense of what they were saying. She had been watching Jason and Missy while Barbara ran up to the store when the police car pulled up in her driveway across the street. Bethany started over to see what they wanted, carrying Jason on one hip and holding Missy's hand. As she crossed the street, Barbara drove up. Bethany heard the words. *"I'm sorry . . . Are you family? . . . An automobile accident . . ."* She knew what the words meant, but she was sure she was missing something. She kept shaking her head and telling them no, they were wrong.

Barbara showed her identification to the officers and told them she'd take care of everything. She pulled Bethany back into the house and gave her a pill and sat with her until she was asleep. When Bethany woke, it was with the awful knowledge that something terrible had happened, but like now, it always took a few minutes to remember what it was. It took her another minute to realize where she was, and she felt another layer of despair settle over the others. Now she didn't even have Barbara and Jason and Missy. Now she really had no one.

She pulled aside the covers and dragged her legs over the side of the bed, tugging her nightshirt out from under her. Then she realized there was no reason to get up. There was nothing to do, no one to see to. She fell back against the pillows and pulled the covers over her head. No reason, she thought, closing her eyes against the tears that threatened. She felt the weight leave her body as her eyes drifted shut.

She was back in Athens, in her living room, sitting on the couch, reading, with her feet curled beneath her. Her mother was at the piano playing something by Bach, she thought. Something beautiful, lilting. The front door opened and her father came in. Bethany jumped to her feet, her eyes widening. It was her father, but he was in that awful blue hospital gown and barefoot. His feet looked white and hairy and misshapen somehow. He had needles stuck in each arm with clear plastic tubes dangling from them and that plastic oxygen thing taped to his nose. He was trying to talk, trying to get her mother's attention, but no sound came out. Bethany tried to go to him, but she couldn't move. It was like she'd been turned to a pillar of salt, like that Niobe woman in mythology her father had told her about. Her mother glanced up from her music and saw him in the doorway. She smiled and got to her feet, holding out her hand to him. Then suddenly they were both covered with blood. It was everywhere: the walls dripped with it, the ceiling, and the floor around them was soaked with it. Bethany tried to scream, but it came out a whimper.

She jerked awake. Her heart was pounding in her ears and she couldn't breathe right. Kicking her feet, she was able to sit up and tug the covers up to her chin while trying to block out the vision of all that blood. "Ohmygodohmygodohmygod," she whispered through trembling lips. Her nightshirt seemed thin and the blankets covering her inadequate to ward off the chill. She shuddered and tried to blink the vision away.

After a few minutes, she remembered to breathe slowly and deeply and count the way Barbara had taught her when she felt panicky. As her breathing slowed, she became aware of her surroundings again: the huge bed, the heavy drapes at the window, her suitcase at the foot of the bed. It was morning, and she wasn't in Athens. It was a dream. Not real. A dream. She repeated the words over and over again until she felt like she didn't have to scream.

When a knock sounded at the door, she jumped. A second later, the lady from the night before, the one who gave her pizza, poked her head in the door.

"Good," she said, coming into the room. "I was afraid you were still asleep. It's a beautiful morning." She crossed to the window and threw open the curtains. "You probably don't remember much about last night. You were bushed. That was easy to see." She glanced over her shoulder. "I'm Marabet, your grandmother's housekeeper. Did you sleep all right?" When Bethany continued to stare, she said, "Of course, you didn't. Who can sleep in a strange bed? Well, it'll be more familiar tonight and then you'll sleep for sure. Right now, I think it's about time for some breakfast. What do you say?"

It took a second for Bethany to realize she'd asked a question. "Uh—"

"That's fine." Marabet headed for the door. "You wash your face and jump into some clothes. I'll see you downstairs in about fifteen minutes."

"But I'm—" Bethany heard the sitting room door close. "—not hungry," she told the empty room. Even as she said the words, she realized they weren't true. She *was* hungry. She was starving.

Marabet tapped on Lilah's bedroom door. "You awake?"

"Come in," Lilah called.

Lilah watched as the words Marabet had been about to say froze on her tongue. What came out was, "Where are you going so all fired early?"

Lilah raised an eyebrow. "I have a number of errands to run. Then I'm going to have lunch at Phipps Plaza while I'm there shopping. After that, I have a meeting at Callanwolde with the holiday lights committee. I'll be back some time after that."

Marabet leaned against the doorframe and crossed her arms. "Hiding."

"Hardly hiding. I'll be in plain view of any number of people," Lilah said. She crossed to the dresser and picked up her handbag. "I'm a busy woman, Marabet, and I'll not change my life to accommodate every—situation that arises." She squared her shoulders and gave herself one last glance in the mirror.

When she turned, Marabet asked, "Will you be here for dinner?"

"I'm not sure." She edged past Marabet and opened the outer sitting room door, saying over her shoulder, "I'll call if something comes up, otherwise you can . . ." As she stepped out into the hall, she stopped.

"Ha! Gotcha!" she heard Marabet say behind her.

The entryway of the house rose two floors, so that the upper level of the house was a U-shaped gallery with the bedroom suites and guestrooms opening off the U. Bethany's rooms were directly across from Lilah's, and the girl stepped into the hallway at the same moment as Lilah.

It took Lilah only a moment to recover. "Good morning," she called across the empty space. "You must be Bethany. I'm Lilah Kimball." She made her way around the U to where Bethany stood and offered her hand. After a moment's hesitation, Bethany shook it. "I hope your rooms are all right," Lilah went on, pulling on her gloves. "I understand Marabet fixed them up a bit for you. Well," she said, glancing at her watch, "I hope you'll forgive me for running off this way, but I have an appointment in Buckhead and I don't want to be late." With a brief smile at each of them, she was down the stairs. As her foot touched the last step, she heard Marabet say, "Yep. That was your old granny. Come on, child. Let's have some breakfast."

Bethany watched as Marabet's back disappeared down the stairs like her grandmother's had seconds before. Grandmother. The word left Bethany's mouth feeling empty, but the handshake, the handshake had left her even emptier. The woman was pretty, especially for someone so old, but her face looked hard. Not hard. She looked—cold and, not mean exactly, but stern. She looked stern. And disapproving, like a teacher when she caught you talking in class after she'd already told you not to.

Marabet called up the stairs. "Bethany?"

Bethany sucked in a breath and followed the voice.

The kitchen looked like something out of a magazine, huge and shiny and clean, with pale wooden countertops and lots of glass-fronted cabinets. She remembered the big eating island from the night before. She saw another eating area off to one side in a small alcove surrounded by windows. It had a padded bench and three chairs surrounding an oval wood table. She couldn't see any other houses out the back. It sure wasn't like her house in Athens, with its little yard and neighbors within eavesdropping distance, where she could look right into the neighbor's bedroom from her own bedroom window and could hear everything that went on inside the house. Not that anything interesting ever went on there.

Marabet's voice brought her back to Atlanta. "Why don't you make the toast while I whip us up some eggs and bacon?"

"All right." Bethany looked around. The counters were immaculate—and bare. "Where's the toaster?"

Marabet reached over and slid open a panel on the counter. Recessed into the wall were all the appliances that had been missing: toaster, mixer, blender, and a few Bethany didn't recognize.

"They hide 'em in these houses," Marabet said, stretching up over the cooking island for a skillet, "like they're too fancy to cook or something, but I'll tell you what." She reached into the refrigerator and pulled out the butter. "Even fancy people gotta eat. Now I'm not fancy, but I like to eat, too. A lot," she said with a chuckle, patting her stomach. "Not that it helped me grow any. Not up, anyway. Why, I'll bet you're taller than I am. How tall are you, honey?"

"Uh—I'm not sure. About five-three, I guess. My parents are—were—tall," she added, her voice breaking on the last word. She turned away.

A moment later, she felt Marabet close behind her. "Bethany, I know you're grieving. You don't have to be embarrassed or try to hide it from me unless you want to. It's natural to feel that way. I only just met your papa, but if your mama loved him, that's good enough for me. And I can tell you, child, I'm grieving for your mama."

Bethany couldn't speak, and she couldn't look at the woman. She blinked back the tears that were burning her eyes and nodded—what? I understand? Thank you?

Marabet gave her arm a pat. "There," the woman said, putting the butter on the counter beside the bread. "I knew you were taller than me." She walked over to the stove and started laying bacon strips in the skillet. "I'm such a shrimp. Five-two at my last physical. Used to be five-three back in the old days. Either the doctor's measurer's gone wacky, or I'm the incredible shrinking woman," she added, poking at the bacon with a spatula. "But they say you shrink when you get old, and I've been doing a lot of that lately. Getting old, that is."

Bethany listened as the voice went on while she mechanically made the toast. It was soothing. Some people talked and talked and drove you crazy, like Gina in the sixth grade, but this lady—Marabet—had a voice Bethany could listen to all day. It was comforting, like a TV on in the background. It soothed her all through breakfast and while they were loading the dishwasher and doing the pots and pans. Then Marabet folded the dishtowel and hung it inside the bottom cabinet. "Now," she said, smiling at Bethany, "how about a tour of the house?"

Bethany shoved her hands in her pockets. "Okay."

Marabet patted her arm. "It's not Disney World, but it's not a walk to the guillotine, either. Come on."

She led the way into the dining room, a long, dark room with a big, heavy table in the center. Bethany counted ten chairs around it. The walls were painted dark green, and the drapes at the windows were green and burgundy and pulled back with gold ropey material. There was a gross picture on the wall of hunters with dead animals across their saddles.

"This is the formal dining room, which blessedly we don't use much. It was your grandfather's favorite room. Depressing, isn't it?"

Bethany felt a sudden urge to giggle as she followed her out of the room and down the hallway.

Marabet led her into another room. "This is the library. It hasn't gotten much use since your mama left. She was the big reader in this family. Well, your granny used to read a pretty good bit, but your mom was the champion."

Bethany followed her into the room and stopped, turning in a circle. Two walls were covered floor to ceiling with bookcases. The third wall was half taken up with a bay window and window seat. Bethany immediately thought of Heidi, curled up in Clara Sesemann's parlor in Frankfurt while she longed for her mountain and grandfather and Peter. Her own longing tightened her throat.

She reached out and touched a book. Her mother might have read this one, or this one, she thought, tracing the edge of the binding. She could almost see her, sitting in the window seat, a book in her lap, lost in whatever world it had opened up for her. "She was a librarian at the university," she heard herself saying. "She loved books."

"She always did," Marabet said. "I'm glad that's what she did. Work with books." There was a moment of awkward silence. Then Marabet cleared her throat. "Like I said, your grandma used to be a reader. The mister wasn't, and I'm sure not. Not that I'm proud of it. Oh, no. I just never got good at it, and it's hard to like what you're not good at. You ever notice that?"

Once again Marabet's voice carried them over the tough spot.

The living room was next. It was two rooms, Bethany decided, with no wall in between. It was big enough for two rooms. One end was filled with couches and chairs, but at the other end was a piano. Bethany drew in her breath. Not just a piano, she saw, walking over to it as if drawn by a magnet, but a shiny black Steinway grand piano. It was closed, but her eyes saw through the wood to the strings and hammers and keys. She smelled the slightly musty smell that all older pianos have, mixed with the scent of lemon oil. She reached out and touched it lightly with just the tips of her fingers.

"You play the piano?" Marabet asked.

She nodded. "A little."

"Will you play something for me?"

Bethany took a step backward. Her dream flashed back into her mind. "Oh—I couldn't. No, p-please," she stammered.

"That's all right, honey." Marabet opened the keyboard and pushed down one key after another. "Maybe later when you feel more comfortable."

"Maybe." Bethany nodded, looking back at the keys. "Maybe later."

Marabet started out of the room. "Your mom used to play the piano really well."

Bethany reached down and closed the keyboard. "Dad always said she played like an angel."

"That she did," Marabet said over her shoulder. "She used to practice all the time. I swear, whenever that child didn't have her head buried in a book, she had it buried in music. Well, that's not true. She did lots of things, but she always found time to practice. I loved to listen to her play."

"You talk about her a lot."

"I do, and it's good to have someone to do it with. She grew up here, so there's a lot of her spirit here in this house. I feel her here."

"I don't."

"No? Well, maybe that's because you didn't watch her grow up here. There's some of her in every room, and there's lots in the attic." She grinned. "Her things are packed away up there. You ought to go poking around. See what you find."

Bethany rubbed her cheek with her hand, feeling oddly unsettled. Why did listening to this lady talk about her mother make her feel uncomfortable? It wasn't like she was saying anything bad. "Maybe. Some time." She looked away. "Would it be okay if I went upstairs now? I mean, unless you need me to help you do something."

"No, honey," Marabet said, patting her arm. "You go ahead. You probably—"

The phone rang, cutting off what she was about to say. "Kimball residence . . . No, Mr. Mulligan, she isn't here. Should I have her call you? . . . All right. I'll tell her when she comes in."

She turned back to Bethany. "What was I saying? Oh, yes. You go ahead and unpack and get settled in. I'll just putter around down here. When you get hungry, we'll whip us up some lunch. Okay?"

"Okay. Sure. When will . . ." She glanced toward the front door. "When will she be back?"

"Probably not until dinner time. We'll most likely have the house to ourselves for the day."

Lynda Fitzgerald

★ ★ ★ ★ ★

Marabet was right, Lilah admitted as she wandered through the mall barely glancing to either side. She was hiding. She had no shopping to do and she didn't have any appointments. She'd even lied about the committee meeting, which wasn't until next month, but when she opened her eyes this morning, she knew she had to get out of the house, and before the girl got up, if possible. Lilah had thought the child would sleep until noon. Wasn't that what teenagers did in the summer? Hadn't she at that age? She tried to think back, but it was too long ago. Then to run into her in the hallway, of all things.

It was what she had dreaded most, that first awkward meeting, but all she felt was relief now that it was over. She had dreaded not knowing what to say, having no idea what the girl looked like. Her appearance had been a big part of it; groundless, as it turned out. She might favor her father, who Lilah never met, but she looked nothing like Elizabeth. Elizabeth had been a blonde, with rich waves that reached halfway down her back, while Bethany's hair was a kind of light brown and almost straight. Her eyes were blue-gray, not Elizabeth's brilliant cornflower blue, and she didn't have her mother's heart shaped face or dimpled chin. Bethany wasn't an unattractive child, but there was nothing exceptional about her that Lilah could see. She was just—ordinary. A marigold, where Elizabeth—

Stop torturing yourself! Elizabeth was gone. She had been gone for a long time. She had turned her back on everything in her life, and all for the sake of some boy. At one time, Lilah had thought she and her daughter shared a close bond, but Elizabeth put paid to that notion by walking out of the house and out of Lilah's life without a backward glance. Lilah couldn't blame Gerome for what happened. He had asked only one thing of Elizabeth, and even that had been more than she was willing to give. Lilah had managed to survive nicely for fourteen years without her daughter.

Her steps faltered. Nicely? She felt the familiar sense of emptiness leach the color out of the world around her. The season's hottest numbers in the store windows became shapeless garments in drab shades of gray. It was the same overwhelming sense of loss that made food tasteless and made today and tomorrow stretch meaninglessly ahead. Still, in time it would get better. Wasn't that what they said? That time healed all wounds?

"Liars," she hissed, realizing she'd spoken aloud when several people turned to look at her. She returned their stares, her eyebrows raised in challenge, and soon they turned away. Oh, she was in a foul mood. Damn the world and *damn* life. This was not the way it was supposed to happen. She felt deceived and—and cheated.

The thought surprised her. What did she have to feel cheated about?

She wandered into one of the refreshment shops and ordered a coffee she didn't want. Taking it back out into the mall, she found a bench half-hidden behind a cluster of potted schifflera trees. Hiding again, she chided herself. She sipped the lukewarm coffee and made a face. It was the girl. Her sudden appearance had brought it back: Elizabeth's defection, the long years that followed. This wasn't the time to second guess herself. She had to believe they had done the right thing by demanding a modicum of propriety from their daughter. They'd demanded the same behavior from Charles, and look at him. He was a successful accountant, married to a perfectly wonderful woman. Well, a nice woman, anyway. Charles had completed college and gone on to get his master's degree, and he had spent a respectable number of years paying court to Lesa before their marriage. That was the proper way to do things.

No, Gerome had made the right decision, despite the

consequences, and Lilah had gone along with him as she always did. She had agreed with him at the time because she was sure Elizabeth would ultimately see it their way. Then she had expected her daughter would come crawling back when she realized her mistake, but Elizabeth had never made the slightest effort to contact them. Lilah couldn't very well complain about the consequences of her own decision.

Gerome hadn't suffered any consequences, Lilah thought with a surge of bitterness. He had put Elizabeth out of his life and out of his mind and that had been that. Lately she had found herself wondering if Gerome had really been that sure of his convictions or whether he was just a cold, unfeeling bastard without two honest emotions to rub together.

She sat back, stunned by her anger. She had felt nothing for so long that the emotions surfacing in her seemed like they must belong to someone else. She hadn't grieved when Gerome died. At the time, she had assumed it was the suddenness of his death that kept her numb. An apparently healthy man in his early sixties goes to work one morning and never comes home. She had tried to feel something—it would have been appropriate to feel *something*—but she hadn't.

No, that wasn't true. She had felt the initial shock when she got the call from his office telling her of his collapse, and then after his death, confusion. How was she supposed to go on? It wasn't so much that she didn't want to go on; she was just uncertain how to proceed. Gerome had always led the way. It was he who told her what committees she should join and whom to invite to dinner, mostly decisions based on furthering his business. Lilah had complied because she wanted to support her husband and because it was the right thing to do.

She remembered the book her father had given her as an engagement present, *How to Help Your Husband Get Ahead*, by Mrs. Dale Carnegie. She had devoured each page, memorized it, believing every word. In today's light, it seemed like some kind of subversive propaganda piece aimed at keeping the little woman in line. The thought make her squirm. Then, after Gerome's death, Charles had stepped into the gap, at least where financial matters were concerned, and Marabet took care of the house. That left Lilah with precious few decisions to make and gave her the freedom to live in a big house and drive a big car and spend Gerome's money at these depressingly gay, overpriced stores buying things she didn't need or want.

She squeezed her eyes tightly shut against the thought. She was sick to death of second guessing old decisions and sick of herself and—yes, sick to death of life.

No matter, she thought, grimacing as she swallowed the last of the tepid coffee. She wouldn't do anything about it, any more than she'd done anything about her life up to this point. She'd just go on getting up each morning and doing nothing all day and hating it until she got lucky and God took the decision out of her hands and struck her dead; and then, being the person she was, she'd probably whine about that, too.

She stood and crushed the empty cardboard cup in her hand, tossing it at a trash receptacle. It hit the edge and fell to the ground. She reached down to pick up the cup. Then she straightened, kicked the cup under the bench, and walked off without a backward glance.

Chapter 4

Bethany raised the lid from the keys and ran a finger across them. It was an old piano with beautiful ivory keys, only slightly yellowed with age. She knew that most pianos today had plastic keys or keys made out of some other kind of wood made to look like ebony and ivory, but these were *real*. She could feel it.

Was this the piano her mother had learned on? Her fingers twitched with wanting to play. Some part of her wanted to put her feelings into music, to just let them pour out of her, to play until she was all drained, the way she had played after her father's death, pounding out songs that wept so that she wouldn't; but she couldn't bring herself to do it. Not here. Not in this house.

She touched middle C, bringing it soundlessly to the key bed, trying to feel her mother's presence in the room the way Marabet did. She wanted to feel her here, needed to, but it was no use. Restlessly, she got up from the bench and closed the lid. Maybe she'd be able to feel her up in the attic.

Lilah's steps were firm as she entered the house two hours later. She had made up her mind on the drive home. Things that were going to change. She would not continue to hide, either away from home or within it. This was her house and her life, and she would not see it made more difficult by a temporary situation that was outside her control. She stuck her head in the kitchen. "Marabet, please plan to have dinner in an hour. We'll eat in the dining room."

"Without me," Marabet said. "That room gives me indigestion."

"As you wish," Lilah said. She pulled off her gloves as she started up the stairs, determination propelling her forward.

"Tom Mulligan called," Marabet called up the stairs after her.

Lilah turned. "Tom? Did he say what he wanted?"

"Just wanted to know how you were doing."

"What did you tell him?"

"I said you'd call him back. You will, won't you?"

Lilah turned and headed up the stairs. She had a strange relationship with Thomas Mulligan, her attorney. He had been her husband's attorney until Gerome's death. He had handled everything for Lilah during that difficult time. She should feel gratitude, but instead these calls just to see how she was doing made her uneasy.

She put Tom out of her thoughts, turning her mind to the situation with the girl. Bethany was here until other arrangements could be made. It was awkward, but there was no reason why they couldn't share a living space for that short a time. She would be polite and, hopefully, the child would respond in kind. After all, they were two civilized people.

She was in her bedroom when she heard a sound in the attic. As she stepped back into the hallway, she saw Bethany coming down the stairs, clutching something to her chest. "What were you doing up there?" Lilah demanded in a voice that surprised even her.

She could see Bethany stiffen before she opened her mouth. "Marabet said it was all right. She said I could look through my mother's stuff."

Lilah felt her stomach twist, but she kept her face expressionless. "I would rather you didn't," she managed to get out. "It's dirty up there, and much too stuffy to be healthy. You should be outside doing—something."

The girl's anger was tangible. "Playing?"

Lilah felt herself flush. She tried to think of a response and failed. "I've told Marabet dinner is to be at seven. Will you please be downstairs then?"

Bethany nodded once without speaking. Then she turned and walked away with great dignity.

Lilah closed her sitting room door behind her, troubled by her own reaction. There was nothing private up in the attic, nothing secret. What harm could it do if the child poked around? Still, it bothered her, the thought that the girl had been going through Elizabeth's things. Lilah knew there were boxes up there, although she'd never allowed herself to go through them. When Elizabeth left, she had taken only the clothes she was wearing. Marabet had carefully packed away the rest of her things, thinking Elizabeth would come back for them or send for them, but she never did. Marabet had announced to Lilah in one of her more incautious moments that it showed how badly they'd hurt Elizabeth, that she'd rather go naked than ever contact them again.

Lilah shook off the memory. She simply had to stop questioning herself. It was nonsensical to pick apart her every thought and decision. It was her house and her right to say who did what in it.

Bethany pushed her sitting room door closed behind her. Then she slid down it until she was sitting on the floor. "I hate her I hate her I hate her." Tears burned her eyes as she looked down at the picture she still cradled in her arms. Brilliant blue eyes smiled up at her out of a face surrounded by wild and glorious golden waves. Happiness radiated from the frame. Goodness. Kindness. Bethany remembered the first time she had realized how beautiful her mother was.

"I wish I looked like you," Bethany said, studying her mother's face as Elizabeth brushed mascara on her lashes. Bethany was eight years old. Her hair was straight and brown, her eyes blah brown or green or sort of blue. Her mother—her mother was a fairy princess, with her clouds of golden hair soft around her face.

Elizabeth put down her mascara wand, turning her whole attention on Bethany. "Why, you silly goose? You're beautiful just the way you are. You're unique. Did you know that? No one else in the world is just like you."

"I don't want to be unique. I want to be like you."

"And you will be someday. You'll be like me and your daddy both, but all that will come together and become you, that special Bethany Freemont." When Bethany looked away, Elizabeth took her by the shoulders and turned her back to the mirror. "What do you see there?"

Bethany peeked, and then averted her eyes. "Stringy ugly hair and—and . . ." Her voice trailed off.

Elizabeth put her finger under Bethany's chin and turned her back to the mirror. "Do you know what I see? I see the promise of beauty to come. I see the future. I see all that's good in the world, all that makes life worth living. That's what I see." She pulled Bethany to her, hugging her tightly. "You're perfect just the way you are, sweetheart. Your daddy and I want you just the way you are. Don't be so impatient. Beauty comes later, from time and experience. Your job isn't to worry about the future and what it will bring. Your job is to be what you are and let the future take care of itself."

Bethany choked on a sob. That was before her daddy got sick, when he used to bring his students over and he let Bethany listen while they talked and her mama made them all cookies and still thought the future would bring all those wonderful things. "But it didn't, mama," she whispered, as the tears she'd been fighting all day spilled from her eyes. She bit her knuckle so that she wouldn't sob out loud. Then, hugging the picture once more against her as if it were the woman herself, she lay down on the carpet and wept silently.

At seven sharp, Lilah went downstairs. When she entered the dining room, the girl was already seated at the table. It struck her as silly, suddenly, that the two of them should be eating at a table that seated ten. Still, maybe the formality of the room would keep things civil. "Hello, Bethany," she said as she entered the room. "I'm glad to see you're prompt," then wondered where the inane and slightly insulting words had come from.

"Hello," Bethany said without smiling.

Lilah sat down at the table and shook out her napkin, placing it in her lap. She glanced at Bethany. Her eyes looked red and swollen. Had she been crying? Sleeping? Her napkin, Lilah noticed, was already in her lap. At least she had manners. Then she caught herself. Of course Bethany had manners. She was Elizabeth's daughter. The thought was as unwelcome as it was uncomfortable.

The awkward silence was broken when Marabet entered the room carrying two salad plates.

"Are you sure you won't join us, Marabet," Lilah asked, trying to control the pleading note that tried to creep into her voice.

"No, thank you." Marabet gave her a chilly smile, placing the salad in front of her and then Bethany. "I'm serving steak au poivre. I hope that will be all right."

Lilah groaned inwardly at the master-and-servant act. "That will be fine."

"I was going to serve hamburgers and fries, but it didn't seem right in here," she added, looking around with distaste.

Lilah thought she saw a fleeting smile on the girl's face. "Maybe another night," she said, picking up her salad fork.

When Marabet was gone, the silence hung as heavy as the

outdated drapes at the windows. In the old days, Lilah had hosted dinner parties with any number of virtual strangers and had never had any trouble coming up with suitable conversation. Now she frantically searched her mind for something to say.

"What grade are you in, Bethany?"

Her voice seemed to startle the girl. "Eighth."

Lilah nodded as if she were really interested. "Do you like school?"

"Yes, ma'am."

Okay, Lilah, she said to herself as she chewed a piece of lettuce, *what's next? You can't talk about home or family.* "What's your favorite subject?"

Bethany glanced away and Lilah was certain she rolled her eyes. She knew she would have in her place.

"English."

"Do you like to read?"

"Yes, ma'am."

"Well, we have lots of books in the library. I'm sure you'll find something in there to read."

"Marabet showed me."

"Did she give you a tour of the house?"

"All except the attic," Bethany said, looking straight at her for the first time. "She told me to look around up there by myself."

The words were clearly a challenge. Lilah was spared answering by Marabet's entry. The steak au poivre, she noticed, was served on her fine china.

"Will that be all?" Marabet asked, straight-faced.

Master and servant all the way. "Yes, thank you, Marabet."

Silence descended once again. The meal seemed to go on interminably. Lilah considered and discarded any number of conversational gambits. She couldn't talk about Bethany's life in

Athens. She couldn't ask the girl about her future plans. She had none. They'd exhausted her education in four sentences. In the end, she faked an interest in her food, seldom raising her eyes. What would Emily Post have said about that? She noticed that the girl did little more than push the food around on her plate. The child was rail thin. Surely she should eat, but Lilah didn't know how to suggest it without it sounding like an order. If mentioning her getting some fresh air had caused such a reaction, she couldn't begin to imagine what telling her to eat her dinner would bring. A screaming tantrum? Was she short-tempered? Again it struck Lilah that she knew virtually nothing about the girl, and she realized with something like sorrow that she had no desire to change that.

Finally the meal was over. Lilah felt a wash of relief when Bethany declined dessert and excused herself to her room. Lilah followed suit, despite her earlier determination to tough it out. She wasn't hiding. Exactly. She was just eliminating the strain on all of them by removing her presence.

Once upstairs, she stopped just inside the door to her bedroom and stared. What she saw was a cold and neutral room which, at the moment, seemed nothing more than a reflection of her life. She glanced back into the sitting room. It was bland, but the bedroom bothered her more. Unadorned beige walls. Light brown curtains. A nondescript beige bedspread covered the bed. In the deep recess of a bay window sat a small round table and chair that served only to catch dust. The large dresser, her husband's, took up much of one wall even though his clothes had been removed and given to charity long ago. Slowly, still surveying the room, she slipped out of her dress and crossed to the closet to hang it. The huge walk-in closet was still half-empty. Out of some kind of overblown respect for his space? No, she thought, because she had never felt the slightest motivation to change it.

Of Words & Music

Had Gerome liked the décor? She had never asked him. He wasn't an easy man to talk to, or to live with, if she was honest with herself, but he had been her husband all the same. Why did people have so much trouble understanding that? She remembered years ago when their attorney, Tom Mulligan, had asked Lilah why she put up with him. Tom was present when Gerome had one of his nastier attacks of temper. She couldn't even remember what it was about, but Gerome had called her stupid and slammed out of Tom's office, leaving Lilah stranded. Tom was furious. "Why in the hell do you put up with him?" he had demanded.

Lilah was shocked and even a bit scandalized that her husband's attorney would ask her such a thing. "Because he's my husband," she announced. "Gerome may get angry from time to time, but that doesn't make him a bad man. Everyone gets angry. I certainly don't think you have any right to criticize him." Tom had raised his eyebrows, but had said no more. He had insisted on driving her home, although she could have taken a taxi. At least he hadn't made any more inappropriate remarks about her marriage. Why was it so hard for people to understand that she honored her marriage vows? Her marriage hadn't been perfect, but whose was? Still, she took great pride in the fact that it had worked for thirty years.

"Lasted," the evil demon in her mind whispered. "Not worked. Lasted."

Tying a wrapper around her, she walked into her bathroom and turned the faucets on full. Then she sat down at the dressing table and pulled the pins out of her hair. She picked up her brush and began her nightly ritual. One hundred strokes, just like her mother had taught her. Looking in the mirror, she saw an aging woman peering back at her, brown hair streaked with gray, neck not as firm as it used to be. The hands that had been her secret vanity all her life had age spots now, and she knew without looking that her ankles were discolored with spider veins.

She felt another surge of irrational, undirected anger. Putting down the hairbrush, she pushed herself to her feet and walked back into her bedroom, looking around. It looked exactly as it had throughout her married life, and she didn't like it at all.

Bethany heard the water running in another part of the house. One day was gone. How many did that leave to get through? Too many. She almost dropped the picture she was cradling when the knock sounded on the sitting room door. She was about to get up from the floor when Marabet stuck her head in. "You decent?"

She hesitated a moment when she saw Bethany on the floor, and then slipped in the opening balancing a tray, sitting it on the little table in front of the loveseat.

Bethany stared. Hamburgers. Fries. Chocolate chip cookies and milk.

"I thought you might be hungry," Marabet said, grinning at her.

"I was. I mean, I am." Bethany grabbed a fry and looked back at Marabet. "You're a feeder."

Marabet sat down on the loveseat and took a cookie. "I'm a what?"

"A feeder. My mother used to say people fell into categories. There are enablers and avoiders and dictators and—" She grinned. "And feeders or nurturers or something like that, and a bunch of others I can't remember. You're a feeder."

"Well, I guess I am that." Marabet munched on her cookie for a minute. "I don't suppose she ever talked about me?"

The hamburger stopped halfway to Bethany's mouth. She put it back on the plate. "No. I'm sorry. She never said anything."

Marabet seemed to shake herself. "Now wasn't that the silliest question? Of course she didn't talk about me. That would have meant she talked about home, and she wouldn't have done that."

"No, she never talked about—anyone." She looked down at the picture in her lap, her food forgotten.

Marabet motioned at the picture. "Did you find that in the attic?" When Bethany nodded, she said, "May I?" Bethany handed it to her, and Marabet held it at arm's length, studying it. "She was a beauty, and that's the truth. Eat, girl, or you'll hurt my feelings." When Bethany picked up her hamburger and took a bite, Marabet went on, "Prettiest girl I ever saw, but not just pretty. She was kind to a fault. Kind to everyone. You know?"

Bethany chewed and nodded.

"Got that from her mama," Marabet went on, ignoring the choking sound Bethany made. "Lilah Kimball was always kind to everyone. I knew her in high school. Course she wasn't Lilah Kimball back then. Lilah Andreson. She was my best friend, even though I was as poor as she was rich. Yep. That was me. The girl from the wrong side of the tracks. Lots of Lilah's friends looked down on her for befriending me, but she didn't pay them any mind. Not a snobbish bone in her body."

Bethany swallowed. "She doesn't seem like that now."

"Well, she is. Of course, life throws funny curves at people sometimes. Makes them act different than they would otherwise."

"You mean me."

"No, I don't mean you, missy," Marabet retorted, taking another cookie. "I mean all kinds of things. Like her husband. He didn't always approve of—oh, what did he call it?—her liberalism, I think it was. Said she should stick to her own class."

"Why did she marry him?"

"Oh, who knows why anyone marries anyone? Why did I

marry my Jessie? Well, maybe I do know why. He was the handsomest man you ever saw. Real manly, you know? But he was bad as the day is long. Up and left me. Took my car and my savings and even my house," she said with a twinkle in her eye. "We lived in a trailer. One day I came home from work and it was gone."

Bethany stared at her open-mouthed. "That's terrible!"

Marabet chuckled and shook her head. "Well, it was, but now it's just a memory of one of those curves life threw at me. Anyhow, Lilah heard about it and jumped right in and made me move in with her."

Bethany's mouth turned down at the corners. "As her servant."

"Not as her servant. I insisted on that myself. She wanted me to be a long-term houseguest, but I couldn't very well do that, could I? Mr. Kimball would never have stood for it, and I don't blame him a bit for that. It's not healthy for somebody to do nothing at all. I had never worked except in a laundromat. Figured I'd rather fold her laundry than some stranger's."

"She makes you live behind the kitchen."

Marabet grinned. "You think that was her choice? She's tried to get me to move upstairs for years, but I like it where I am." She chuckled. "Right next to the food."

Bethany chewed for a minute. "What's she like?"

"Your grandma?" When she nodded, Marabet put the picture on the table and sat back against the chair, munching her cookie and studying the ceiling. "What's she like? She's got good and bad like anyone else. Right now she's hurting too much to be like herself."

"Hurting from what?"

"From what? Good heavens, child, she's hurting for the same reason you are. She just lost her daughter."

"She didn't care about her!" Bethany said angrily, dropping

her half eaten-hamburger on the plate.

Marabet leaned forward, laying a hand on Bethany's arm. "You're wrong about that, Bethany. She loved your momma something fierce. She hadn't seen her for a long time, but that didn't mean she loved her any less."

Bethany scowled at her but made no effort to move Marabet's hand. "She never called. Not once in all those years."

Marabet nodded, her face sad. "That's true, child, but that phone works both ways, you know."

For a long minute, Bethany considered her words. Finally, she looked up. "What happened? Mama never would talk about it. All she said was that her parents wanted her to live their way and she preferred to live her way."

Marabet sank back again and seemed to be weighing her words carefully. "It's an old story, I guess," she said. "Your mom wanted romance, and your grandparents wanted her to be sensible."

Bethany bristled. "Are you saying she was wrong to marry my father?"

Marabet shook her head. "There's no wrong about it, child. Your mom was a girl with all the stars of the sky in her eyes, and, oh, your daddy! He was a man to please the eye. He waited in the kitchen that night she told her folks about her plans, so I had plenty of time to check him out and, believe me, if only I'd been thirty years younger." She glanced at Bethany. "Anyway, she must've took one look at that man, and all her notions of propriety went right out of her head. Married him two months after she met him. Your grandparents wanted her to wait a while to be sure, but your mama wasn't having a bit of it. And—well, harsh words were spoken by all of them. Then off she went and changed her life and her name and that was that."

Bethany chewed her lip. "It seems like a stupid reason to never see your family again."

"I couldn't agree more."

After a minute, Bethany picked up a cookie and nibbled on it. "What about my grandfather? Didn't he miss her?"

Marabet let out a long, slow breath. "Your grandfather was—he was—" She broke off as the phone rang. "Who in the world?" She got stiffly to her feet and crossed to the desk. "Kimball residence." "Oh, hello, Miss Greenlea. Yes, Bethany's fine. She's right here. You want to talk to her?"

She held the phone out to Bethany.

Taking as long as she could, Bethany stood and brushed the crumbs from her shirt. Finally, she crossed the room and took the receiver from Marabet. "Hello?" She watched Marabet slip out of the room, leaving the tray and pulling the door closed behind her.

"I'm sorry it's so late, Bethany," Felicity said. "I wanted to call earlier, but I just got free. How is everything going?"

Bethany traced her initials on the desk with her finger. "Fine."

"How are you settling in?"

"Okay, I guess."

"Do you like the house?"

"I guess so. It's big."

"It certainly is. How are you doing with your grandmother? Have the two of you had a chance to talk."

Bethany lay her palm down over the initials, then raised her hand to see if it made an impression. "We talked some at dinner."

"And?"

Silence. Then, "I like Marabet. The housekeeper. She's really nice."

"She seemed nice when I met her last night."

"She was just up here in my room. She brought me some food."

"I thought you said you had dinner with your grandmother."

Bethany gave a little laugh. "Marabet brought me a second dinner. She believes in feeding people."

"Well, there's nothing wrong with that."

Bethany heard voices through the phone and a piano playing softly. "Where are you?"

It was a moment before Felicity answered. "I'm at a restaurant. My friend is playing here."

"Your boyfriend, the music teacher?"

"Yes. His name is Elliott. He's the one playing the piano. Can you hear it?"

Bethany heard the smile in her voice. "Yes. It sounds beautiful."

Felicity laughed. "Yes, it does." She paused, then said, "Would you like for me to stop by tomorrow? If you'd rather, I could wait a couple of days. It's up to you."

Bethany really didn't want her to come at all—it just reminded her of where she was and why—but she didn't think "none of the above" was one of her choices. "Maybe in a few days, if it's all right. There's no reason for you to come now."

"If you're sure that's what you want. You have my phone numbers if you change your mind or if anything comes up."

"I'm sure."

"All right then. Goodnight, Bethany."

"Good night."

It was nine-thirty when the phone rang again. Lilah was curled up in bed trying to read, but the words seemed unable to make it from the printed page to her mind. She was more than ready to lay the book aside. She picked up the receiver at the same time as Marabet answered downstairs. "I have it, Marabet," Lilah said, and waited for the click when Marabet disconnected. When she didn't hear it, she said again, "Thank you, Marabet. I'll take it," and was rewarded with a loud click in her ear.

"Why do you put up with her, mother?"

"You're calling awfully late, Charles," Lilah said, ignoring his question. She could hear the sounds of traffic in the background. He must be calling from his car.

"Just left a client's. IRS audit next week. We're getting ready. So, how was your first full day of motherhood—or grandmotherhood, if there is such a word?"

"I don't believe there is," she said, settling her bedcovers over her. "Did you call to harass me, Charles?"

"Heavens no. Just morbid curiosity. What's she like? Did she call all her friends long distance? Is she into dolls or boys? I can't remember what twelve was like."

"Whether you can or not is immaterial. You were never a twelve-year-old girl." She settled the phone on her shoulder. "She seems nice enough. A bit confrontational, perhaps."

"She came by that honestly. Got it from her mother, I'd say." There was only the sound of traffic and the hum of phone lines. After a minute, Charles said, "I'm really calling to invite Lesa and myself to dinner tomorrow night. We're free and it might be fun to meet the child. Think you could get that housekeeper to ruin something for us?"

Lilah tried to think of a good excuse to say no, but none was forthcoming. "Seven o'clock?" she said finally.

"I wouldn't miss it for the world. See you then."

She hung up the phone and waited for the knock. "Come in, Marabet."

Marabet came into the room and sat on a corner of the bed. "What did his highness want?"

"Charles," she answered pointedly, "wanted to invite himself for dinner tomorrow night."

"Just him?"

"And Lesa, of course."

"Of course."

"Seven o'clock. In the dining room."

"It's your indigestion."

"Lamb?"

"Sounds delicious."

"I'm glad you approve."

"Sit down," she said as Marabet got up to leave. "Tell me about your day."

Marabet sat back down on the bed. "Mine or Bethany's?"

"Marabet," Lilah cautioned, her voice exasperated.

Marabet sighed and sank back down on the bed. "Not bad, all things considered. We had breakfast after you left."

"She ate?"

"Of course she ate. Why?"

Lilah picked at the bedspread. "I was just concerned. She ate very little dinner and she's so thin. We wouldn't want Miss Greenlea to think we're starving her."

Marabet's mouth twitched. "I don't think there's any danger of that."

"What then?"

"Oh, I showed her around the house. She went up to her room for a while. Then we had lunch, which she ate gobs of," she added before Lilah could ask. "She walked around outside for a bit. Then she went up to the attic."

"I don't want her up there."

Marabet sat back. "Why not?"

"Because it's . . . dirty up there."

Marabet raised one eyebrow. "I beg your pardon. It is not dirty."

"It's stuffy."

"And your real reason is?"

Lilah pushed the book off her lap. "I don't want her rummaging through Elizabeth's things."

"Why not?" Marabet demanded. "They're her mother's

things, too."

"She is—was my daughter. I want her things left alone."

"They certainly have been left alone this last decade and more. Why would you care? You've never given them so much as a glance."

Lilah averted her eyes, picking at the bedspread. "Because I do."

Marabet stood, hands on hips, and regarded Lilah. "You're jealous."

Lilah looked up, startled. "That's absurd."

"No it's not. You're jealous of Bethany's relationship with Elizabeth. You want to keep her all to yourself."

"What in the world are you talking about?" Lilah demanded, sitting straighter.

Marabet's voice softened. "I'm talking about you hanging on so hard to Elizabeth's memory that you can't even share it with her own daughter." She crossed to the door, then stopped and turned back. "I think that's a big mistake, Lilah. Bethany's loss has been as bad as yours. Worse. She's got no parents now, and she's still a child. She can't go and do like we can. She has to go the way we push her, and you want to deny her the one little scrap of her mother's history we can offer. Not letting her even get close to her own mother's things is more than unkind, it's purely selfish—and it's not at all like you."

Marabet turned and walked out of the room, pulling the door closed behind her.

Lilah stared after her.

No, she thought, picking at the bedspread again. Marabet was wrong. There was no jealousy or possessiveness involved in her decision. It was obvious that the things in Lilah's attic belonged to Lilah. Bethany didn't need to nose around in Elizabeth's possessions. They were from a time before Bethany was even born, and she didn't need them. She had all her memories in her house in Athens, and she'd have those once again when everything was settled. Surely she didn't need all the rest.

She reached behind her back and punched her pillow back into shape. Then she picked up her book and stared at the page without seeing it. It had been a day of unwelcome emotions, and this latest was no exception. It felt a little like anger, and maybe a little like shame.

Chapter 5

Bethany's eyes popped open the instant Marabet knocked on the door. Her first thought was of breakfast. It was seconds later before the desolate feeling of loss washed over her.

"Another beautiful day," Marabet said, coming into the room and throwing open the drapes. "I thought I'd make something special for breakfast. How about blueberry pancakes with whipped cream and some sausage? Fifteen minutes?"

She was gone before Bethany could open her mouth. She couldn't help but smile at the energy of the tiny woman. She paused at the window and looked out. There was the squirrel again, poised on the branch, tail twitching and paws moving as he stared back at her. That's what Marabet was like. The squirrel. Never still, determined, and *fun!*

Her stomach growled. Pancakes and sausage, she thought as she jumped out of bed. She stopped only long enough to splash some water on her face and pull her hair back in a ribbon before she slipped into shorts and a t-shirt and headed downstairs, the smell of browning sausage drawing her like a magnet.

They were halfway through breakfast when Lilah entered the kitchen. She had dressed casually in slacks and a silk blouse. She was also wearing makeup, but she feared it didn't hide her puffy eyes. With an effort, she rearranged her face into a smile. "Something smells good, Marabet. Is there any left?"

Marabet got up from the table and headed to the oven, where

Bethany had seen her tuck another plate of pancakes. "No appointments this morning?"

Lilah's smile held. "None that can't wait until I eat." She got a fork and knife out of the drawer and took a napkin from the holder. Then she joined them at the table, where Marabet was setting her plate on a hot pad.

"Good morning, Bethany," she said, acknowledging the girl for the first time.

Bethany glanced up and then back down at her plate. "Good morning."

Silence fell as they each began eating.

When the tension in the room had reached the painful level, Lilah said, "What do you have planned today, Marabet?"

"I thought I'd clean the attic," she answered without raising her eyes from her food.

Lilah barely missed a beat. "That reminds me, Bethany," she said, not quite looking at her, "I wanted to tell you it's all right for you to go through the attic if you want. Marabet assures me it's not at all dirty, and she should know," she added with a sideward glance at the housekeeper. "Maybe you could open one of the windows up there and let in some fresh air."

Bethany looked from one woman to the other, then down at her plate. "Okay."

There was another silence. Lilah took another bite. She sipped her coffee. "What other housekeeping chores did you have planned?" she asked Marabet.

"I thought I'd clean the silver and air out the dining room for tonight."

Lilah gave her a sweet smile. "What a nice thought. That will be lovely."

Again silence. She looked at Bethany. "And you? Will you spend some time outside today?"

She knew the words were wrong as they left her mouth, and

the girl's sullen expression confirmed it. "If you want."

"It's—healthy, is all." The words were lame, out of sync, as were all the words she spoke to her. She simply could not talk to the child. It was useless to try.

"Well," she said, pushing back her plate, "I hate to eat and run, but I'm going to do some shopping this morning. I'm thinking of redoing my bedroom, and I thought I'd go get some ideas." She rose and took her plate to the sink.

Marabet's head swiveled around. "Redoing your room? Why?"

"Because it's ugly," Lilah said over her shoulder as she left the room. "I may not be back for lunch."

"Because it's ugly," Marabet grumbled when Lilah was out of earshot. "Like it hasn't been ugly for the last thirty years. Finally she notices," she added, picking up her plate and heading for the sink.

Bethany followed her. "Is it really ugly?"

"Not ugly," she muttered. "It's—boring. Just plain boring."

"The rest of the house isn't boring. It's pretty," Bethany said, looking around her.

"Oh, sure. The Germ hired a decorator to do the downstairs because someone might see it. He personally handpicked all the things for their rooms upstairs."

"The germ?"

"Never mind. Forget I said that."

After a minute, Bethany ventured, "My rooms are pretty."

Marabet's face softened. "That's because your mother redecorated those rooms not long before she left for college." She stared out the kitchen window as she rinsed off the plates and handed them to Bethany to put in the dishwasher.

Bethany thought of the rooms, done in a muted blue and green plaid, with splashes of red and yellow here and there. Yes, she decided, the rooms looked like something her mother would like. She grabbed a dishrag and wiped off the breakfast table.

"So, what's next," she asked, draping the cloth over the divider between the two sinks.

Marabet made a face. "Well, I guess since I opened my big mouth, I'd better clean the silver."

"Can I help?"

"It's not much fun. Don't you have something you'd rather be doing?"

Bethany's eyes went involuntarily to the ceiling, then quickly back to Marabet. "Maybe later. I'll help you now if you want me to."

Marabet draped an arm around Bethany's shoulders, giving her a tiny squeeze before herding her into the dining room. "I won't turn down the help, and that's a fact. There's not much I hate like I hate cleaning musty old silver."

Lilah pulled the car into an empty space in the Phipps Plaza parking deck. There was a bounce in her walk that even Marabet and Bethany couldn't entirely eliminate. She had awakened this morning determined not to spend another night looking at that room. Once her eyes had been opened to how ugly it was, she almost couldn't wait until morning to begin changing it. She didn't want to hire a decorator. This was something she wanted to do herself. She wouldn't do it all in one day, of course. It would take weeks of intense shopping. Maybe longer because she was unaccustomed to shopping for household goods, but she would keep at it until she was satisfied. She was not hiding, she told herself as she made her way into Lord & Taylor and headed toward the home furnishings department. She was doing something constructive.

She saw what she wanted almost the minute she walked into the department. It was in one of the partitioned rooms where they displayed coordinates. The half-size bed was covered with a puffy quilt sporting subtle yellow and blue flowers on a white background. Matching curtains hung at the fake window, backed by sheers of a blue so pale it was almost white. Solid throw pillows that picked up the colors in the quilt were tossed artfully on the bed, which was turned back to display bed linens of buttery yellow. Lilah could imagine slipping between the cool sheets after her bath, pulling the coverlet up to her chin on chilly nights.

As she walked around to view it from another angle, a saleswoman walked up. Dressed in black with a single strand of pearls at her throat and high heels on her feet, she could have been a model. Lilah winced at the thought of what her feet must feel like after a day at work.

"Pretty, isn't it?" the saleswoman asked, admiring the room. "Fresh as spring."

Lilah smiled at her. "You're exactly right. It looks like spring."

"It would look cool all summer. The quilt is featherweight, of course. Comfortable even in August."

"I'll take it," Lilah said, smiling.

"The quilt?"

"All of it."

"All?" The saleswoman looked back at the display. "The pillows and sheets?"

"And the drapes and sheers, too. All of it," she repeated, snapping open her purse and pulling her charge card out of her wallet. "Queen-size bedding and eight floor-to-ceiling curtain panels."

The saleswoman beamed. "Of course. I'll just make sure we have it all in stock and get you a total," she said, taking the charge card and glancing down at it. "Can I get you some coffee while you wait, Mrs. Kimball?"

Twenty minutes later, receipt in hand, Lilah headed down the escalator feeling even lighter than when she came in. Quite cheerful, in fact. The bedroom ensemble would be delivered by four o'clock, the bubbling saleswoman had assured her. Lilah was certain she must work on commission, and she hoped she had made good money off the sale. It would help pay for the podiatrist she was going to need later on.

She was almost to the door when she heard her name. She turned and couldn't stifle a groan as she saw Melba Turnbull bearing down on her. She had known Melba for twenty years and disliked her for most of them. There was nothing evil about the woman. She was probably fairly typical for an aging southern belle of her background. Her appearance certainly was typical: a bit overweight, overdressed, with overly styled hair of an improbable blonde color that had all the flexibility of a helmet. Lilah found the combination distasteful, but she managed to keep it out of her face.

"Lilah, *dear!*" Melba took her hands and squeezed them. "I'm so very glad I ran into you. I've *so* wanted to call you." Her voice oozed southern, her manner, insincerity. She glanced at her watch. "I have just enough time. Let's go get us some coffee."

"I—"

"Now, don't you even think of saying no," Melba said, taking her arm and pulling her toward the restaurant. "You've turned into such a recluse these last few years! *Everyone* has been asking what's become of you." Her eyebrows snapped together. "And then when I *heard!*" She barged into the restaurant, ignoring the hostess and taking a table near the door. "Two coffees," she said, as the hostess caught up with them. "Nothing to eat."

The hostess sighed and took back the menus she had laid on the table. "Certainly, ma'am," she said.

Melba once again captured Lilah's hand, her face a study in sympathy. "Why didn't you call? That's what friends are for, you know. For times like these."

"What are you talking about?" Lilah said, reaching for the

sugar bowl as an excuse to take back her hand.

"Your precious *Elizabeth!* That's what I'm talking about. We were all simply devastated. None of us had any idea. We still wouldn't if Donnie—you know, Caroline's youngest—if he hadn't packed Caroline's birthday gift with newspaper. He's still at school. UGA in Athens, you know. On his third major. He'll probably still be a junior when he's forty-five. At least that's his plan, if you ask me. But never mind about him," she said, waving the subject away. "Caroline smoothed out the paper to save it for recycling. You know she's an absolute fanatic about the environment, like the little bit of paper she recycles is going to save some rain forest—" She gave a short laugh, then frowned. "And there it was in the obituaries. Well, it took her a minute. What caught her eye was your name, you know. She didn't know Elizabeth's married name. Survived by her mother, Lilah Kimball, and her daughter, whatever her name is. Anyway, Caroline simply couldn't believe it! The paper was over two months old then and we hadn't heard word one about it. How terrible for you, you poor darling!"

She caught Lilah's hand again and squeezed it. "How you must be suffering!" Then, "Was she divorced? It didn't mention a husband."

Lilah felt exposed, humiliated and angry at the same time, incensed at Melba's morbid curiosity about the husband, the pretense of sympathy. She retracted her hand. "No, Melba. Elizabeth was a widow," she said, her voice icy.

Melba's eyes widened. "Then the child, the daughter. Oh, the poor *dear.* An orphan. What will become of her now?"

"Bethany is staying with me for the time being."

"Bethany," Melba breathed out. "Isn't that just the sweetest name? It must be such a comfort having her there." She tasted her coffee and made a face. "Why can't you ever get decent coffee in one of these places?" She pushed her cup away. "It's simply tragic. There's nothing as terrible as losing a child."

"She was thirty-two."

"Still, the parent shouldn't be burying the child. It should be the other way around, don't you know. Poor *Lilah,* and that poor little orphan!" She shook her head sadly, glancing over Lilah's shoulder at the wall clock. "Oh, but look at the time!" She jumped to her feet and dropped a dollar bill on the table. "I'm late again, but there's never enough time, is there? It was so wonderful to see you, darling. You really must get out. It's the best thing, you know. And we'd all love to meet—uh?"

"Bethany," Lilah said through clenched teeth.

"Of course. Bethany. Sweet." She leaned down and kissed the air beside Lilah's cheek. "You call me if you need anything, you hear now? I'm always there for you." Giving Lilah's hand a final pat, she was gone.

Lilah sat for another minute, staring down into her cup, until the hostess came over. "Can I get you anything else, ma'am?"

Lilah looked up at her, startled. "Oh. No. Thank you." She reached into her purse and pulled out a five-dollar bill, dropping it beside Melba's single.

But I didn't, she thought as she stared into her cold coffee, her elation pricked like a balloon. *I didn't bury my child.*

With the impact that robbed Lilah of her breath, the memory of that first phone call from Felicity Greenlea flooded her consciousness.

Lilah hung up the phone and turned to Marabet, who was standing at the door. "That was a woman with social services. She said there was an accident." Lilah hesitated a minute before adding, "Elizabeth was killed."

Marabet reached out and grabbed the doorframe. "Oh, dear God, no!"

It was a moment before Lilah could continue. "There's more," she related in a flat voice. "It seems her husband died two years ago." She paused. "And—there's a child."

Marabet straightened. "A child?"

Lilah nodded. "A girl. Twelve years old. Apparently she has nowhere to live." With that, Lilah rose from the chair and left the room. It was much later, when she was at the dressing table brushing her hair, that she heard a tap on her door.

"Do you want to talk about it?"

Lilah looked at her in the dresser mirror. "There's nothing to talk about."

Marabet's voice rose half an octave. "Your daughter's dead, and there's nothing to talk about?"

Lilah's words came out stilted. "Elizabeth has been dead to me for many years."

"Oh, bullshit!"

Lilah threw her brush down on the dresser. "That's enough!"

Marabet backed out of the room, slamming the door. A moment later, she flung it open again. "What about your granddaughter?" she demanded. "Are you just going to pretend she doesn't exist?"

Just that quickly, Lilah was back in control. "I'm not going to pretend anything. I told the social worker I'd call her in a few days and make an appointment to discuss the child and what's to be done with her."

"What's to be d-done with her?" Marabet sputtered. She opened her mouth and closed it a number of times before she finally said, "Maybe you can put her in a flour sack and drown her in the river," and slammed out of the room again.

Still later when Lilah was in the kitchen making tea, Marabet came out of her room. "What kind of accident?"

Lilah closed her eyes for a moment, hanging her head. Then she put the teapot on the counter and turned to face Marabet, folding her arms in front of her. "An automobile accident."

"What happened?"

"I didn't ask for particulars."

"When?"

"Three months ago."

"Three months ago? Did someone bury her?"

Lilah fought the urge to scream. She took a deep breath. "Yes. A neighbor who was a close friend arranged the funeral."

"And you weren't invited."

"Marabet, please don't make this worse than it already is."

Marabet stared at her for a long time as tears slipped down her cheeks. "I don't think that's possible."

"Can I get you anything else, ma'am?"

Lilah looked up to see the waitress regarding her curiously. At the same instant, she realized her cheeks were damp. "No. Thank you," she said, dabbing her face with her napkin. "There's nothing you can get me. Nothing at all."

Bethany stood at the top of the stairs, looking around her. The attic was huge. It spanned the length of the house and was divided into rooms with a wooden framework but no walls. She glanced over her shoulder down the stairs. Even though they had told her it was all right to look around, she still felt like a trespasser, like any minute a hand would descend on her shoulder and she'd be hauled off to jail for being there. In the end, the pull of her mother's history won out. Bethany knew so little about it. Not that her mother had outright refused to talk about it. She just postponed or sidestepped those conversations. Her mother had been very good at avoiding things that bothered her.

She switched on the overhead light and moved into the area she'd begun to explore the day before, the one where she'd found the picture of her mother. There were boxes stacked head high. The first two she looked in were full of books and those big old records people used to play. It was in the third box that she'd found the picture, along with a bunch of photo albums, all carefully preserved in tissue paper and tied with a string. Once she had unwrapped the top picture and came face to face with her mother's bright smile, she'd been unable to look further. Now she opened the flaps with determination and looked inside.

There were more pictures. She pulled them out and stacked them around her, curling her legs under her as she gingerly unwrapped one after another. Looking at the pictures propped up around her in a makeshift gallery, she felt an ache deep in her chest. They didn't overwhelm her as the first one had, maybe because she hadn't come on them unexpectedly. In each photo, the camera had caught the girl who had grown up to be her mother. She had the halo of golden curls and a less formed version of her mother's elegant features. She had the smile trembling with life and the eyes that seemed to sparkle even in the black and white photographs. In one picture she was standing beside a little horse—a Shetland, Bethany remembered hearing them called. In another, she was dressed in a pink tutu and balanced precariously on her toes. The pride of that little ballerina glowed out of the frame. There were lots of pictures of her at the piano, her posture straight as she played, oblivious to the camera.

There were several with a boy. He looked older than her, and he looked pouty and maybe a little mean. Bethany remembered her mother telling her about an older brother. She'd dismissed him with, "We were oil and water. We never could stay in a room together for more than five minutes." Bethany, in those lonely moments that every only child knows, had thought that if she had a brother, she'd make an effort to get along with him. The boy was a head taller than her mother in the pictures, his hair darker and straight. The photographs were posed and stiff. "My uncle," she murmured, looking at each photo and trying without success to feel some kinship.

Under the photos were four vinyl-covered school yearbooks. Bethany flipped through each one, finding her mother's class picture and then reading the signatures from her classmates with short messages like, "Remember Mr. Franklin? He never knew it was us!" and "Your notes made Algebra fun!" The yearbooks with all their notes made Bethany angry. Her mother should have been here with her to go through these so she could explain away the mystery of the words. Now they would always be a mystery. Unexplained, unshared, like too many things.

By the time she had gone through all the yearbooks, the sun was over the house and peeking in the west windows. The attic caught that heat and held it. Bethany thought about opening a window, but then her stubborn streak kicked in. There was also a big fan in one of the end windows, but the same orneriness prevented her from turning it on.

She put the yearbooks back in the box and pushed it against the wall. Then she pulled out another and looked inside. Her breath caught in her throat when she realized what she was looking at. Diaries. Half a dozen diaries. She reached in and pulled one out, then dropped it back in the box guiltily when she heard the attic door open. She exhaled in relief when Marabet stepped into the room.

"I figured you'd be up here. Lord, child," she said, fanning herself, "it's an oven in here. Why didn't you turn on the fan?"

"I didn't notice," Bethany answered, lying only a little.

"Didn't notice! It's a fair wonder you didn't expire!" She crossed to the window and flipped a switch on the wall next to the fan, which roared to life. "There. Now it will be cooler when you come back up. Ready for a bite of lunch?"

Bethany closed the flaps on the box with the diaries, but left it where it was. "Sure."

Marabet came back and looked down at the pictures Bethany had arranged around her, her face softening. "Aren't they just wonderful?" When Bethany nodded, she said, "You should put some of them in your room. Then you'd have her all around you."

Bethany looked toward the door. "She wouldn't—I mean, it would be okay?"

"Of course it would be okay. What could be wrong with putting pictures of your mama around?"

"There aren't any anywhere else in the house."

"Well, you're wrong there," Marabet said, starting for the door. "I have lots of them in my room. I'll show you after lunch."

Stepping into Marabet's room was like stepping into another house altogether. It was warm and lived in, from the braided rug on the floor to the pale flowered wallpaper covering three walls of the sitting room. The furniture looked comfortable and worn. Along one wall, a bookcase was stuffed with videos and statuettes and stuff. All around the room were framed photographs. "See what I mean?" Marabet asked, walking over to the bookcase. "I like memories I can touch," she explained, picking up one of the pictures.

Bethany followed her in and looked down at the picture she was holding. Here her mother was dressed in a gold cap and gown, her smile brighter than the sunlit day on which it was taken. "Her high school graduation picture," Marabet said unnecessarily. "I didn't get a college graduation picture."

"I have one," Bethany blurted out. Then, "In Athens."

"Maybe we can get me a copy made of it. I sure would like that."

There were half a dozen other framed photographs of her mother around the room, some duplicates of the ones Bethany had found in the attic. She reached over and picked up a black and white picture of two girls standing beside a swimming pool, grinning broadly at the camera. One was tall, with flowing dark hair and long legs. The other was short, with cropped hair and a square figure the bathing suit did nothing to enhance. "Who's this?"

Marabet chuckled. "That's your granny and me," she answered, shaking her head. "Weren't we a sight? Don't know why I keep that old thing around."

"It's—cool," Bethany said, putting it back on the shelf.

"It was cool all right. Darn near froze that day. It was mid-April and couldn't have been sixty degrees out. Lilah had a new swimsuit and wanted a picture in it, so she dragged me over to pose with her. Mutt and Jeff, we were. I looked like a fireplug, straight up and down with arms and legs sticking out. Always told Lilah she just kept me around to make her look better by contrast." When Bethany squirmed uncomfortably, Marabet poked her with an elbow, "That was a joke, child."

"Oh." Bethany grinned and looked at the photo again. "She was pretty."

"She sure was. As dark as Elizabeth was light. Both pretty women—" She looked at the girl. "Like you."

"Me!" Bethany blushed. "I don't look like either of them."

"No you don't, but you're pretty all the same."

Unable to think of anything to say, Bethany picked up another photograph, this one of Elizabeth and a tall young man.

"Her and her brother, Charles."

"What's he like?"

Marabet hesitated before answering. "You'll find out tonight. He's coming to dinner."

"He is?"

"He and his wife, Lesa, your aunt," she said, making a face. "She's pretty harmless. Doesn't say a word to anyone. Not that he'd let her. Likes to hear himself talk." When Bethany grinned, she added, "He's a lot like his father was. Jam full of opinions."

"You don't like him?"

Marabet turned toward the door. "It's not for me to like or dislike him. He's Lilah's son and your uncle. Whatever else he might be is no concern of mine."

Bethany hesitated a second before following her, thinking that, her concern or not, Marabet definitely didn't like him.

Lilah couldn't bear to come home in the black mood that had descended on her after her run-in with Melba. Instead, she stopped by a paint store to look at wall colors. Then she'd spent several hours in a flooring showroom choosing new bedroom carpet and arranging for its installation. Her last stop was Beverly Hall Interiors, where she looked at furniture without making any final decisions. The earlier sense of euphoria hadn't returned, but she was very nearly in good humor by the time she pulled into the driveway at four-thirty.

When she came into the hall, Marabet was halfway up the stairs, dragging the bagged quilt behind her. "Let me help you," she said, grabbing more bags.

Marabet squinted down at her. "I thought you were just going to get ideas," she huffed. "Pretty heavy ideas."

"I did get ideas," Lilah said, taking the bag from her. "I also got some new bed linen."

"And pillows. And who knows what else."

"I know what else." Lilah smiled at her. "Wait until you see. They're really pretty."

"I hope they're prettier than pretty. I got a look at the bill. Your son is going to have a stroke when he sees it."

Lilah ignored her. They crossed the sitting room and went into the bedroom. Lilah unzipped the bag, pulling out the quilt and laying it over the bed for effect. Then she turned to Marabet. "What do you think?"

A wide smile spread over Marabet's face. "I think it's like a breath of fresh air."

"Isn't it? And look at this." She pulled the throw pillows out of another bag and tossed them against the head of the bed. "Isn't it wonderful?"

Marabet nodded. "It's an improvement for sure," she looked around the room, "but it doesn't look like it belongs in here."

"I know," Lilah said. She grabbed the bag with the sheets. Ripping them open, she said, "Once I get the walls painted and the new carpet installed—"

"New carpet?"

Lilah looked over at her. "Yes, new carpet. Why not?"

Marabet stepped back. "No reason in the world. You just never bothered much with things like that before."

"I know," Lilah said, sitting down on the new comforter and running her hand across it, "and I have to wonder why. I love pretty things."

Marabet took the sheets out of her hands. "Maybe you forgot for a while what you really do love."

Lilah looked at her without speaking.

"Let me wash these for you before I put them on the bed," Marabet said, turning away. "We don't want you breaking out from fabric dyes."

Lilah stood and reached for the sheets. "I'll wash them myself. You have a dinner to prepare."

"Don't remind me."

That caused a little smile, a few rays of sunshine through the clouds. "Bethany knows they're coming?"

"I told her, but not what to expect. Let her find out for herself she's going to be on display like some freak at a side show."

"It won't be that bad," Lilah said as they left the room and started down the stairs.

Marabet gave her a sidewise look. "You think Master Charles is going to be disposed to like her?"

"Well . . ."

"He won't. He's just coming to size up the competition."

"The competition? What in the world are you talking about?"

Marabet followed her into the kitchen and then down the basement stairs to the laundry room. "You really don't see it, do you?" she asked, measuring detergent into the washing machine.

"Apparently not."

She turned to Lilah. "Charles doesn't want to share. He never did. Not anything. That's why he hated Elizabeth so much—"

"He didn't hate—"

"All right. Dislike. Words, that's all they are. That's why he never tried to get you to like Lesa, and why do you think he hates me so much? All right, dislikes," she corrected, waving her hand in the air. "Did you ever wonder about that?"

"Well, yes, but I . . ." Her voice trailed off. After a minute, she shook her head. "Surely you're wrong. I know Charles is a little difficult." She ignored Marabet's snort. "But I can't believe that he's that way because of some infantile jealousy."

"There's nothing infantile about it. It's grown up jealousy. He was happy as a clam when Elizabeth left. Never even pretended he wasn't. So don't expect him to welcome his long lost niece with open arms. He's only coming here to size Bethany up, the way he'd size up the threat of a gorilla about to be let out of a cage at the zoo."

"Oh, that's ridiculous. I don't believe it for a minute."

"Good." Marabet took the sheets from her and stuffed them into the washer. "Then it won't make you uncomfortable, but I bet you it'll make Bethany plenty uncomfortable."

As Lila watched, Bethany squirmed in her seat. She had to wonder how much longer the child could sit there and pretend to be interested in what they were saying. Or what Charles was saying, she amended. He was monopolizing the conversation.

He usually did, she suddenly realized, only usually she didn't mind. It saved her the trouble of keeping it going. Tonight, though, his monologue was wearing thin even on her, with his ceaseless chatter about investments and tax shelters and all of his important clients. It was almost as if he were showing off for the girl—or was that just the extension of the idea Marabet had planted in her head?

When he and Lesa arrived, he looked Bethany over as if she were a lab experiment gone badly, without a hint of a smile or any effort to shake her hand. "So you're Bethany," he said. That was it. Lilah thought she had taught him better manners than that. He immediately launched into a monologue about the IRS and audits his clients were undergoing—subjects certain to be of no interest to a twelve-year-old. Once in a while, Lilah had caught him glancing at Bethany out of the corner of his eye, looks that might suggest she had something smudged on her face.

Lesa had been more polite, if only with her silence. She smiled at Bethany and murmured something Lilah hadn't caught before she scuttled over to the sofa and sat down.

Lilah caught herself seeing Lesa through Bethany's eyes: ordinary, not tall or short or fat—well, maybe a little thick around the hips, as Marabet loved to point out. Brown hair and narrow face, she looked like a portrait out of a history book: sepia, colorless and meek, and totally lacking in animation, with her legs crossed at the ankle and her hands folded in her lap. Not for the first time, Lilah wondered what Charles saw in her, although observing him tonight she might wonder the opposite as well.

Lesa was taking peeks at Bethany, but her observation didn't appear critical. She looked curious, but as if she thought curious wasn't polite.

There was a break in the talk as Charles went to fix himself another drink. To Lila's surprise, Lesa looked over at Bethany. "Are you all settled in now?" she asked softly.

Bethany shrugged. "Pretty much."

"You lived in Athens, didn't you?" When Bethany nodded, she said, "I went to school at the University of Georgia. It's a wonderful school."

"That was long ago and far away, my dear," Charles put in, returning to his spot at the mantel, "and I think you bandy the word wonderful around pretty loosely. They have a decent accounting program and maybe one or two others that are passable, but for the most part it's your typical southern school. More sound than substance." He turned back to Lilah. "Speaking of substance, mother, I want to get with you next week about the Warren Harris Building. I still think that would be an excellent investment for you. The AJC is calling it a prime development."

Lilah felt a stab of impatience. Now Lesa might not speak again for another six years, and she'd found herself curious to hear what she would say. "All right, Charles," she said grudgingly, glancing at her watch, "but right now let's have dinner."

As they moved into the dining room, Bethany seemed to hang back. She stood at the table until Lilah motioned her to a chair. There were only four of them at a table for ten, so they sat clustered around one end. Charles sat next to Lilah, who was at the head of the table, while Bethany sat next to Lesa on the other side. It didn't escape Lilah's notice that Bethany sat as far away from her as possible.

The salads were already on the table. Lilah noticed that the silver gleamed, even in the dim light. Bethany seemed intimidated by the amount of cutlery on the table and watched Lesa to see which fork she picked up before imitating her. She must not be used to formal dinners.

Charles was talking about the Dow Jones or something

equally stimulating now, talking only to Lilah and ignoring the others as if they weren't at the table. Then Bethany surprised her by leaning over slightly toward Lesa, saying, "I think UGA is wonderful, too. My father was a professor there."

Lesa visibly brightened. "Was he?" she asked softly. "How wonderful for you. What did he teach?"

"History. Western Civ."

"I'll bet you're good at history, then."

"I wish," Bethany answered. "I'm okay at early history, but when you get up around the First World War, I just lose it."

"My downfall was American History."

"My dad said that's because it's over-taught. He said they spend as much time on American history from the colonies to the Civil War as they do on the history of civilization from prehistory to the world wars."

"I never thought of it quite like that . . ." Lesa's voice trailed off as she realized she was the only one in the room speaking. She glanced at her husband.

"Go on, Lesa," Charles said, his voice overloud. "Give us your take on history."

Lesa's features tightened as she flushed.

Lilah thought she saw a flash of anger—belligerence?—something cross Bethany face. "We were talking about *teaching* history," the girl said, raising her chin. "Do you think American history is over-taught?"

Charles regarded her steadily. "Actually, I never thought about it. I mean, really, who cares?"

He turned back to his mother, but before he could speak, Marabet entered the room from the kitchen, pushing a wheeled cart. The smell of lamb followed her in and wrapped itself around Lilah's head. She didn't like lamb. Charles liked lamb, which was why she had suggested it. Now she wished she'd made another choice. Marabet pushed the cart to the table and placed the serving dishes in the center. There were oven browned potatoes, too, and asparagus and corn. At least she could enjoy the rest of it—or use it to hide the lamb chop.

"This looks wonderful, Marabet," Lilah said as Marabet started out of the room.

"I thought you'd want to serve yourselves." There was a challenge to her words.

"That will be fine. Thank you."

When Marabet nodded and left the room, it looked like it was all Bethany could do not to jump up and run after her. Were they developing a relationship? Lilah hoped not. It would be so much more difficult for her when the child left.

Charles took each of their plates and put food on them. Even that familiarity seemed sinister now, as if he were attempting to control what they ate. Marabet had definitely planted a garden of unhealthy ideas in her head. Still, Lilah accepted her plate graciously, and fell to cutting her lamb chop into tiny, easy to hide bites.

For a few minutes, no one spoke. Then Charles said, "This is almost edible, mother. Is Marabet taking cooking lessons?"

"Marabet is an excellent cook," Lilah answered, her voice cool. She turned to Lesa. "I didn't realize you went to the University of Georgia, Lesa. What was your major?"

Lesa swallowed, choked a little, and then swallowed again. "I majored in elementary education," she finally managed to get out.

"A useless major," Charles interjected. "Teaching is one of the worst paying professions there is."

Lilah saw the color creep up Lesa's neck and face. She felt like throttling her son. What in the world was the matter with him? Or was he always this way?

She was about to make some kind of remark when Lesa put down her fork and said, "It's a good and rewarding profession, but you're right. It doesn't pay well. It doesn't matter anyway, since you don't want me to work," she said, darting a glance at him.

"Why in the world would you?" Charles asked, spearing a bite of lamb. "It's not like we need the money, and you have plenty to keep you busy. I might add that this is hardly a conversation we need to be having at my mother's dinner table." He stared at her until she looked down at her plate.

It could have been his father speaking, so familiar was the tone of voice, the facial expression. Lilah felt a sharp stab of kinship with the woman and wondered what she might be like in a one-on-one situation. Maybe she'd make an effort to find out.

Conversation lagged then. Charles and Lesa left immediately after dinner. Bethany disappeared upstairs. Lilah helped Marabet with the dishes, but even Marabet seemed subdued. Had she heard the fiasco in the dining room? Probably, Lilah decided. Marabet didn't miss much.

In the end, she headed up the stairs to her room feeling unsettled by Charles behavior, by Lesa's ready acceptance of it, by Bethany witnessing it, and by her own inability to salvage the situation somehow. She crossed her sitting room and opened the door to her bedroom. She stopped then and stared, a little smile tugging at her mouth.

She'd forgotten all about it. It looked just as bright and cheerful as it had in the store. Marabet had made the bed with the new linens and comforter, which was turned down now and inviting her to climb under its softness. The pillows were plump in their new shams, and throw pillows marched across the head of the bed like little square soldiers on parade. The curtains hung in the windows, close enough to the right size—if they lowered the rods an inch, they would be perfect—and all that beige and brown was gone. In the garbage, for all Lilah cared.

She felt giddy suddenly, light, as if the cheerfulness of the flowers had seeped into the center of her being. The next instant, she felt guilty, ashamed that such a trivial thing as bed linen could elevate her mood. Then guilt gave way to flowers, and her smile widened. She crossed to the closet with a lighter step, unbuttoning her shirt as she went. She opened the door and reached in for a hanger—and stopped. Her smile grew even wider as she grabbed a handful of clothes and moved them to the other side of the closet. Then another, and another. She spread the clothes out so that both sides appeared equally full. Satisfied for the moment, she undressed and wrapped herself in her robe, heading for the bathroom and a long soak.

She was climbing out of the tub when she heard a tiny sound from somewhere above her. From the attic, it had to be. She toweled herself quickly and slipped back into her robe. As she stepped into the hallway, she saw Bethany coming down the attic stairs with several books clutched to her. The girl stopped short, her mouth open, when she saw Lilah.

"I thought I heard a noise in the attic."

"I'm sorry. I tried to be quiet."

"No, I just wondered who was up there. What were you doing?"

"Getting something to read."

"In the attic?"

Bethany nodded.

Lilah waited a moment for her to go on. She didn't. "Well—don't stay up too late."

"Are you setting a bedtime for me?" Bethany asked, her chin jutting in the air.

Lilah gritted her teeth. "No," she said shortly. "I am not setting a bedtime. Just don't stay up all night. It isn't healthy."

"All right," Bethany said. She turned and walked down the hall and into her room.

Lilah walked back into her own room, shutting the door behind her. What was it about that child that made it impossible to communicate? Not that it mattered, since the girl would only be there a short time. It was frustrating, though. Other people seemed able to talk to her. She'd heard her talking with Marabet easily and freely. Even Lesa, who didn't talk to anyone, had been able to chat with her at dinner, but Lilah couldn't seem to say a word to her that didn't inspire a negative reaction. Nothing she said was taken in the vein in which it was intended. They had no words, no common language with which to open and sustain a conversation, and Lilah could see no way to span that chasm. That was exactly what she intended to tell that social worker.

Chapter 6

Lilah was just coming out of her room when Marabet answered the door. She could hear her say, "Miss Greenlea, I'm so glad you've come. Mrs. Kimball will be down shortly. Come on into the living room and sit down. Would you like some coffee? Bethany's upstairs. She's doing really well. Settling in nicely. Should I get her, or do you want to talk to Mrs. Kimball first?"

"Why don't I talk to Mrs. Kimball first," Felicity answered. Then their voices faded as they moved into the living room.

Lilah gave them a minute, then she started down the stairs.

"Mrs. Kimball." Felicity extended her hand when Lilah entered.

Lilah gestured to the chair. "Please sit down. I believe Marabet is bringing coffee?" She sank into the chair across from her.

"Yes. Your message said it was important?"

"Not so important that we can't wait for our coffee."

Felicity seemed at a loss for words. Lilah couldn't blame her. She knew her message had been cryptic, but she didn't believe in putting off unpleasant tasks.

"Marabet seems like a remarkable woman," Felicity said finally.

Lilah smiled. "Marabet is one of a kind."

"Has she been with you long?"

"Quite a while," Lilah answered. "I've actually known her since we were girls."

"That's—" Felicity broke off as Marabet entered the room

carrying a tray in both hands, laden with a coffee service and a platter overloaded with cookies.

"Here you go," Marabet said, pouring the cups of coffee. "You help yourself to some cookies. I baked them just a little while ago."

Lilah took one of the cups of coffee and handed it to Felicity. "Thank you, Marabet. They look wonderful."

Marabet walked around behind Lilah's chair. "That's all we need right now, Marabet. Thank you."

"You're welcome."

Lilah glanced over her shoulder. "Why don't you close the door on your way out."

Marabet stiffened. "Yes, ma'am."

Lilah sighed inwardly. Another offense to add to the list. They were piling up quite nicely. She held out the plate of cookies to Felicity. "Please. Won't you try one?" She put several cookies on a plate and handed it to her. "Marabet is an excellent cook."

"Bethany mentioned that. It's a wonder you're able to stay so slim."

"I can tell you it's not due to my sensible eating habits," Lilah said, taking a cookie and nibbling on it. "I'm afraid I have a weakness for sweets, and Marabet caters to it shamelessly." She took a sip of coffee. "I know you'll want to talk to Bethany, but I thought we should talk first."

"Where is Bethany?"

"I imagine she's either in her room or in the attic. I'm afraid she spends much of each day up there going through boxes packed with my daughter's things."

"I'm sure it's a comfort for her to have her mother's things around her."

Lilah didn't miss the emphasis she laid on the word "mother." Had she been talking to Marabet?

"Most of their possessions are still in the house in Athens," Felicity said. "It didn't seem wise to make any arrangements until we knew where Bethany was going to be living."

"The house," Lilah repeated.

"Yes. They had a small house. There's furniture, and of course, your daughter's clothes and a lot of Bethany's things. The bank has been good enough to work with us to keep the house intact until disposition could be made. We are aware from papers we found at the house that your daughter owed no money other than the mortgage. She had a car, but it was paid for and, well, the accident . . ."

Lilah winced at the visual image.

"There wasn't a lot of savings, but enough to pay the mortgage for several months. As you're her nearest living relative, you will probably be called on to decide about that, and the furniture. Of course, Bethany will want to keep a lot of personal items, pictures, clothes, but we haven't gotten that far yet."

Lilah was nodding. "I see. If you need additional money to maintain the house until Bethany is settled, please let me know. I can have my attorney make arrangements."

Felicity put the cookie down on the plate. "How is Bethany doing? Your housekeeper said she's settled in."

"I'm afraid Marabet said that because it's what she wants to believe." She sat back in the chair, resting her elbows on the chair arms. "The fact is that Bethany isn't happy here. Oh, she enjoys looking through—Elizabeth's things, but she keeps to herself most of the time. As I said, she's either in the attic or in her room."

"Maybe we could get her involved in some summer activities."

Lilah felt a jab of impatience. "It's more than that. The girl dislikes me, and I find that I can't feel any kinship with her. We barely speak, and neither of us seems equal to the effort. Everything I say angers her, and her entire attitude irritates me. She's as much a stranger to me after a week as she was the first night in the house."

"There are family counseling programs—"

"I don't want family counseling, Miss Greenlea," Lilah said sharply, then caught herself. "I am telling you why this situation won't work. When you came here a week ago, you asked if I would care for Bethany for a short time while you searched for relatives where she might be placed permanently. I agreed to that and to nothing more. I'm keeping my end of the bargain. I trust that you will keep yours as well." She stood. "Now I'll have Marabet send Bethany to you."

Felicity jumped to her feet. "I'd like to see you both together if possible."

Lilah stopped in mid-stride. "All right," she said without turning.

The living room door opened before she reached it.

"I'll go fetch her," Marabet said.

Lilah shook her head. Then she came back into the room and sat on the edge of the chair, tense and silent.

Bethany came into the room with Marabet right behind her. "There's some cookies there, honey. Do you want some milk?"

"No thanks, Marabet. I'm still stuffed from lunch."

Bethany stole a glance at her grandmother, her face wooden. Then she looked at Felicity. "Hi." She dropped down on the sofa.

"Hi, yourself," Felicity said with a smile. "How are you doing?"

Bethany looked over at Marabet, who was hovering in the background again, then at Lilah. "I'm okay."

"Just okay?" Felicity asked gently.

Bethany looked down at the carpet. "I'm fine."

Felicity nodded. "That's good. Your grandmother tells me you've been going through some of your mother's things in the attic."

Bethany's head snapped up. "They said I could," she answered, glaring accusingly at Lilah.

"I'm sure they did," Felicity said. "Do you and your grandmother look through them together?"

"No."

Felicity looked at Lilah before turning back to Bethany. "I think it's wonderful that they're here for you to look through. Have you found anything interesting?"

Bethany shrugged. She resumed her study of the carpet. "Oh, you know. Yearbooks and stuff like that. Pictures."

A long silence. "It must be fun to look at that old stuff."

"It's all right."

Bethany thought maybe she'd leave now, but then Felicity said, "Well, why don't you show me the yard?"

Bethany shot a look at her grandmother, then looked back at Felicity. "Why?"

Felicity was smiling. "Because I'd like to see it. Will you?"

Bethany got to her feet. "Okay, but there's nothing interesting out there."

Felicity turned to Lilah Kimball. "Thank you for seeing me, Mrs. Kimball. I'll probably head out after Bethany gives me the tour."

That earned a nod. "Thank you for coming, Miss Greenlea," was the cool reply.

Bethany led the way out the front door. She knew why Felicity wanted to see the stupid yard. It was so she could get her alone, so she could ask her questions without her grandmother there. She didn't say anything as they walked around the house toward the back. Directly off the kitchen, there was a patio of old stone that looked like it had been there forever, and a magnolia tree as tall as the house. A stone path wound through the massive oaks and towering pines. The rich odor of sun-warmed earth and growing things filled the air.

"This is really beautiful," Felicity said. "Does your grandmother have a gardener?"

"I don't know," Bethany answered, kicking at a pinecone.

"She couldn't possibly maintain all this by herself."

Bethany shrugged.

Felicity gestured to a bench built around one of the oaks. "Want to sit?"

"Okay."

"It's nice out here," Felicity said after a minute.

"It's okay. *She's* always telling me to go outside," she said, glancing at the house.

"Who?"

"You know. Her."

"You don't call her Grandmother?"

Bethany shook her head.

"Did she tell you not to?"

"She didn't tell me anything. She doesn't like me. It's okay," Bethany added quickly. "I don't like her either."

"You must have talked some this week."

"Yeah. She told me to go outside."

"Ah. Well, she probably thinks it's healthy. Don't you like to be outside?"

Bethany looked around. "There's nothing to do out here."

"Sure there is. You could watch the squirrels or pull weeds or stretch out in the sun or climb trees."

Bethany stared at her.

"What, you don't like squirrels?"

"I don't climb trees."

"Oh. I see. You probably think you're too old to climb trees."

When Bethany didn't respond, Felicity stood and put her handbag on the bench. "But I'm not," she said, stepping up on the bench seat and hoisting herself onto a low branch, then reaching for a higher one and pulling herself upright.

Bethany stared at her open-mouthed. Then she burst out laughing.

Felicity grinned down at her. "Chicken. I dare you."

"I'm not a chicken," Bethany said, standing and taking a couple of steps backwards, "and I don't take dares."

"Uh-huh," Felicity said, reaching for a higher branch and pulling herself up. "Chicken. Chicken. Cluck, cluck."

Bethany still hesitated for a minute, but the taunt was too much for her. She jumped on the bench and scrambled up the tree like one of the squirrels she watched out her window. In seconds, she was higher than Felicity. Felicity caught up with her and dropped down into a sitting position on a broad limb, laughing as she clutched the branches on either side of her.

Bethany plopped down beside her. They held onto smaller limbs for balance as they sat side by side, swinging their legs. It was cool up in the branches, or as cool as anywhere in Atlanta in June. From up here, Bethany could see in the second floor windows. She felt like a peeping Tom. It was kind of fun. "Where'd you learn to climb trees?" she asked.

Felicity pulled off a leaf and smelled it. "Growing up. I was the oldest of five kids. The only place I could get any peace and quiet was up in the tree in our backyard. An avocado tree," she mused. "I ate a lot of avocados over the years. That was in Florida," she added. "They tell me it's too cold here to grow them." She smelled the leaf again and tucked it behind her ear.

"You're from Florida?"

"Uh-huh. Orlando. My folks moved up here when I was fifteen, and I hated it. I didn't know anybody. I was so lonely I thought I'd die."

Bethany felt another bit of tension melt. "What about your brothers and sisters?"

"Oh, they were more trouble than company."

"I think it'd be nice to have a brother or sister," Bethany said, looking away.

"It has its moments, I guess," Felicity said, pulling off another leaf and tucking it behind Bethany's ear, "but I used to think it would be nice to be an only child."

They grinned at each other.

"So, what else did you find in the attic?"

"What?" Bethany asked in alarm.

"Come on, gal," Felicity said, nudging her with an elbow. "You don't expect me to believe you've spent a week looking at old yearbooks, do you."

Bethany examined Felicity's face minutely. After a minute, she said, "Diaries. I found her old diaries."

"Wow!"

"I know. It's so cool! There must be twenty of them." She thought for a minute. "You don't think it's wrong that I'm reading them, do you?"

"I think it's great that you're reading them. I'd love to get my hands on my mother's old diaries. So what's in them? Juicy stuff?"

"Nah. Nothing like that. I'm only up to when she was a little older than me. I'll tell you what, though, she sure did fight with her dad a lot."

"Did she? About what?"

"Everything. He was always telling her stupid stuff like to act like a lady and remember who she was and stuff like that. She hated it."

"She did?" Felicity swung her legs, then grabbed a limb for balance. "Did she fight with her mom, too?"

"No. There's nothing bad about her in there. Yet."

"How many more do you have to read?"

"A bunch. About ten. Maybe eleven."

"So you sit up in the attic and read the diaries."

"Yeah. I was going to bring them down to my room, but she almost caught me. I'm afraid that if she knows I have them, she'll take them away."

"But she said you could go up there."

"Not at first," Bethany said, snapping off a twig. "She said she didn't want me up there. Then I think Marabet said something to her, because she changed her mind."

A jet soared overhead. After a minute, the sound faded.

"Marabet's pretty cool, huh?"

Bethany broke off a leaf, nodding. "She's great. She told me I don't have to be ashamed of grieving for my mother. She talks about her all the time. At first, it bothered me. I don't know why."

"Maybe because she knew a different Elizabeth than you. A younger Elizabeth, before she was a mom. She shared different stuff with her than you did."

Bethany considered it for a moment. "Yeah. Maybe. Anyway, now it's great. Marabet's room is full of pictures of my mom."

"She must have cared for her a lot."

"She did."

"I'll bet she misses her."

"She does, but she doesn't talk about that. She just talks about the happy stuff, things my mom did when she was a kid."

"Oh yeah? Like what?" Felicity asked, leaning back against a branch.

Lilah stood at the kitchen window and watched them sitting up in the tree together, Bethany animated as she talked; Felicity smiling. She didn't need to hear the words; their faces said it all. She hadn't known what to expect from this visit, but it certainly wasn't this—this camaraderie between the two of them. Obviously, the woman wasn't telling Bethany that it wasn't going to work. Lilah had left it open ended, but she hoped the social worker knew that she was serious. This wasn't working. It could only be harmful to delay the inevitable.

She felt Marabet walk up behind her.

"Looks like they're having a fine time of it up there."

Lilah flinched. "I wanted to ask about dinner."

Marabet turned. "What about it?"

"Have you given any thought to what we're having?"

"Nope."

Lilah wanted to strangle her. "Will you do so? Soon?"

"Yep." As Lilah turned to go, Marabet said, "Maybe if you'd learn how to climb trees, you could talk to her."

Lilah felt her back grow rigid. "I know how to climb trees," she said, "and how to talk. I just choose not to." She started from the room.

"Uh—Lilah?"

Lilah turned, ready for battle. "Yes?"

"Why don't you close the door on your way out."

Chapter 7

The phone rang. A moment later, Marabet's voice came over the intercom. "His highness is on the phone."

"Thank you, Marabet."

Lilah put aside the gardening magazine she'd been looking through. It had been years since she'd done anything in the yard. She had a lawn service that came once a week to mow and edge and trim the shrubs, but there'd been a time when she enjoyed doing the pretty part—laying out flowerbeds, planting annuals. She wasn't sure when she'd quit or why, but then the magazine caught her eye at the pharmacy, and she felt a sudden yen to don her gardening gloves and plant something. She picked up the phone. "Hello, Charles."

"I've been getting bills from all over town, mother," he said without preamble. "What in the devil are you up to?"

"I'm redecorating my bedroom."

The phone hummed. "Why?"

Lilah felt an immediate flash of irritation, which she squelched. "Because it needed it. Why do you ask?"

"Six hundred dollars for a bedspread? Don't you think that's a little excessive?"

She could visualize him sitting in his home office in the high backed leather chair she had given him when his father died, his desk bare except for the tidy stack of her recent bills. She almost smiled. "I don't think so. I liked it, and I can afford it."

"I'm well aware of that, mother, but don't you think you're

going hog wild?"

"Did you get the bill for the carpet yet?" she asked nastily.

"Carpet? You're having carpet installed?"

"Next week. You'll have to come by and see it."

"Your bedroom carpet is in good shape."

"Was. Now it's being replaced. Really, Charles," she said, her impatience coming through in her voice, "I don't know why you're questioning these expenditures."

"As your financial advisor, it's my job to keep your spending on track."

"As my financial advisor, you know that I spend very little except for the upkeep on the house, but your concern is duly noted." She was struck with a thought. "Actually, I'm glad you called. I've been meaning to call Lesa. Is she there?"

"Lesa?" He sounded like he'd never heard the name before. "Why?"

"Because I'd like to talk to her."

"About what?"

"About lunch. Will you tell her I'm on the phone?"

"Are the two of you having lunch?"

"Charles, tell Lesa I'm on the phone."

Lilah arrived at the restaurant a full fifteen minutes early, not knowing what to expect from midtown traffic. She had suggested Bacchanalia for lunch, one of the old converted red brick buildings just off Fourteenth Street, really a warehouse dressed up in party clothes. As she passed the little shops in the entrance lobby, the yeasty smell of freshly baked bread and ground coffee reminded her how long it had been since breakfast. Early as she was, she could see Lesa already seated at the reserved table, sipping her water and trying not to look from side to side. Lilah had felt something akin to pity when she'd invited Lesa to lunch the night before. The woman had been no less stunned than

Charles. "Um . . . certainly . . . if you want to. Is—uh—anything wrong?"

"No, nothing's wrong. I just thought it would be nice if we could meet and chat. Tomorrow at noon?"

Lesa's acceptance had been fraught with suspicion, and Lilah couldn't blame her. They'd shared very few social occasions since the wedding six years ago, other than the occasional dinner and the dutiful Thanksgiving and Christmas visits. Of course at those, Charles was ever present

"I hope you haven't been waiting long," Lilah said with a smile as the waiter seated her and handed her a menu.

"No. Not at all. I'm always a little early," Lesa said with a nervous laugh. "I hate being late, so I get places early and then I don't have to worry about it. Charles says I worry too much."

So Charles was already at the table with them. "I'm the same way," Lilah said. "I've always looked on that as being considerate." She looked at the waiter. "I'd like a glass of white wine. Sauvignon Blanc, if you have it. Would you like a drink, Lesa?" she asked, turning to her daughter-in-law.

"I'd like the same thing. Please."

Lilah unfolded the napkin and spread it across her lap. "Have you had lunch here before?"

"No, I—no."

Lilah looked down at the menu. It could be a very long lunch. "I can recommend the salmon, and the veal is excellent. I haven't had the shrimp, but I imagine everything they serve here is delicious."

They studied their menus while the waiter brought their drinks. Lilah ordered the shrimp and Lesa, dutifully, the veal. Lilah didn't know if Lesa even ate veal. She had never served it to her and Charles. Marabet didn't like veal, and what Marabet didn't like, she didn't buy. It was a little bit of food tyranny that amused Lilah more than it irritated her.

"I'm glad you agreed to have lunch with me," Lilah said when the waiter was gone. "I've been remiss. We should have gotten together long ago and done this."

"I know you're busy."

"Not so much busy as disorganized."

"I don't believe that," Lesa said, looking shocked.

Lilah took a sip of wine. "Well, inefficient, then. I think of calling and then something comes up. The time slips away. Like this week. If Charles hadn't called last night, I probably would have let it slide again."

Lesa stared down at her glass. "I was surprised."

"I don't doubt it. Listening to you at dinner the other night talking about where you went to college, I realized how little I know about you."

"I'm sorry I was so argumentative. Charles said—"

"Charles says quite a lot," Lilah said, her voice sharp. She forced herself to relax. Jumping down Lesa's throat was not the way to get her to open up. "I didn't find you argumentative at all. I found you interesting. You said you majored in elementary education?"

Lesa's eyes lit up. "Yes. I know what Charles said about the salaries being awful is true, but teaching is so important. A teacher has the opportunity to open the world for a child. She can guide their interests, expand them as human beings. There are no bounds, really."

Lilah sat back, listening as Lesa talked on, becoming more animated with every word. The waiter served their salads. Lesa picked up her fork and took a bite or two, but Lilah would have sworn it was a wholly unconscious movement. Lesa's face flushed slightly as she warmed to her subject. Her excitement made her look ten years younger and immeasurably more attractive. Caterpillar to butterfly in the space of one short salad. Their entrees were served, and she was certain Lesa was totally unaware of what she was eating. They could as successfully have dined at Burger King, as long as education was the topic of conversation.

"Watching children develop is fascinating," Lesa said. "The world is endlessly exciting to them. They see magic in a seed growing, in how paste sticks two pieces of paper together." She suddenly stopped talking; looking down at her empty plate, then up at Lilah in mortification. "Oh, I'm so sorry. I've just rambled and rambled. That was so rude of me. Charles says—"

"You haven't rambled at all," Lilah said, cutting her off. "What you're saying is intriguing. I've enjoyed every word." She motioned the waiter over. "Coffee?" she asked Lesa.

"All right. If you're having some."

"Two coffees," Lilah told the waiter. Then she sat back in her chair and turned to Lesa. "As strongly as you feel about children, I'm surprised you don't have a house full."

Lesa froze, the light leaving her face as if some inner candle had been extinguished.

"I'm sorry, Lesa," Lilah said, sitting up straight. "That was a thoughtless thing to say. Please forgive me."

"Forgive you?" Lesa asked, looking confused. Then her face cleared. "Oh. I see what you mean. No, there's no reason that Charles and I can't have children. He just doesn't want them quite yet."

"Quite yet?" Lilah repeated, incredulous. "What in the world is he waiting for? You've been married for six years. He's financially secure; he has a home, a lovely wife."

Lesa rewarded that with a blush. "He says he'll know when the time is right."

"*He'll* know? Lesa, the last I heard, it took two to make a child. What about when you know? Don't you want children now?"

Lesa picked up her water glass and took a sip. When she

looked up, her face was troubled. "It would be nice," she finally answered, "but more than that, I want my marriage to be happy."

Lilah looked at the younger woman and suddenly saw herself as she had been early in her married life. Single-minded. Earnest. Determined. It was a terrifying vision. She chose her next words carefully. "A happy marriage takes two happy people. Forgive me, but I remember Charles saying he didn't want you to work in your chosen field. He doesn't want you to have children. What does he want you to do?"

Lesa didn't answer immediately. She poked at her empty plate with her fork until Lilah thought she might have gone too far with her question. Finally, Lesa looked over at her. "He wants me to be—like you," she answered slowly. "He's told me so many times how much of an asset you were to his father, keeping a wonderful home, entertaining clients, helping him build his career. He wants me to be like that. And I—try," she added quickly, "but I don't think it comes naturally to me like it did to you."

Lilah was stunned. "It wasn't natural for me," she blurted out. "It was hard work, and it was completely stifling." Where did that come from, she wondered? She looked up as the waiter brought their coffee. When he was gone, she said, "It was a miserable job, Lisa, but I had a couple of consolations. I had two lovely children."

Lesa looked uncomfortable and unhappy. "It's worth it to me to sacrifice to make my marriage work," she said, defensiveness edging her voice.

Again, Lilah was struck with a sense of déjà vu, and it wasn't pleasant. She wanted to shake Lesa, but what for? What was she doing that Lilah herself hadn't done? Her next words came to her unbidden. "I understand what you're saying, Lesa, but don't try to emulate anyone else. Especially me. I did what I did because I really believed it was the right thing to do, and now it's over and I'm glad." Lesa's misery was so apparent that she softened her words, "I suppose it's all right to sacrifice some things in the interest of marital harmony. I certainly did. Just make sure that you don't sacrifice yourself while you're at it."

She'd said more than she had intended, and she had the uncomfortable feeling that Lesa had heard a great deal more than she wanted to. This was not the way she wanted to end their first solo meeting together, but it was too late to do anything about it. She certainly seemed to be having trouble communicating these days. Too little in one direction; too much in the other.

The waiter appeared to clear their plates. He put a small dessert in front of each of them.

Lesa looked up at him in confusion. "I didn't order dessert."

"It comes with the meal," Lilah said quickly, and thanked the waiter. She searched for a conversational gambit to cover the woman's embarrassment. "Well, I think I'm going to Hastings Garden Center to find some flowers for the yard after this. It's been years since I planted anything."

Lesa latched onto the neutral subject like a safety line in the rapids. "I was there last week. They have some beautiful hostas, and I found some gorgeous lavender."

Lilah felt a small stirring of relief. "Well, then, why don't you come with me?"

Bethany closed the diary slowly, and held it to her chest. She sat propped up against one of the cardboard boxes, her legs folded under her. Her hair was pulled back in a ribbon, and she wore her usual shorts and shirt—fluorescent green today. It was hotter than ever in the attic, even though she had the fan on and all the windows open. She could feel the sweat in the creases behind her knees. It was easier to think about how hot she was than how sad she felt.

Every time she finished one of the little books, it was like she was closing the door on another part of her mother's life. It was silly. It was all in the past anyway, gone, and there was nothing to say she couldn't read them again. It was just that this particular part of the past in its plastic covers was done. She had four more to go. If she didn't slow down, she'd have them all finished in a week. Then she would have nothing to look forward to.

She was up to the part where Elizabeth was going into high school, and she was beginning to know this girl who grew up to be her mother. There wasn't much about boys. Oh, there were whole paragraphs about heroes in books, but not real boys. She'd had plenty of friends. They'd gone to movies and the malls—shopping centers, Elizabeth had called them. They had dances on Friday nights at the school gym. There were a couple of boys Elizabeth always danced with, more because they were good dancers than because she especially liked them. She wrote a lot about the classes she liked and not so much about those she didn't. It seemed funny that Elizabeth had hated studying history and had married a history professor.

She wrote a lot about her family. Charles, her older brother, was a jerk according to Elizabeth.

"I don't know why Charles doesn't tease me and my friends like Gina and Annalese's brothers do. I think I could take that okay. Charles sticks his nose in the air and pretends he's better than we are. What a pompous dork he is!" And another time, *"Charles hung around during my whole birthday party. No one wanted him there. He didn't talk to anyone, just looked down his pointy nose at us. Marabet said to ignore him, and I try. But it's so hard. He's horrible!"* Even having only spent one night in the man's company, Bethany found herself agreeing.

Most of what she wrote about her father early on was affectionately disdainful.

"Daddy said Marabet had to call me 'Miss Elizabeth' like she was some kind of kitchen maid or something, so I started calling her 'Miss Marabet.' He had a fit! I laughed and laughed." Later, it wasn't quite as affectionate. "Daddy yelled at mama again today about Marabet. He said Marabet was a terrible maid, and he was tired of it. Mama didn't say anything, but I could tell she was really upset." "Daddy had a hissy fit when I came downstairs in my bathrobe. There was a plumber in the kitchen. He told mama that if she wouldn't raise me to act like a lady, he'd send me away to school where they would. Mama pretended like it didn't bother her, but later I saw her crying."

She wrote a lot about her music. It seemed to be the most constant thing in her life. She wrote funny stuff about her teachers.

"Mr. Andrews wears a hairpiece! I'm sure of it!!! I'm sure I saw it slip when he was pounding away on that Chopin Etude today, but I forgot all about it when he started playing Beethoven. I wonder if I'll ever be able to play that way." "Mrs. Sunderling told me I had to concentrate on my music more, but how can I concentrate when all I can think about is that mole on her cheek. It has hairs growing out of it. Yuk!"

Lilah Kimball was in those memories, too.

"Mama sat there and listened to the whole lesson. She always does. That's so neat, because if I forget something, she'll remember it." "Mama and Marabet came to my recital. Mama said I played better than anyone, but she's always saying things like that and Marabet's just as bad." "Daddy told me it was silly to keep taking piano since I'd never do anything with it, but mama told me later that I could take lessons as long as I wanted. She's always on my side." "I was playing some old pieces today and when I looked at mama, she had tears in her eyes. I asked her what was the matter, and she told me she was crying because she loved me and because my music was so beautiful. I don't think it's that beautiful to anyone else."

This didn't sound like the Lilah Kimball Bethany knew, the one who'd sent her daughter away because she'd wanted to get married. When had she gotten so mean? When had she started hating her daughter?

Bethany stretched her legs out in front of her. She carefully wrapped the diary in the special tissue paper she'd found it in and replaced it in the box. She started to pick up another, but she changed her mind. She felt restless. Edgy. She didn't want to sit up here and read anymore.

She got to her feet. Her grandmother was out somewhere like she usually was during the day, and Marabet had run up to the store. She'd asked Bethany if she wanted to go, but she'd said no. It felt good to have the house to herself, if only for a little while.

She wandered downstairs and turned to go to her room. Then she changed her mind and went down the lower stairs with the vague idea of fixing herself a snack. Her legs refused to cooperate. They took her into the living room and up to the piano bench. She opened the lid and there was the sheet music she'd known would be there, music she knew her mother had studied because she had taught it to Bethany. The inside of the bench smelled musty, but it was the good musty of old paper. It reminded her of her mother and all their lessons together. Marabet was right, she thought. She, too, could now feel Elizabeth the girl in the house. After reading eight of the diaries, she could see her moving from room to room, dropping her books on the hall table after school, curled up in her big bed with a friend, giggling long after they'd turned the lights out. It wasn't her mother she was sensing, but someone younger, sillier. Someone who hadn't learned to always pretend everything was all right.

After a minute, she pulled out the bench and sat down. She ran a finger over the key cover, and then opened it. The black and white keys beckoned to her. Her fingers itched to play something. For the last six years she'd played almost every day. Until her mother died. Since then, not at all.

She got up and went to the window. No cars in sight. Would she hear them if they drove up? Probably, if she played softly, she decided.

She pulled a book out of the piano bench, Bach's Well-Tempered Clavier. She had the same Urtext version in Athens. She opened the front section of the piano lid. She had never played a grand piano before, and it took her a minute to figure out how the music holder flipped up to hold the music. She opened the book to the first piece, Prelude in C. She knew it even without the sheet music. It had been one of the first Bach pieces she ever learned. It was a soft blend of broken chord sounds that moved gradually across the keyboard.

She started playing very slowly, her foot on the soft pedal as well as the sustain pedal. Her ears at first were more attuned to the driveway outside than to her own music, but gradually the sound of the blended notes swelled in the room, in her until she could feel it reverberating through her. Within a couple of minutes, she was lost in the flow of sound, so much so that she didn't realize Marabet was in the room until she looked up at the end of the piece.

Bethany jumped up from the bench. "I'm sorry. I didn't know you were back."

Marabet walked over and put her hands on Bethany's shoulders, pushing her gently back down on the bench. Her eyes were bright, and she was smiling. "Please don't quit. I can't tell you how good it was to walk into the house and hear that old piano again. It took me back a ways. I love that song. Elizabeth used to play it for me. What's the name of it?" she asked, sitting down on the bench beside her.

Bethany looked over her shoulder into the hallway.

"She's not home, honey. She'll probably be a while longer. Why don't you play something else for me? You play as pretty as your mama used to."

"I don't play nearly as well as she does—did."

"You play as well as she did fifteen years ago, and that's a fact. So give yourself credit where credit is due. What else can you play?"

Lilah climbed out of the car, pushing the trunk release. She felt inordinately pleased with herself. She'd bought white and pink begonias to brighten up the area beside the back walk and lavender impatiens for under the breakfast room window. At the last moment, she had added three huge bleeding heart plants in peat lined baskets to hang in the shade of the oak limbs. By the time she and Lesa had finished shopping, they'd been laughing at themselves for traipsing along Hastings' cluttered aisles of plants in high heels and stockings. Both had runs in their hose and mud on their shoes. Both also had smiles on their faces by the time she'd dropped Lesa back at her car with a promise that they'd do something again soon.

Lilah looked down at her mud-flecked suit and smiled as she lifted a flat of begonias out of the trunk. Halfway around the house, she stopped, almost dropping the flowers. The piano piece. She knew it. Beethoven's Fur Elise. Elizabeth had played it for one of her many recitals. She had practiced the same song for months, and Lilah had heard it and heard it until she thought she'd scream. After the recital, the song had rolled around in her head until she nearly did scream. Now the sound of it cut through her like a knife.

The music was coming from the living room. Lilah forced her way through the foundation bushes to the window, unaware that she still carried the flat of flowers in her hands. Seated at the piano was Bethany, eyes closed, her face blissful. Lilah had thought her plain before, but right now she looked almost beautiful with the light from the window shining on her, creating planes and shadows on her face. Marabet sat next to her on the piano bench, as Lilah had so often sat next to Elizabeth. She didn't realize her hands had formed fists until she heard the plastic flat crack.

At that moment, Marabet's eyes were drawn to the window. She made no movement. She just looked at Lilah, her face expressionless. Lilah stood watching, unable to look away. Then the song ended, and she turned from the window.

She moved with slow steps to the back patio, where she gingerly placed the flowers on one of the stone benches around its perimeter. When she straightened up, her mind flashed back to the summer of Elizabeth's last recital. She'd been seventeen, ready to go off to college and conquer the world. Her goal had been to play Mozart's Sonata in A with at least six of its variations, and she'd spent almost a year working on the pieces. One day Lilah came home—it must have been from some gardening center because she'd been carrying flowers just like today—and she heard Elizabeth playing the sonata. She'd stopped, just like today, and listened to her play through the sonata and all six variations without a single mistake. But that day, Lilah had knocked on the window and waved. Elizabeth had come running out the front door and flung herself in her mother's arms.

"Did you hear me, mama? Did you hear it all? I was brilliant! I can't believe I did it. Oh, how I pray I can get through it at the recital! Do you think I can? Oh, of course *you'd* think so, but *can* I? Is it too much to play? Do you think the audience will get antsy? But you don't get the whole effect unless you play at least six of the variations. But only the six. Everybody plays that old Rondo ala Turka at the end, but no one knows what it's the end of. They've all missed the best part!"

And on and on. They'd walked into the house together, their

arms around each other's waists, the flowers forgotten entirely until Gerome had come home and demanded to know why the car trunk was still open and a flat of wilted flowers was sitting on the front steps. Then the two of them had rushed out to rescue the flowers, giggling together like schoolgirls.

Now Lilah sank down beside the flowers feeling ancient. Exhausted. Her skin ached like she was coming down with the flu. She felt her shoulders slump and had no energy to straighten her posture. She looked back in the direction of the car and thought of the other flats of flowers and the hanging baskets in her back seat. The car seemed miles away, the flowers too heavy to lift. She could get Marabet to bring them around—the woman had more energy than Georgia Power—but that was too much like admitting weakness—or defeat.

With supreme effort, she pushed herself to her feet and trudged back to the car. She'd get the damned flowers to the back if it killed her, and right now she wasn't at all sure it wouldn't.

They were in the kitchen when Lilah finally came inside. Marabet was at the sink washing green beans, while Bethany sat on one of the stools at the cooking island, her feet hooked around the legs, slicing potatoes.

"How was your lunch?" Marabet asked, glancing up at the clock.

"It was very nice," Lilah said. She crossed to the refrigerator and pulled out the pitcher of iced tea. "We went flower shopping afterward."

Marabet raised her eyebrows. "Flower shopping? Like flowers for outside?"

Lilah mirrored her look. "Yes. Flowers for outside."

"You went out and bought flowers?"

Lilah could see Bethany watching her out of the corner of her eye as she diced the potatoes. "Why are you so surprised?"

she asked. "I used to buy flowers all the time."

"Not for a long time, you haven't. Are you going to plant them yourself?"

"I thought I might. There aren't that many of them. Why, do you want to help?"

"Me? With these old knees? Perish the thought. Bethany might give you a hand, though," she said, her eyes on the green beans in the sink.

Bethany stared down at the cutting board, her knife frozen in mid-air.

Lilah had been reaching in the cabinet for a glass. She pulled one down and pressed it against the ice dispenser on the refrigerator. The ice falling into the glass sounded like gunshots. "Certainly," she said at length. "If she wants to."

Another silence while Lilah poured her tea.

"Okay," Bethany said, resuming her chopping, "if she wants me to."

Marabet beamed at them. "Good. I'll dig out a couple of pairs of gloves and some trowels in the morning. It's supposed to be a pretty day. You two will have a wonderful time."

Chapter 8

Morning came too soon. Bethany dreaded the day ahead. She didn't mind the work. She had always liked helping her mother in the yard. It was the thought of spending hours in *her* company. It would take forever to plant all those flowers on the patio, and it would seem like longer. Reluctantly, she climbed out of bed. She was dressed in shorts and a tank top, fluorescent orange this time, before Marabet knocked on her door. "Come on in, Marabet. I'm up."

Marabet stuck her head in the door, smiling broadly. "That's great, honey. What would you like for breakfast this morning?"

"I'm not very hungry."

"Okay. Ham and eggs with English muffins. Maybe some orange juice. Ten minutes?" And she was gone.

Bethany looked after her, unable to keep from smiling. Whatever kind of witch her grandmother might be, Marabet was just too, too cool.

The kitchen was bright with sunlight, and the early morning breeze ruffled the curtains at the windows. Bethany set the table as a matter of routine now.

Lilah joined them just before they sat down to eat. "Morning," she said, crossing to the coffee pot and pouring herself a cup. "Nothing for me, Marabet."

She was dressed in khaki workpants and a shirt, and looked about as enthusiastic as Bethany felt.

"Looks like the two of you are ready for a big day of yard

work," Marabet said, serving up three plates and carrying them to the table.

"I don't want—" Lilah began.

"Can't do a hard day's work on an empty stomach," Marabet placed the plates on the table. "It isn't healthy. Sit down and eat," she added. It was more an order than an invitation

Lilah and Bethany both obeyed, neither looking at the other. They ate in silence, which Bethany expected to last the whole day, and they both cleaned their plates.

When Marabet finished eating, she put down her fork and looked from one to the other, smiling. "I'll take care of the dishes. I put the gloves and hand shovels on the bench. Why don't the two of you get started before it gets too hot outside."

Lilah and Bethany rose from the table like automatons and headed for the door. Bethany followed Lilah's rigid back, thinking back to when she used to help her mother. They had made a game of it, seeing who could make her flowers look the prettiest. Her dad had always been the judge, which was why Bethany almost always won. Usually, by the time they got back inside, they were sweating and covered with dirt from head to toe. She stole a glance at her grandmother. She couldn't imagine her getting dirty. She couldn't imagine her sweating. She couldn't imagine—

"Let's start with these pink ones," Lilah said.

"Begonias."

Lilah looked at her in surprise. "You've planted flowers before?"

Did she think Bethany had been raised in a box? "Yes, ma'am. With my mother. She loved flowers." She felt a flash of satisfaction when Lilah flinched.

"Oh. Well, of course. Well, then . . ." Lilah handed her a flat of begonias, motioning to the other side of the terrace. "Why don't you put these over there? Not too close, though. But you probably already know that."

Bethany took the flowers and walked away. Nine to twelve inches apart. Everyone knew that. She must think Bethany was a dunce. She set the flat down on the terrace and knelt down. The stones bit into her knees. Why hadn't she worn jeans? No way was she going to admit she hadn't thought of it. Wouldn't *she* just love that? The dumb girl was too dumb to wear jeans. No. She'd rather bleed to death.

She stabbed her hand trowel into the dirt and yanked a begonia out of the flat. The top snapped off in her hand. Had she seen that? She glanced over. No. *Whew.* It probably wasn't dead. It would still probably bloom if she planted it, but then *she'd* see it. Bethany dug a deeper hole and buried the whole thing, pulling another begonia out of the flat and planting it right beside it. Now she'd never know—unless she counted them. She dug another hole and eased another plant out of the plastic container.

The child was angry. Lilah could tell that, and she didn't totally blame her. Of course the girl knew about flowers. Elizabeth had loved flowers. She probably had a garden at that house of hers. Lilah watched as she went down on her knees on the terrace. The stones had to be tearing her skin to shreds. Why hadn't she worn long pants, like jeans or something? Not that she dared mention that she go change. She winced as Bethany yanked a begonia out of the flat, snapping off the stem. Then she quickly looked away, pretending not to see. The child was already furious. No need to make it worse. She could always buy more flowers.

She heard a car coming down the drive and had to restrain herself from crying out in relief. She stood, wiping her hands on her pants and heading around the side of the house.

Lesa was parked in the driveway, leaning into the trunk of

her car. When she straightened, she was smiling shyly and clutching a large plastic bag. "I remembered last night that we didn't get any mulch for the flowers. I thought maybe you already had some, but I had to get mine and so I thought . . ."

"Come on around, Lesa. I'm grateful you thought of it. It's too late in the year to put these in without heavy mulch." She looked over Lesa's shoulder. "Let's get these bags around back."

"I'd be glad to stay and help you," Lesa said as they reached the terrace. She caught sight of Bethany on her knees. "I mean, if you need help."

"Oh. Well . . ." Lilah looked over at Bethany.

"That's okay," Bethany said, dropping her trowel on the terrace. "If you want to help, I mean." She stood, not looking at either of them. "I have a bunch of stuff I need to do inside."

"If you're sure," Lesa said faintly.

Bethany pulled off her gloves and dropped them on the stone bench.

After she was gone, Lesa looked over at Lilah in dismay. "I hope I'm not intruding. I didn't think—I mean . . ."

Lilah shook her head ruefully. "She was hating every minute of it and making sure I knew it, and I can tell you, that was taking every bit of the pleasure out of it for me. No," she offered Bethany's discarded gloves to Lesa, "I'm glad you came. Now you can help me decide. Should I put all the begonias in this border, or should I put a few of the white ones in the flower bed under the window?"

Bethany let herself in the front door, hoping that Marabet wouldn't hear her come in. If she did, she'd probably just send her out again, and then what would she do? She tiptoed down the hallway, but stopped as she passed the living room. She looked longingly at the piano, poised on the gleaming hardwood floors like a beacon drawing her in. She had thought that playing the day before would get it out of her system, but it had only made it worse. She stood there for several minutes, imagining Elizabeth the girl sitting on the bench, her long blonde hair curling and waving down her back as she practiced hour after hour. She wished she could feel as free to sit down at the piano and play until she couldn't play anymore.

Instead, she turned and headed up the stairs, stopping in her room long enough to change into clean shorts and a shirt before heading up to the attic. It was already hot up there, heat trapped from the day before. She immediately went to the windows and pushed them open. She could hear Lesa and—*her*—laughing as they planted the flowers. The sound gave her a hollow feeling in her chest. She decided not to turn on the fan because she didn't want them to know she was up there.

Marabet had brought up a bunch of throw pillows and propped them up against the boxes like a makeshift sofa. Bethany flopped down on one beside the diary box and took out the next book, unwrapping it carefully. It was fancier than the others. They'd had plastic covers and little flaps that locked with a key, although none of them was locked. This one was cloth bound, with a ribbon bookmark. She opened the cover and settled back against the box.

September 12

I love high school! It's so different from what school was like last year. The teachers treat us like we're grown up. They give us our homework assignments and just expect us to do them. And miracle of miracles, I do! I have a crush on Mr. Sturgis, my Algebra teacher. How could someone so cool teach a yucky subject like Algebra? Anyway, I'd die if he found out. Or if anyone else did. Melissa and Trina would tease me forever! No, I'll never tell anyone, but he's so cute! I won't even tell mama, and I tell her everything!

Bethany lay the book face down in her lap, resting her head against the box and closing her eyes. Elizabeth had really loved the woman who was her mother. She had loved her and trusted her, and that made what happened so much worse. It must have broken her heart when her mother turned her back on her. What kind of a mother would do that to her daughter?

She opened her eyes again. For a minute, she watched as the filtered light coming in the window cast shadows on the boxes opposite, shapes without definition or meaning. She could hear the voices downstairs in the background, talking, laughing. They, too, were meaningless. Just words. The older voice sounded like someone nice. But it was only a voice. Only words.

A tear leaked from the corner of her eye, and she brushed it away unconsciously. She felt close to her mother up here, surrounded by things that had been hers. She'd gone through the other boxes. Some were filled with dresses. Others with winter coats and sweaters. She'd been tempted to try on some of the stuff, especially the fancy party dresses, but she'd been afraid someone would come in while she was doing it. One day she'd slipped on one of the coats, hugging it around her and imagining her mother wearing it, but it had been too hot to keep it on for long. It made her feel sad, too, so she'd folded it carefully and put it back in the box. She only wished she could put her feelings in a box the same way and seal it up with tape.

She picked up the diary and began reading again.

September 13

I told mama anyway, about Mr. Sturgis, and she didn't laugh at me. She said it was good to have positive feelings for someone who was teaching me something important. She reminded me that I'd had really good feelings about Mr. Andrews last year. She's right. I'd forgotten all about that. She said that part of what I was feeling is admiration and, if he was handsome, so much the better. She's wonderful. Not like Julia's mother. Julia's mother told her she was a silly fool and boy crazy. Mama would never say anything mean like that. She's so neat.

"She's not neat," Bethany said aloud. "She's a—a bitch, and she abandoned you!" She slammed the book shut and dropped it on the floor, grabbing up one of the pillows and hugging it against her. Mothers weren't supposed to do that. They were supposed to be there always, not go away. How could they leave you when you needed them? Somehow they should be there. It wasn't fair. It just wasn't fair.

She brought the pillow up to her face, crying silently into the soft fabric. Tears and tears and tears. She didn't know where they all came from, but it seemed like they'd never stop. But finally they did stop. Bethany felt drained and exhausted, but angry at the same time. She heard laughter again from outside. It only made her madder. She tossed the pillow down and got to her feet, crossing to the switch that controlled the fan. Defiantly, she switched it on.

Lilah looked up at the attic window when she heard the fan kick on and closed her eyes for a minute. She looked back to see Lesa watching her.

"Bethany?" she asked.

Lilah nodded. "She practically lives in the attic. I think she only comes down for meals."

"What does she do up there all day?"

"I don't know. Probably fancies herself some kind of modern day Cinderella." She bit her lip, averting her eyes. She dug into the ground with her spade, harder than necessary. "I'm sorry. That wasn't very kind. I'm not certain what the fascination is, but I can guess. I have things packed away up there. Elizabeth's things." It felt strange to say the name aloud.

"Is that what she's doing? Going through her mother's things?"

"Probably," Lilah said, pulling off her gloves. "Who knows? She doesn't talk to me. She talks to Marabet some, but only when I'm not around."

"Do you think she might be afraid of you?" Lesa asked, some of the old timidity back in her voice.

"I don't think it's fear. There's too much belligerence in the girl for that. I think she just doesn't like me, and I have to admit that I can't seem to feel anything for her. It may not seem natural, but it's the truth. Marabet likes her, and that bothers me, too. I hate for her to get attached to the child since she's not going to be staying." She pressed her fingers in the small of her back and arched backwards. "I'll be glad when the state makes other arrangements for her."

"Do you think—I mean, would it help if she came to stay with—well, with Charles and me?"

Lilah looked at her in surprise. "Do you think Charles would go along with that?"

Lesa averted her eyes. "I could ask," she answered in a small voice.

Lilah watched her for a minute. Lesa seemed sincere enough, and she certainly loved children. It might just solve a multitude of problems, and what could it hurt? "If you're sure you feel comfortable with it, I certainly wouldn't mind. Let's go fix some iced tea and you can call."

Inside, Lilah could hear the deep throated whine of the vacuum running in the front of the house. She washed her hands before taking down two tall glasses.

Lesa wiped her hands on her pants and walked over to the phone. She dialed a number and waited while it rang. "Hi, Toni," she said into the receiver. "This is Lesa Kimball. Is my husband busy? Oh. Oh, no. Don't disturb him. Will you ask him to call me when he's free? At his mother's house. Thank you."

"Come sit down," Lilah said, bringing the two glasses over to the table. "We deserve a break."

Before Lesa could move, the phone rang. She looked at Lilah, who nodded, and Lesa picked up the phone. "Kimball residence. Oh. Yes. Just a minute." Lesa covered the mouthpiece. "It's Thomas Mulligan."

Lilah sat up straight. "Tell him . . . tell him . . ." She sighed and reached for the phone.

"Hello, Tom."

"Lilah, how are you? Did I catch you at a bad time?"

"I'm fine, but I'm afraid I'm a little busy right now."

"Oh?"

"Yes. My daughter-in-law is here. Actually, we were expecting another call."

She heard Tom's chuckle come through the phone line. "You aren't very good for a guy's ego, my dear, but fortunately I'm made of strong stuff. I won't keep you. I just wanted to ask how you were. You'll call me if you need anything?"

"Of course, Tom," Lilah said, not meeting Lesa's curious gaze, "and thank you for calling."

Before Lesa could say a word, the phone rang again. Lilah handed it to Lesa. "Yes, Charles. It's me. What am I—? Well, I just dropped by." She glanced at Lilah. "We're planting the flowers we bought yesterday. There's something I wanted to ask you. I was thinking—I mean, your mother and I were talking and—" She took a deep breath. "I wondered if we could have Bethany stay with us for a while," she blurted out.

Lesa winced visibly at his response. Lilah couldn't make out the words, but she could hear his voice from across the room. "No, she—No, I was the one who suggested—" Then, her voice miserable, "Yes, she's here. Just a minute."

Lesa looked apologetic as she handed Lilah the phone. "He wants to talk to you."

"I gathered," Lilah said wryly, taking the receiver. "Yes, Charles."

"What are you up to, Mother?"

"What do you mean?"

"Now I understand why you invited Lesa to lunch. You're trying to pull a fast one, aren't you?"

"You're making no sense, Charles," she said, congratulating herself for not adding "as usual." "What does Lesa having lunch with me have to do with anything? Just for the record, though, I asked her to lunch because I wanted to get to know her better." She looked over at Lesa. "And I'm glad I did. I like her very much."

"Sure you do. This sudden liking you've taken to her couldn't have anything to do with wanting to dump that brat of Elizabeth's on us, could it?"

Lilah felt her temperature rise to near the boiling point. "I'm afraid you're getting me confused with you, Charles. I don't operate from motives as shabby as that."

There was a long silence. Then Charles' voice, cool, "Let me speak to Lesa."

Lilah considered refusing, but in the end, she handed over the telephone.

"Yes, Charles." Lesa listened for a minute. "No, I won't stay." She hung up the phone and glanced at Lilah, then quickly looked away. "I should probably be going."

"What did he say?"

"Oh, nothing important. Just not to wear out my welcome."

Lilah's mouth opened, and then shut. "Wear out your welcome? Honestly. What is the matter with him?" Before Lesa could answer, Lilah patted the chair beside her. "Come sit down, Lesa. Let's have our tea."

"If you're sure . . ."

"I'm sure. Come on. Sit down."

Lesa took the chair across the table from her. "I apologize for the way he acted," she finally said.

"No," Lilah said. "*I* apologize for the way he acted. I thought I'd raised him better than that."

"But you did. I mean, he isn't always like that."

"No, but he's getting more like that every day."

Lesa looked troubled, but she didn't say anything.

"What is it?" Lilah prompted.

"It's just that I don't understand what he has against his sister."

"Someone far more objective than I suggested that he's jealous of her."

"But she's—" Her eyes widened and she covered her mouth.

"I know." Lilah gave Lesa a smile she hoped was reassuring, "but that doesn't seem to make any difference. He's always felt that way. I don't know why. I don't think he was slighted as a child. He was certainly his father's favorite." She stirred her iced tea absently with a finger. "Gerome catered to him outrageously, despite my protests. As far as he was concerned, Charles couldn't do any wrong."

Lesa nodded. "I remember."

"That's right," Lilah said, wiping her finger on a napkin. "I'd forgotten Gerome was still alive when you and Charles were married." She shook her head. "I've been a terrible mother-in-law to you."

"No, you—"

"I certainly have. I've neglected you miserably, and I have no excuse except that . . ." Her voice trailed off as a host of unwelcome thoughts teased at her mind. She realized that Lesa was staring at her. "Well—I have no excuse, or at least, none that matters. I don't know what Charles said to you, but he accused me of buttering you up so you'd take Bethany."

Lesa flushed.

"And nothing could be further from the truth. I asked you to have lunch with me yesterday because I was really interested in what you said at dinner the other night. It made me realize how little I knew you and that I wanted to know you better. There was no ulterior motive, and don't let Charles try to convince you otherwise."

"He—" Lesa glanced over, then away. "What you said about his father. It's true. Charles thought the sun rose and set in him. He changed after his father died."

"He acts like he's trying to become his father," Lilah stated flatly.

The two women stared at each other, both startled by the idea.

Lesa recovered first. "He does—act—like him, doesn't he?"

"If you mean he's behaving like a petty tyrant, then yes, he is acting like him. Gerome had a number of good qualities, but patience and tolerance weren't among them. Neither were forgiveness and kindness, now that I think about it. But enough about him," Lilah said, getting to her feet. "Gerome is dead and so will those flowers be if we don't finish getting them in the ground."

Lesa looked at her and giggled.

Lilah chuckled, and then laughed outright. "I guess that didn't sound much like a grieving widow, did it?"

"Not much."

"Well, Gerome has been gone a long time. So, are you game to help me finish?"

Lesa got up and picked up her gloves. "Are you sure you want me to?"

"Absolutely. Think of it as an act of mercy. I'll die if I have to plant all those flowers by myself."

Bethany woke to a car engine starting up in the driveway. She couldn't believe she'd fallen asleep on the floor. The sun was coming in the west windows now, making it almost too hot to breathe in the room. The ribbon had come out of her hair, and long strands were stuck to her damp face. She pushed it back, rising to her feet and stretching her stiff muscles, unable to decide if she was going to die first from the heat or hunger. One of them for sure.

As she turned to go downstairs, the door opened and Marabet stepped inside. "I wondered if you were ever coming down," she said, looking at the pillows scattered on the floor, the cloth-bound diary lying prominently on one of them.

Bethany gasped, and her gaze flew to Marabet's face.

"Oh, good. You found the diaries," Marabet said, her voice mild. "I was hoping you would. Seems like there are a few more somewhere around here." She walked over and poked among the stacks of boxes, moving one and then another. "Here they are," she said, pulling out a small carton from behind the others. "They wouldn't fit in with the others, so I had to give them their own box."

Bethany was still trying to recover from being found out. "It's okay?"

"For you to read them?" Bethany nodded. "I don't see why not. Your mom wouldn't mind. She read me parts of them herself."

"She did?"

Marabet smiled. "Your mom wasn't much of one for secrets."

"She was when I knew her."

Marabet thought about that. "Maybe she got that way later. People change when they get older. Still, I'm sure it's fine."

Bethany picked up the smaller box and, lovingly, placed it next to the box containing the rest of the diaries. "Did you pack all this up?" she asked, gesturing at the stacked cartons.

"I did, and it was the saddest day of my life. Second saddest day," she corrected. "Course, I thought she'd be back as soon as everyone cooled off. And speaking of cooling off, why don't we go downstairs and do that. Are you hungry? It's past lunch time, but I didn't want to bother your grandmother until she got finished with her flowers. She's in her room now, probably taking a shower. She was dirt from head to toe. I'll fix enough for three, and we'll see if she comes down to eat."

Bethany trudged down the stairs after Marabet. "You're awfully nice to her, even when she's not nice to you."

"That's how it is with friends," Marabet said over her shoulder. "With real friends, anyway. Lilah's been through a lot, just like you. I'd be the first to admit she isn't always the most pleasant person lately, but she's coming around. Just look what she's doing in her bedroom."

"What? New sheets?"

"New everything. New sheets. New furniture. New carpet. Maybe the next day, a new life. It's kind of symbolic, don't you know? At least, that's how I see it."

Chapter 9

Lilah came downstairs the next morning with a spring in her step and a bundle of clothes tucked under her arm. She stopped abruptly when she saw Marabet at the door arguing with two workmen in blue coveralls. "What's going on?" she asked, coming up behind Marabet.

"Carpet delivery, ma'am," the taller of the two men said, holding up a clipboard. "This lady—"

Marabet's voice rolled over his. "I tried to tell him he wasn't supposed to be here until tomorrow, but he says it's today."

The man held up the clipboard. "Says right here. Thursday. That's today."

"I asked them to deliver it on Friday," Lilah said, taking the clipboard from him. She looked where he pointed. It clearly read Thursday. "I'm afraid there's been a misunderstanding. We aren't ready for you. You need to come back tomorrow."

The man took off his cap and wiped his forehead before replacing it. "Sorry, ma'am. Schedule's full up. Our next opening is—" He lifted a page on the clipboard and looked at a calendar, "Next slot is a week from Wednesday. Course, if that's what you want, we can do it then."

Lilah looked from the man to Marabet. From Marabet to the long, plastic-wrapped rolls on top of the van in the driveway. She wanted that new carpet. In her mind's eye, she could see how the pale green carpet would look against her new bedding. Well, so be it. "Go ahead and install it. Marabet will be here.

She can answer any questions you have."

She turned and started toward the kitchen.

Marabet was right behind her.

"What do you mean, 'Marabet will be here.' Where will you be?"

Lilah headed straight for the coffee pot, pouring herself a cup. "I'm going over to help Lesa plant her flowers. Then we're going shopping for my new bedroom furniture." She turned around and bumped into Marabet.

"Today?" Marabet demanded, taking a step back. "You're going to leave me here to deal with all this mess by myself?"

Lilah felt a stab of guilt, but she held firm. "Lesa is expecting me. I promised her." She looked at her watch. "In fact, I was hoping to be over there by now. I'm sure you'll be able to handle everything just fine."

"Oh, sure. You go plant flowers and go shopping. Don't give me a thought, except that we were going to empty those closets if you'll remember, and I was going to give them a good cleaning before the rug went down."

"And I told you that was silly. They're just going to mess everything up again. You'll need to empty the closet, but just lay the clothes across the bed in a guestroom. Bethany can help you. We can clean up after all the furniture is back in." She put her coffee cup in the sink.

"Fine. Leave. It'll serve you right if they brought the wrong color carpet. If they did, I'll tell them to put it in anyway. If they brought orange carpet, you can just live with orange carpet."

Lilah bit back a smile. "I'm certain they have the right color." She picked up her purse and tucked a rolled-up bundle under her arm. "Everything's set. I'll be at Lesa's for the morning at least, and then we'll be out of touch for most of the afternoon."

"Fine," Marabet said shortly.

"Fine," Lilah repeated in the same tone, but there was still a trace of a smile on her face.

An hour later, she climbed into the driver's side of the car and tossed her dirty clothes in the back seat. "That didn't take long at all," she said as Lesa slid in on the passenger side.

"Not with two of us working. It would have taken me half the day alone."

"It seemed only fair, since you spent yesterday helping me." Lilah started the car. "Are you game for a bit of furniture shopping?"

Lilah made a point of steering the conversation away from Charles during the drive, which wasn't difficult as long as she kept bringing the subject back to elementary education, but Charles still had a way of slipping into the conversation. During the short ride, she learned that Charles had chosen their house, their furnishings, maid service, and even their cars.

"He doesn't do the grocery shopping, does he?"

Lesa colored. "No . . . but he does check the list."

"Busy as he is running your lives, I'm surprised he has time to do any accounting," Lilah said, feeling a surge of resentment toward her son.

Lesa's lower lip trembled a bit. "He says I spend too much. He's probably right. I do impulse shop. I don't mind that he checks my purchases. It really matters to Charles, and it doesn't matter to me."

Lilah winced, hearing words she'd used herself, words she'd hidden behind for decades. *It doesn't matter. It's not important. I don't mind.* Lies, every one of them, but there was no way she could tell her daughter-in-law that. Besides, at some level, Lesa already knew.

She was relieved when they arrived at Miami Circle, a decorator shopping Mecca off Piedmont Avenue. Lilah hadn't been there in years, but she hoped with their eighty-plus shops, she might find something she could use in her bedroom. On her last trip, she had been overwhelmed by too many choices and Marabet scandalized by the prices; and they had thrown in the towel after the third shop. She was hoping Lesa was made of sterner stuff.

Almost the minute she walked into the first showroom, Lilah spotted what she wanted. The bed was queen-sized; a four-poster with an openwork headboard fashioned out of some kind of bamboo-like wood and stained a pale yellow. Near it was a bow-shaped dressing table. At either side were nightstands. There was even a wardrobe. Each piece differed enough from the others to look unique and yet, together they all worked. A discreet glance at the price tag attached to the headboard told her it cost much more than she had planned to spend. She felt a smile tug at her lips.

She walked straight to it and ran her hand over a headboard. She heard Lesa making appreciative sounds beside her. "Do you like it?" Lilah asked.

"I love it. It's beautiful."

"You don't think it's too frivolous?" She saw Lesa hesitate. "Tell the truth, now."

Lesa looked over at her apologetically. "It does seem . . . I mean . . ."

Lilah smiled. "I agree." She turned to the salesman who was just beginning to move toward them. "I'll take it."

"The complete set?" he asked, his eyes gleaming.

"Every stick." She sat down on the bed and bounced up and down a couple of times. "Does the mattress come with it?"

"It certainly can," he answered, smiling. "If you'll just step over here, we'll look in the computer and see when we can arrange delivery."

Fifteen minutes later they were in the car headed back to Lesa's house. Lesa looked at her watch. "That only took an hour. You shop fast."

"Not usually," Lilah said, flipping on her turn signal. "This bedroom just seems to be coming together by itself. It was the same thing when I bought the new linens. I walked into the department store and there they were, staring at me." She glanced over at Lesa. "I had no idea what I wanted when I walked into that store today. I would never have guessed that a light colored set like that would appeal to me, but I can visualize it with the new quilt. You'll have to see it and let me know what you think. Not today, though," she added with a grimace. "I have carpet installers at the house, and I'll bet everything is turned upside down. In fact, I imagine Marabet is cursing my name at this very moment for deserting her."

Marabet was nowhere to be seen when Bethany came back in the house. She had slipped outside as soon as Lilah left because that was the only place she could stay out of everybody's way. The yard was actually pretty neat, like a little woods of her own surrounded by a tall stone fence. Well, not her own, but she could pretend it was her own, just like she pretended Marabet was her real grandmother and that she lived here with her, just the two of them, and she helped her every day to take care of things in the house and then she would come outside to her own private woods. It seemed more like a woods than a yard. There were places where you couldn't even see the house. Massive trees cast much of it in shadow, making it a lot cooler than the attic. Maybe she'd bring one of the diaries out here to read, or maybe one of the books out of the library.

The quiet was heavy, broken only by the singing of the birds and the low hum when an airplane soared high overhead. Squirrels scampered along the fence, pausing to watch Bethany as she passed. The ground underfoot was soft, made cushiony by years of fallen leaves and pine needles. She'd spent a while sprawled on her back, staring up at the sky, impossibly blue through the treetops, as she braided pine needles. She knew the Indians had woven them into mats and baskets in the old days, but she'd never figured out how to do that. Instead, she made zippers of them and spread them out on the ground in a tidy row before wiping her hands on her shorts and heading on her way.

While she was exploring, Bethany had stumbled on lots of places, little nooks hidden from view that would be perfect for curling up in and reading. There were even some trees that looked like they'd be fun to climb, now that she remembered how much fun climbing trees was. She recalled how her grandmother had tried to get her to go outside when she first arrived, and she couldn't understand why she had said no. Just to be mean? Probably. She was feeling mean all the time back then. And now? She wasn't feeling mean now. She was still sad sometimes, though, and the woods helped to make the sadness go away. So did pretending.

She wished she could live here forever. She wished this was her house and her woods. She wished . . . she wished so many things.

Hunger finally drove her indoors. She'd forgotten all about breakfast in all the confusion, and she was pretty sure Marabet had as well. There were still lots of bangs and thumps coming from overhead. At one point she heard Marabet yelling at someone. That gave Bethany an idea. She had ham sandwiches and soup ready when Marabet finally came into the kitchen.

"Well, look at this," Marabet said, coming over to the table. "Aren't you sweet. You fixed us lunch."

"I thought you might need some food," Bethany said, coloring under the praise.

"I do," Marabet said, giving her shoulder a squeeze, "and

about ten aspirins. The racket they're making ripping up carpet and tearing off baseboards has my head about to split wide open. And the mess. There's furniture all over the place," she said, sitting down at the table. "The attic stairs are completely blocked. I don't know if you can even get into your room with everything they've shoved in the hall."

"That's okay. I thought since she's not home, I might practice the piano a little bit—if you don't think it will make your head hurt more."

Marabet reached over and touched her arm. "Probably do it more good than the aspirin. Music's always soothed me. You just have yourself a long session after you eat. If you think you can hear yourself play over the racket they're making up there," she added, gesturing toward the ceiling. "Lilah won't be back till later, and I think I'll lie down for a while after lunch. Okay?"

Bethany's smile widened until it threatened to split her face. "Okay!" She jumped up and started out of the room.

"Honey, your lunch—"

"I'll eat it later." Then she turned back. "The dishes—"

"I'll get the dishes," Marabet said, waving her away.

Bethany spun around and raced down the hall. At the living room door she stopped, looking in at the piano. It was so, so beautiful. Slowly, she walked into the room and took a handful of music out of the piano bench. Then she opened the piano lid and set up the music stand. Smiling, she lifted the key cover. For a minute, she just ran her fingers lightly over the keys. She pushed one down without sound. Smooth. Butter. It was like pushing a knife through soft butter.

She leafed through the books on the music rack, trying to decide what to play. Then she realized she had time. Hours and hours! She would start with her scales to warm up. The twelve major scales. Then the chromatic scale. Then she'd see.

Time vanished as music filled the house. A while later, she

opened the Mozart Sonata in A to the first page. Her mother had been teaching her this one just before—just recently. It was a beautiful piece. At least it was when her mother played it. Bethany had only memorized the first part. They had been planning to start on the first variation soon. After glancing over the sheet music to refresh her memory, she took a deep breath. Then she brought her hands down on the keys. In minutes, she was lost in the music. She couldn't see the notes because of the flood of tears that the music released, tears that streamed down her face. It didn't matter. Marabet was taking a nap and no one else in the house would notice. On the movie screen of her mind, she could see her mother playing the piece, could feel her sitting beside her, encouraging her, loving her. She could feel her warmth and smell her perfume.

Lilah let herself in the front door. With the garage blocked by the carpet vans, she'd had to leave her car in the driveway. She expected chaos, but what she heard when she stepped into the foyer stopped her in her tracks. All the air left her lungs; the room got darker and began to spin. She steadied herself against the wall. She was unable to move as the music ended. She barely noticed when Marabet walked up beside her.

Bethany turned toward her, her face flushed and tear-streaked. When she saw Lilah, her expression changed to horror and she paled. "Oh!" She jumped up from the piano bench. "I—I—I'm sorry." She brushed past Lilah and ran for the stairs.

Marabet reached out toward her, but Bethany didn't stop.

Marabet looked from her to Lilah. "You're early," she said, her words an accusation.

"Yes," Lilah said, not taking her eyes off Bethany's retreating back. "We—uh—finished early." She started for the stairs, only to realize the upstairs hallway was blocked with old carpet and furniture. She looked around for a moment, dazed. Then she saw the library door open. She crossed to it and went in, closing the door behind her. She sank down into a chair, numb. No, not numb. No one who was numb could feel this level of pain. She leaned her head back against the chair, powerless to stop the anguish that washed over her.

Some time later, an hour, two hours, she heard a tap on the library door.

"Come in, Marabet."

Lilah still sat in the chair with her purse in her lap.

Marabet's face was pinched with worry. Lilah didn't have the energy to tell her she was all right. Was she all right? What was all right anymore?

"I made some coffee," Marabet said, putting the tray down on the side table. "I don't know about you, but I could use some." She poured two cups, clearly not expecting an answer. "Those workmen are gone. I'll go tidy up a bit while you drink your coffee. We'll save the big jobs for tomorrow."

Lilah ignored the coffee. "Did you tell her that Elizabeth used to play that song?"

Marabet shook her head. "No, but I think Elizabeth taught it to her. She taught her a lot of them. I've heard her play them."

"Does she—play a lot?"

"Not too much. She's afraid you'll be mad at her if she plays when you're home, so she waits until you go out."

Lilah closed her eyes. Was she such an ogre? "I suppose you think that somehow makes me selfish."

"No, Lilah," Marabet said. "I think that makes her considerate." When Lilah didn't speak, she added, "She loves to play. She's really good."

"Yes, she is," Lilah said without opening her eyes.

She heard Marabet stand. "I'll take my coffee and go tidy up. What time would you like dinner?"

"I don't want anything."

"You have to eat," Marabet insisted.

Lilah's eyes snapped open. "No, I do *not* have to eat. I do not have to eat if I'm not hungry, and I do not want any dinner."

"Okay," Marabet said, holding up her hands and backing out of the room.

Finally, Lilah went up to her bedroom, closing the door soundlessly behind her.

All Bethany's tears seemed finally spent. She was sitting on the floor, hugging her mother's picture to her chest. She didn't look up until Marabet placed the tray on the table, then her eyes widened. Two ice cream sundaes. Cookies. Half a cake.

"I thought we'd have the good stuff first," Marabet said, setting out two plates. "Then if we're still hungry, we can have something healthy."

Bethany's lips trembled. She dropped the picture on the couch and flung herself into Marabet's arms. "Oh, Marabet, I love you!"

Marabet wrapped her arms around the child, hugging her tightly. "I love you, too, sweetheart," she crooned, rocking Bethany from side to side. "I love you more than you can know."

Bethany pulled back and looked at her. "You're crying."

"Not me," Marabet said, sniffling. "Must've gotten something in my eye."

Bethany smiled a watery smile. "Yeah. Me too."

"So," Marabet drew in a deep breath, "do we pig out on chocolate, or do we go downstairs and eat broccoli?"

Bethany's smile widened despite the tears still trickling down her face. She picked up the knife. "I'll cut the cake."

Chapter 10

Lilah opened her eyes, then quickly closed them to block out the sunlight streaming in her window. What time had she finally fallen asleep? Four-thirty? Five? She half opened her eyes and squinted at the clock on her bedside table. Nine o'clock. It felt like the middle of the night. She closed her eyes and then opened them again. The glare wasn't quite as bad when you expected it.

She watched the branches of the tree outside her window sway in the morning breeze, the pale blue sheers at the window softening their outlines and giving them an otherworldly appearance. Reality filtered. It seemed like that was how everyone viewed life, through the filter of their own perception, a perception that colored everything they saw. You could pretend to look at life objectively, but that was just another filter, blue, say, instead of green.

Her filter had been rose-colored, clichéd as it sounded. She had refused to see the direction her life and her marriage were taking. Gerome must be the man for her. Hadn't her own parents assured her it was so? As the years passed and disappointment set it, she had believed it to be maturity. Deny reality. Try to be the perfect wife and mother. Everything will be all right eventually, won't it?

Was that filter the color of obedience? Stupidity?

Spending time with Lesa, seeing this young woman who had modeled herself after Charles' perception of his mother, had stripped off those blinders and had forever changed the color of her memories. What color were they now? What color was anger, resentment? Surely it was brown. People associated the color red with anger, but red was a happy color. Brown. Or was brown the color of futility? Was anger purple? An ugly color, purple, muddy and confused. And grief. What color was grief?

She looked around her room, with its pale yellow walls, its cheerful quilt and curtains, its lovely pale green carpet. Her room was the color of happiness and lightness of being, joy, and some time during the long night, she had decided she wanted happiness in her life as well. It would take a lot of work, a lot of relearning, but surely it couldn't be much harder than keeping her head buried in the sand even as she slowly suffocated.

She pushed back the covers and sat up on the side of the bed. She didn't know how much time she had left in this life. Longevity was an issue that couldn't be avoided once you passed the half-century mark, but however much she'd botched the first six decades of her life, she intended to make the most of what she had left. She wanted to *live*.

She was relieved that both Marabet and Bethany were in the kitchen having breakfast when she went downstairs. It saved her having to face them separately. "Good morning," she said, deliberately meeting each pair of eyes. "May I join you?"

"Sure," Marabet said, putting down her fork. "What can I get you?"

"Not a thing. You can sit right there and finish your breakfast. I'm quite handy enough in the kitchen to fix my own toast." She poured herself a cup of coffee while the bread was toasting. Then she carried both to the table. She hoped Marabet wouldn't notice her hand shaking as she took a sip of coffee and turned to Bethany.

The girl was looking at the table, pretending to nibble on a piece of toast and clearly uncomfortable.

Of Words & Music

"I enjoyed listening to you play that Mozart piece yesterday, Bethany," Lilah said, her voice wobbling only a little. "I haven't heard it since your mother played it for me."

"I didn't play it very well," Bethany mumbled, her cheeks reddening.

"I thought you played it extremely well," Lilah said. It was hard to force the words out of her mouth, but she was determined. "It's not an easy piece. I remember Elizabeth crying and carrying on that she'd never learn it."

Bethany glanced at her. "She did?"

Lilah nodded. "It took over a year for her to learn the andante and the six variations. She blamed it on the song, the piano. She even blamed her piano teacher for not teaching it to her right."

"She never told me that."

"I'm not surprised. Would you admit that to your daughter?"

They smiled at each other.

Marabet made a choking sound that turned into a cough. "I remember that," she said, her voice hoarse. "Claimed he'd confused her by telling her to use the wrong fingers or something like that."

"She had a thing about fingering," Bethany said, her breakfast forgotten. "She used to tell me she didn't care what fingers I used to play a piece, but to always use the same fingering once I learned it. She was right, too. I accidentally changed once during a recital, and I ran out of fingers halfway through a bar."

It was one of the longest sentences Lilah had ever heard the child utter, and she felt a ridiculous sense of pride. "I've done that, too," she said, nodding.

"You play the piano?" Bethany asked, surprised.

"Not well like you do."

"Did you take lessons?"

"Yes, I did, for several years when I was—oh, a little younger than you. I haven't played in a long time."

"Did you like it?"

Lilah smiled. "I loved it."

"Why'd you quit?"

"I got older and was more interested in other things."

"She quit because she hated to practice," Marabet said. "I remember her complaining."

"Everyone hates to practice," Lilah countered.

"I don't!" Bethany blurted out. Then she looked embarrassed. "I mean, I always loved practicing," she said sheepishly. "Mama used to get mad at me for practicing instead of doing my homework."

Lilah tried to picture Elizabeth rearing this child, disciplining her, but it was beyond her powers of imagination. Elizabeth had been little more than a child herself when she left. Then she realized Bethany was watching her, and she tried to remember what they'd been talking about. "Were you having trouble with your grades?" Lilah asked.

Bethany made a face. "I made As and Bs."

"I think that's plenty good," Marabet said.

"She wanted me to make all As."

Lilah remembered feeling the same way herself. "Every mother wants her children to make all As, unrealistic as it may be." She nibbled at her toast. "How about you? The way you play, you must have had formal lessons."

"I did. For three years."

"Why did you quit?"

Bethany looked down at the table. "Daddy got sick, and there wasn't any money for piano lessons." She looked up again, her face registering defiance and something more complex. "But mama taught me just like a real teacher."

Lilah felt sudden tears prick the backs of her eyes, but she tried to keep her smile steady. "She must have done a very good job. I hope you'll play and practice as much as you want. It will be a pleasure to hear you."

"Are you sure? Scales and all?"

Lilah smiled and nodded. "Scales and all."

She looked over at Marabet, but Marabet seemed intent on her breakfast.

Lilah was emptying drawers into boxes when Marabet came upstairs.

"This is starting to look really pretty, Lilah," she said, coming into the room.

"It'll look even prettier when the new furniture gets here," Lilah said, not stopping. "Have the delivery people called?"

Marabet nodded. "They're on their way. Could you use a hand?"

Lilah looked at the clothes spread out on the bed. "I could use ten hands, but I'll settle for two if that's all you have." She grabbed another sweater and folded it into the box beside her. "Did you tell them they have to take this old furniture with them?"

"I did, and they agreed. Relax." Marabet pulled out a drawer and dumped its contents into a box. "I was wondering if you wanted lunch before or after the furniture people come."

"After. Definitely. I'm much too excited to eat."

"That's good. I didn't want to interrupt Bethany's practicing anyway." Silence. "She's been practicing all morning."

"I've heard."

"It sure is good to have music in the house again."

"It is."

Marabet dumped another drawer into the box. "It seems a shame the girl had to give up her lessons when her father got sick. She's really good."

"She certainly is," Lilah agreed.

"You know," Marabet said, pulling out another drawer, "I

just had a thought. It would be great if she could pick up her lessons where she left off."

"I don't know," Lilah said, frowning down into the half-full box. "I doubt her teacher would drive all the way from Athens."

"I wasn't talking about that. I—"

Lilah laughed aloud. "I know very well what you were talking about, Marabet. You're about as subtle as a runaway truck." She started to fold her lingerie into the box, then changed her mind and dumped it in. "I don't have any real objection to Bethany taking piano lessons. It'll give her something to do while she's here."

Marabet let the drawer she was holding dangle from her fingers, spilling bras onto the new carpet. "While she's here."

Lilah's smile faded. "Yes, Marabet. While she's here."

"But—"

They both turned toward the window as a truck pulled into the driveway. "I have no objection to her taking piano lessons while she's here, although I'm not sure how to find a teacher for her."

"I'll find someone."

"Good," Lilah said, distracted.

There was a knock at the front door. Lilah looked around the room in dismay. "I'm not ready for them. Will you go let them in while I get all of this into the other room?"

Lilah was surprised that Marabet waited until dinner to broach the subject. "Bethany, your grandmother thought you might want to take up your piano lessons again. What do you say to that?"

Bethany looked at Lilah in surprise.

"Actually, it was Marabet's idea," Lilah corrected, "but I think it's a good one if you think you'd be interested." When Bethany's face lit up, Lilah went on. "I know the house isn't really geared for a person your age. I thought it might give you an interest. You know, something to do while you're here."

Bethany's smile faltered and then died altogether. She stared down at the table.

Lilah wasn't sure what she'd said. She looked at Marabet, but Marabet was intent on the child. "Marabet said she could call around and find a teacher who's available if—"

"No." Bethany lifted her chin, looking directly at Lilah. "Thank you. That's very—nice, but I don't think so."

"Bethany—" Marabet began.

"Are you sure, Bethany?" Lilah interrupted. "It would give you something to fill your days."

"I—No. Excuse me." She stood up from the table and carried her dishes to the sink. Then she walked out of the room, her back rigid.

"Well," Lilah said, blotting her lips on her napkin, "I don't think Bethany liked your idea."

Marabet's face flushed alarmingly as she looked at Lilah through narrowed eyes. "Are you really as unfeeling as you're acting?"

"What are you talking about?"

"You can't see?" Marabet looked toward the door where Bethany had disappeared. "That child is in such pain, and you just keep on hurting her."

Lilah threw her napkin on the table. She was sick and tired of her every action being criticized. "I did what you wanted," she said in irritation. "I offered her piano lessons."

"Right." Marabet's voice rose. "You offered her piano lessons the same way you told her to go outside and play and *allowed* her to go up to the attic, to keep her busy and out of your hair *while she's here.*" She regarded Lilah steadily. "I swear to God, I'm ashamed to call you my friend."

With that, she stood and went into her room, slamming the door.

A minute later, Lilah banged into the room behind her. "What exactly have I done that's so wrong?" She stood just inside the door, hands on her hips.

Marabet stood across the room, mirroring her stance. "You're acting like that girl's a casual house guest."

"She is a house guest."

"But not casual, Lilah. I don't care what you decide to do about it, that girl out there is Elizabeth's daughter and your granddaughter."

"I know that."

"Do you?"

"If this is about Bethany staying—"

"This is not about Bethany staying," Marabet said, her voice shaking with anger. "This is about another human being's happiness. Right now, at this minute! You act like that's not any concern of yours, like you're too good to be bothered with it."

"I said I'd do what I can to help the girl while she's here. I'll even help out financially after she's gone if need be."

"Oh, sure. You'll do anything money can buy. Right?" She spun away and spun back. "I always thought Charles got his callousness from that unfeeling Germ that raised him, but I'm beginning to think he got it from you."

"Don't you talk about my family that way," Lilah said angrily.

"Or what?" Marabet countered. "Are you going to pull that employer-employee crap on me? Well, let me tell you something, Lilah. You may pay me wages, but I'm no damned servant. If you want me to leave, just tell me, but don't you even think of trying to pull rank on me after all these years."

Lilah's mouth dropped open. "I don't want you to go anywhere, Marabet. You're my best friend."

"Am I?" Marabet was visibly shaking. She sat down on the couch arm. "I've known you since you were a girl, and I thought we were friends. But you've changed, and I'm not sure I want

Of Words & Music

to claim the person you've become as my friend."

Lilah sagged against the door jamb. "That's not fair."

"Isn't it? I watched you get beaten down for years by your husband. Oh, not physically," she said when Lilah started to speak. "I know he didn't hit you, but words are weapons, just like fists." She leaned forward. "I saw how he hurt you year after year, and it broke my heart because I couldn't do a damned thing about it. I'd have thought that living through that and knowing how much it hurt you, you would've gotten more sensitive over the years, but now I see you kicking someone when she's down. And not just anyone, but a girl who's just lost both her parents. I wouldn't have believed you'd treat even a casual stranger that bad."

Lilah opened her mouth to speak, but Marabet charged on. "I've watched you wrap yourself up in some kind of—of cocoon these last fifteen years, ever since Gerome decided your daughter wasn't welcome in your life. No. Even before that. Since you married him. I've watched you pretend that everything was all right when it was terrible. I've watched you pretend not to grieve over losing Elizabeth when she died. You said your life was a big pretense. Well, you're right. It was, and maybe it still is. I always thought you'd pull yourself back together, especially when Gerome died, but I was wrong. You're just as closed off as ever. Did living with him kill every feeling inside you?"

Lilah looked away.

Neither woman said anything for a long time. There was no sound in the room, in the house. Just their breathing, ragged, but slowing now. Finally, Lilah said, "It's true that I have some . . . problems to work through. I—I hope I haven't become as unfeeling as you say. If you say I am, then I really have to consider it because you've never lied to me and because, whatever you say, you are my best friend." She saw tears fill Marabet's eyes, but she continued. "I know Bethany means a lot to you, although I wish you hadn't gotten so attached to her. I can't feel the way you do about her, Marabet. I'm sorry. I can't even pretend to, but I meant it when I said I'd do anything I could for her. I know you think these piano lessons will be good for her, but you heard her yourself. She doesn't want piano lessons. We can't force her to take them."

"No, we can't, but I think she refused because of how they were offered, like some kind of charity thing. I would have thrown them back in your face, too."

"I didn't mean it that way."

"Maybe not, but Bethany's a real sensitive girl. She doesn't have a home or a family anymore. She has nothing but what you give her and what the state decides she can have. Can't you put yourself in her place for a minute and imagine how that feels?"

"I . . . guess I can't." Lilah looked at the floor, then back at Marabet. "Why do you feel so strongly about her taking piano lessons?"

"It means something to her. Music means a lot to her. It's almost the only thing she has left in her life. You saw her face when she was playing. If we can give her even a little bit of heaven after the hell she's been through, well then, I think it's that important." She shook her head. "I don't know how I can convince her that you're sincere about this—" She looked up at Lilah. "If you really are."

Lilah swallowed. "I am."

Marabet shook her head again. "I'll have to think about it and talk to her, but I'll only do that if you really mean what you said about doing anything you can."

"I do mean it. I feel sorry for the child. I'll do whatever is within my power for her while she's here."

"And you won't renege if I commit you."

"No, Marabet," she answered wearily. "I won't renege."

"You promise."

"I promise."

"You told her what?" Lilah sat straight up in bed.

"I told her you wanted to take piano lessons with her." Marabet perched on the end of Lilah's bed, leaning against the footboard.

"Are you out of your mind?" Lilah asked in a strangled voice.

"Is that a problem?"

"Is that—yes, I would say that's a problem."

"Why?"

"I'll tell you why," she sputtered. "Because I have no intention of taking any kind of lessons."

"Lower your voice. She might hear you."

"I don't care—"

"You said you'd do anything within your power."

"I certainly didn't mean—I meant—" Lilah stammered. "What in the world possessed you to tell her such a thing?"

"It was the only way I could convince her you really wanted her to take lessons."

Lilah crossed her arms. "Okay. I can't wait to hear this. How did that convince her?"

"I told her your reasons were kind of selfish, that you'd wanted to take lessons for a long time, but you thought you were too old. I said you wouldn't feel so silly if you were taking them with her."

Lilah closed her eyes and shook her head. "You really are out of your mind."

"I don't see why."

Lilah ticked her reasons off on her fingers. "Because I don't want to take piano lessons. I am too old. I'd feel totally ridiculous. I don't have the time. I certainly don't want to take lessons with someone else." She started on the fingers of the other hand. "I have no intention of doing so."

"You said you'd do anything within your power."

"I didn't mean this."

"What'll it cost you?"

"I don't know. What do teachers charge these days?"

"I don't mean money. What will it really cost you?"

"My dignity."

"Oh, pooh! You have enough of that to spare. It'll cost a little time, and you have plenty of that to spare, too."

"I won't do it."

"You said you wouldn't renege."

"You had no right to commit me."

"You promised."

"Forget it."

"You *promised.*"

"I said forget it, and that's my last word."

Chapter 11

"What time is our teacher coming?" Bethany's voice sounded unnaturally loud in the tense stillness of the room.

"Felicity said four o'clock," Marabet answered.

"Is she coming with him?"

She nodded. "To introduce you."

Bethany stole a glance at her grandmother, who was sitting stiffly in her chair, studying the fireplace. She had come downstairs just a minute ago and marched over to her chair like a queen to her throne, not looking at either of them. Maybe she was mad because Bethany remembered that Felicity's boyfriend was a music teacher or—or—who knew what? Earlier, Marabet had asked Bethany to be patient with her. She'd explained that Lilah was embarrassed, and that sometimes that came across like anger. She wished they'd hurry up and get here. Maybe she would relax then.

They all turned toward the window as a car came up the driveway. Marabet got up and went out into the hall. The doorbell rang. Then voices, footsteps.

Marabet led the way into the room. "Elliott Morrison, this is Lilah Kimball," she said, leading the teacher over to Lilah.

Lilah offered her hand, and he shook it. "Mr. Morrison. Felicity." She nodded at the social worker. "Please sit down. Thank you for coming."

Marabet ignored her, steered Elliott over to the couch. "And this is Bethany."

Bethany stood and offered her hand, causing Marabet to smile and Lilah to raise her eyebrows. "Hello," she said shyly.

"Hello, Bethany," he said, shaking her hand. "I've heard a lot about you. Felicity told me you love the piano."

"I do," she said, coloring. "I'm not very good at it."

He smiled. "You'd be amazed at some of the famous pianists who have said the same thing."

"She's wonderful," Marabet interjected. "You should hear—"

"Marabet," Lilah's voice interrupted. "Will you bring in some coffee?"

Marabet turned and regarded her as if deciding. Then she pasted a sweet smile on her face and executed a little curtsey. "Yes, ma'am."

Lilah didn't miss the grin on Bethany's face. "Please, sit down," she said again.

Felicity took the seat beside Bethany on the couch, and Elliott the chair near Lilah Kimball's. "Are you twelve, Bethany?" he asked.

"Almost thirteen."

"I understand you took piano lessons before."

Bethany nodded. "For three years. Then my mother taught me for three years after that."

"That sounds like a solid background."

He turned to Lilah Kimball, but before he could say a word, she asked, "What is your background, Mr. Morrison."

He raised his eyebrows. "Elliott, please. I teach music at Marietta Middle School. I have a degree in Music Education from Kennesaw State, and a master's degree in piano performance."

"Do you?" she asked, raising her eyebrows. "Perform?"

"Only very casually right now. I'm playing three evenings a week at Shelby's. It's a piano bar."

"I know Shelby's," she interrupted. "Fine restaurant. They

have good veal."

"And good music," he countered. "Actually, I haven't tried the veal."

"Nor have I tried the music."

"Perhaps we both have something to look forward to," he said.

As they regarded each other, Marabet entered, pushing a cart laden with cups and saucers, a silver coffee service, and two large platters of cookies and small cakes.

"Good heavens," Lilah said under her breath.

"Learning's hungry work," Marabet said, pushing the cart up beside Lilah's chair. She moved the heavy coffee tray to the table and placed a platter laden with food on either side. Then she moved back behind Lilah's chair, standing like a sentinel.

"Have you played before, Mrs. Kimball?" Elliott asked as Lilah poured the coffee.

"Mmmm." She nodded. "When I was a girl." She handed a cup to Felicity, and then poured one for Elliott. "I haven't touched the instrument in years."

"I'm surprised you want to go back to it," he said.

"I'm not sure I do." She ignored Marabet's glare, picking up her cup and taking a sip. "I thought I'd talk with you and—well, see how things develop."

He sat back in the chair and crossed one leg over the other, balancing his coffee cup on the arm of the chair. "Fair enough."

Lilah said nothing for a moment. Then, "What do you see as the purpose of piano lessons?"

"Fun," he answered without hesitation.

"Fun?" she echoed.

Elliott nodded.

"And that's all one gets out of it? Fun?"

"Oh! I see what you're driving at." He took a sip of his coffee before answering. "Well, I see the purpose of the lessons as fun, but while that fun is happening, what the student gets out of it is immeasurable. I think piano develops determination. It helps the student learn to examine each challenge with a fresh eye and try as many solutions as necessary to meet the challenge successfully. It teaches him or her that anything can be accomplished if it's approached with patience and a willingness to look a bit foolish during the process. It teaches the student to laugh at his or her mistakes while learning from them. It teaches flexibility in thinking."

"All that?" Lilah asked, sitting back.

"Oh, there's more."

"I'm certain there is," Lilah said, taking his measure. "How long have you taught, Mr. Morrison?"

"Elliott. For eight years. I also have five private students."

"And you perform in the evenings. You sound like a very busy man."

Elliott laughed. "Not that busy. Actually, summers can be deadly for teachers who don't write or travel extensively. A weekend off is a treasure. Three months off can get a little tedious." He uncrossed his legs and put the cup and saucer on the table, leaning forward to rest his arms on his thighs. "Lack of time wouldn't be a deterrent to my working with you and Bethany, Mrs. Kimball," he said seriously, "but I would want to know that you actually want lessons before I'd agree to undertake them. Do you?"

Lilah looked intrigued. "I'm beginning to think I might. May I ask you to play something for us?"

Elliott nodded shortly. He rose and crossed to the piano. "Anything in particular?"

"You take requests?"

He smiled at her but didn't answer. He sat down on the bench and let his hands hang loose for a moment. Then he raised them and rested them on the keys.

Of Words & Music

Softly, softly, he played the opening notes of the Moonlight Sonata. So softly that the music was more felt than heard. Slowly, it swelled until it was a presence in the room. The music rose and fell, always controlled, and yet free and blending and interweaving. He went directly into Scarlatti's Sonata in D minor, the light, almost playful minor tones creating a mystery of sound. Then into Bach's Italian Concerto. He finished with Satie's three Gymnopedies.

When the last note finally faded, the room was totally silent. No one seemed to breathe. Then Elliott turned. "Did I pass?" he asked, grinning at Lilah Kimball.

It was a moment before she answered. The room's air shimmered again, only this time a silvery blue. Lilah felt wonder. Excitement. Joy, almost on the sharp edge of sorrow. She could scarcely breathe, but she felt the corners of her mouth tilt upward. "You certainly did—Elliott."

"Well, then," he said, rising and gesturing to the piano bench. "Your turn. And then we'll hear Bethany."

The haze vanished. "Oh, no. I—"

"Me?" Bethany asked. "With all these people?"

"I think that's our cue to leave the room," Marabet said, coming from behind the chair and gesturing to Felicity. "Why don't we go into the kitchen and give them some privacy."

Lilah stopped in the hallway, unwilling to interrupt. She had come to tell Felicity that Elliott was ready to leave when she heard Marabet say, "Did you see Lilah's face? He had her eating out of the palm of his hand. Smitten, she was, the minute he sat down at the piano and began to play. I haven't seen her face look like that since—well, I can't remember when. Maybe the last time she listened to Elizabeth."

"She really loved her?" That was Felicity. "I shouldn't ask that."

"No. It's all right. I can see why you'd think otherwise. She did though. She loved her more than anything."

"Then why . . ." The voice trailed off.

"It's hard to explain. You'd have to know her years ago. Lilah was sweet, lively, fun-loving. Not all that strong-willed back then. Her husband . . . well, he was—oh, hell, he was a bastard. He ruled the roost. Just like Lilah's father."

Lilah took a step back. She'd never heard Marabet talk like this before. She knew she should make her presence known, but she couldn't make herself move.

"Women often pick husbands like their fathers."

Marabet snorted. "Lilah didn't pick him. Not really. Her parents picked him and Lilah went along. Like I said, she wasn't very strong-willed back then."

"Then she's changed."

"She has, and even more since her husband died. Her son's tried some of that strong-arm stuff on her lately, and she isn't buying. But back then . . ." She was silent for a minute, then, "When Elizabeth left, I was honest to God afraid Lilah would do herself harm. She was half dead with grief for months, although most people couldn't tell by seeing her, but she wouldn't have dreamed of going against his orders. And they were orders. He told her that Elizabeth was no daughter of theirs, and they wouldn't have anything more to do with her unless she mended her ways. Those were his exact words, *mended her ways,* like she was some naughty child who'd misbehaved. Lord, how I hated that man."

"Why—"

"Why what?"

"I just wondered why you never contacted Elizabeth."

"I couldn't. I just couldn't. I know you couldn't tell it in there, but Lilah really is my best friend. I couldn't have seen Elizabeth or talked to her and not told Lilah, and if I'd told her, it would have torn her to pieces—and if his highness had found out, I'd have been out on my ear. Then Lilah would've had no one. Oh, Lord, don't you know I've beaten myself up about that. I thought there was plenty of time, don't you see? Elizabeth was only thirty. Lilah didn't seem to be getting any older. Once the Germ—her husband—died, I thought it was just a matter of time. I started working on Lilah. A word here and there. I didn't want to push too hard too fast and have her go stubborn on me. For a year or so, she played the grieving widow. Oh, I don't mean that unkindly. I think she convinced herself that she was. You know what I mean? Her whole life she'd always done what was expected of her. At least until lately. That's why this means so much to me. For Bethany's sake, sure. I love that girl already, and I can't bear the thought of her going away. But for Lilah's sake, too. Lilah needs her and she doesn't even know it, and I think—I think Bethany might be her last chance."

Lilah turned and walked down the hallway and up the stairs without stopping.

Chapter 12

Bethany slipped down the stairs. Lilah had seemed really different after Elliott left. Pensive. She grinned. That was one of her father's words. Pensive. She rolled it around in her mouth and decided she liked it. Pensive. Still, she'd waited a while after the piano went silent, thinking Lilah might have gone in to talk to Marabet, but she was still seated at the piano, leafing through a music book. The light over the piano was on, but the rest of the room was in shadow. Bethany could see half a dozen books spread out on the piano. She turned to leave, but Lilah's voice stopped her.

"Don't go, Bethany. I'm finished here."

Bethany turned back. "I didn't mean to make you quit."

"No." Lilah put the book back on the music holder. "I've hogged the piano long enough. It felt really good to play again." She caressed the piano keys, but then stopped abruptly. "We might think about working out some kind of practice schedule if we're both going to be taking lessons."

Bethany came into the room. "If we play a piece together like Elliott said, we'll need to practice together, too."

Lilah shook her head. "I don't think that would work. You're too far ahead of me. I'll be essentially starting over."

"I thought that song you played for Elliott was great," Bethany said.

"That little piece?" Lilah asked, her voice softening. "That was one of the first sonatinas I learned."

"What was it?"

"Sonatina in C. By Latour."

"It's really fast."

Lilah nodded. "It is fast. I worked on it forever. I thought I'd never teach my left hand to play as fast as my right."

"It sounded perfect. Do you have the music?"

Lilah stood and opened the piano bench, riffling through the music. "Not here. It must be up in the attic somewhere. Maybe I'll look—"

"I'll look for it tomorrow," Bethany said quickly, feeling a flicker of panic. She hadn't put anything away upstairs. Then, embarrassed, "If you want me to."

"All right," Lilah said, straightening up and closing the bench. "Marabet can probably give you some idea of where to start." She made a move as if to leave, then she stopped. "What did you think of Elliott?"

"I think he's dreamy."

Lilah smiled. "I can't argue with you there, but I meant his piano playing."

"Oh, isn't he amazing? All those trills! I've never heard anyone play like that except on a record. Mama used to have all these old records . . ." Her voice faltered.

"I remember," Lilah said. She cleared her throat. "Well, Elliott will be back tomorrow for our first official lesson, so I'll let you get to your practicing."

"Are you sure it won't bother you?"

"Quite sure. I probably won't even be able to hear it in my room."

Lilah closed her sitting room door and the door leading to her bedroom, but still the music reached her, song after song that Elizabeth used to play. Haunting her, tugging at her heart, punishing her, and the worst part of all was that the punishment was unintentional. She couldn't very well go down and ask the girl not to play the only songs she knew. Of course she would know Elizabeth's pieces.

Lilah found herself reading the same paragraph over and over. Finally, she put down her novel and took off her reading glasses, chewing on one of the ear pieces as she listened. Bethany was good, really good, although she didn't seem to realize it.

It had felt strange to play in front of someone else, especially that virtuoso teacher. She agreed with Bethany. Rarely had she heard the piano played so beautifully. The girl was right about his looks, too, Lilah thought with a smile. She might be twice his age, but she had eyes in her head. No, his face was not going to be hard to look at. He reminded her of someone, but she couldn't place the resemblance. He had spunk, too. She'd used her best you're-a-peon-and-I'm-king-of-the-castle manner on him, and he'd tossed it right back at her. Interesting man. Since she'd agreed to these ridiculous lessons, at least for the present, it helped that the teacher was going to be a pleasure to work with.

She picked up the novel she'd discarded, trying to block out the sounds from below. She'd get used to it. Pretty soon it wouldn't bother her at all.

Bethany came racing down the stairs as soon as she heard the front doorbell. She skidded to a stop just inside the living room. "Hi," she said, shy again.

Elliott smiled at her. "Good morning. Ready for your lesson?"

"I guess so."

"Did you get a chance to review any of your old pieces last night?"

She nodded. "Most of them."

"Most? How long did you practice?"

Bethany glanced away. "A few hours."

"That's great, but did you give your grandmother any practice time?"

"She gave me more than enough practice time," Lilah said, coming into the room. "Good morning, Elliott. I'm afraid I don't share Bethany's love for practicing. Or her endurance," she added with a wry smile.

"Then we'll just have to work on that love of practicing," Elliott said, returning her smile. "That will help build the endurance." He looked around him. "Can we bring another couple of chairs over here?"

The words were barely out of his mouth before Marabet came into the room. "Why don't I bring in a couple from the kitchen? Those over there are too heavy to be moving around much," she added, gesturing across the room.

Elliott looked at Lilah and raised his eyebrows.

"You get used to it after a while," she said. "That will be fine, Marabet."

Once they were seated, Elliott at the piano and Lilah and Bethany in the chairs, he said, "I thought I'd work with one of you for half an hour, then both of you together for an hour, then the other for half an hour. I'll want you to sit in on each other's half hour, at least at first. I've found that you can learn almost as much from watching others' classes as from your own. What do you say?" He looked from one to the other.

Bethany shrugged. "Sure."

"Do you really think Bethany and I should work together?" Lilah asked. "Her playing is light years ahead of mine."

"I wouldn't say light years," Elliott said with a smile. "She has a few years on you, but I brought a book of duets for us to look at. Generally one part is more difficult than the other. Bethany could take the hard part, and it would even out."

Lilah looked skeptical. "If you say so."

Elliott grinned. "Trust me. But we're getting ahead of ourselves. First I have a question for each of you. What are your piano goals? What do you want to get out of the lessons? Where do you want it to ultimately take you? Bethany?"

"I don't know," she answered slowly. "I never thought about it."

"Do you just want to play for a few years?"

"No! I want to play—forever," she finished, looking embarrassed at her outburst.

"How good do you want to get?"

"Really, really good," she said earnestly. "Like you," she added with a shy smile. "I know I probably never will be as good as you."

"Don't believe that for a moment," Elliott said, leaning forward, elbows on his thighs, his hands clasped between his knees. "I want to get as good as Horowitz. That's my goal. If I never make it, that's okay, but if I didn't have that goal, I wouldn't play as well as I do now. What about later? Do you want to study music in college?"

Bethany shrugged. "I think so. Probably. If I get to go to college."

Elliott darted a look at Lilah. "Well, then," he said, "I think we have a pretty good idea of where you're going. Piano isn't a short-term goal for you. You want to continue studying music, whether you pursue it beyond college or not. Since the chance exists that you might want to focus on music later, you want to make sure you have a solid background in theory and sight-reading, as well as technique."

Bethany looked bemused. "Okay."

He turned to Lilah. "What about you, Mrs. Kimball. What are your musical goals?"

"Please," she said, raising her hand, "call me Lilah. Since I didn't have any piano goals as of yesterday morning, I'm not sure what to answer. They certainly wouldn't be as lofty as Bethany's." She thought for a moment. "I was truly impressed by your playing, but I was also overwhelmed. I don't aspire to play anything that complex. I used to love to hear Elizabeth play. My daughter. I think I'd like to be able to play those songs. You know, fairly simple things that I could play just for my own enjoyment."

Elliott nodded. "From sheet music or memory?"

She considered his words. "Both, I think."

"Have you ever done any sight reading?"

"No. Never."

"You?" he asked, turning to Bethany.

"Some."

"Okay," he said, sitting back. "I think that gives us an idea of where we're going. Lilah," he said, smiling at her, "I'll get you started on some sight reading. We'll spend ten or fifteen minutes on it during our lesson each week, but I want you to sight read a little each day."

"What should I sight read?"

"I'll bring something with me next week for you to get started on. Now, I think it would be a good idea to get a feel for what each of you can do so we'll know how to proceed. How about scales? Do you both know them?"

Bethany nodded.

Lilah looked doubtful. "Not . . . really."

"Okay. We'll start with Bethany." He stood and motioned for her to take the piano bench.

Bethany sat down at the piano. "How do you want me to play them?"

"Any way you want," Elliott said, taking the chair next to Lilah.

Bethany began with the C scale, playing with both hands flying over the keys, first in the same direction, then in opposite directions. She didn't pause between scales, executing instead some kind of little turn-around. When she'd played for what seemed like a half hour, she stopped and looked up at Elliott. "That's the Russian pattern."

    He grinned at her. "I know it is. Where did you learn that?"

    "My teacher was Russian. He learned it when he was in school there. In Saint Petersburg."

    "I'm impressed."

    "I'm embarrassed," Lilah said. "I didn't know you meant scales like that. I think I only worked on C, F and some other. Maybe G."

    Elliott nodded. "Perfect." When she looked at him in surprise, he said, "That will be your first assignment, Bethany. I want you to teach your grandmother the scales in the Russian pattern. All the scales," he added with a gleam in his eyes.

    "I'll never learn all that," Lilah blurted out.

    "It's not so hard," Bethany said. "Really. I'll show you." She turned to Elliott. "What about the chromatic scale?"

    When Lilah clutched her throat, Elliott laughed. "We'll save that for later. Okay." He picked up one of the books out of his briefcase. "Let's see how you do with sight reading, Bethany. Then we'll all take a look at some of those duets."

Lilah was thoughtful as she walked Elliott to the door. As his hand reached out for the knob, she opened her mouth to say goodbye, but what came out was, "Did Felicity put you up to this?"

    Elliott's hand fell back to his side. "Up to what?"

    Lilah could feel heat spreading up her neck, but she was determined. "The piano lessons. All this togetherness," she added, waving her hand toward the living room.

    Elliott seemed to consider his answer. "She may have mentioned that it would be good for the two of you to work together." As Lilah opened her mouth to speak, he barged on. "But I do think it's important for two people in the same household to be involved in each other's lessons," he added. "I meant what I said about group lessons being beneficial. You can learn a lot from each other's mistakes and triumphs."

"You mean my mistakes and Bethany's triumphs."

Elliott looked down at her with a slight crease between his brows. "No, that's not what I mean at all. You may learn something about execution from Bethany, but you have even more to teach. You have patience. Determination. Experience and wisdom."

Lilah laughed uncomfortably. "I don't see what they have to do with learning to play the piano."

"The two former? Everything."

"And the latter?"

"Maybe nothing," Elliott said with a shrug, "but they have everything to do with living. What good does having experience and wisdom do if there's no one to share them with? They're what you have to teach, Lilah. Don't hoard them."

Lilah couldn't meet his eyes. "Is that all Felicity suggested?"

After a long uncomfortable moment, Elliott said, "All that I intend to share." He opened the door and let himself out of the house.

She stood for several minutes staring at the closed door. It appeared that Elliott was more than a pretty face and an accomplished pianist. He was a very strong and self-confident young man. Lilah found to her surprise that she didn't mind.

She turned and headed back into the living room. She sat down in one of the chairs beside the piano, where Bethany was still seated.

"Ready to start?" Bethany asked, her face still alight with pleasure.

Ready, yes. But willing? "I don't know why I have to learn a lot of scales just to play for my own enjoyment."

"They're really important."

"Why?"

Bethany leaned forward. "They teach you to play the notes evenly. Some fingers aren't as strong as others. Playing scales builds the weaker ones. And fingering. You learn which fingers play which notes in a key, so when you play a song in a certain key, you know which fingers to use. And—"

"All right," Lilah said, holding up her hands. "I give in." Then she shook her head. "Do you really think I'll be able to learn all those scales?"

"Sure."

"How many are there?"

"Twenty-four."

Lilah made a face. "It sounded like a hundred."

Bethany grinned. "That's what I thought, too, when I first learned them."

"It sounded like a song when you were playing them with both hands. And you played them with your hands going in opposite directions."

"Contrary motion."

"It looks impossible."

"It isn't. Really. Some of them are hard, but some of them are easier to play in contrary motion than parallel motion. Like E and E flat."

"Parallel motion. That's both hands going in the same direction?"

Bethany nodded again. "I'll show you if you want."

For a minute, Lilah hesitated. Then she moved to the piano bench, sitting beside Bethany. "I guess there's no time like the present to begin."

As Bethany began to play the C scale, Lilah muttered, "Twenty-four scales. What in the world have I gotten myself into?" But there was a trace of a smile on her face.

When the phone rang, Lilah was just stepping out of her bath. Fragrant steam wrapped itself around her, and she breathed in deeply. She was exhausted from hours at the piano, and yet she felt strangely exhilarated. Who would have thought scales could be so much fun to play? Frustrating, but fun. As she tied the belt on her terry robe, Marabet's disembodied voice came through the intercom speaker on the wall. "It's Lesa Kimball."

Lilah smiled as she picked up the receiver. "Lesa, how are you? I've been meaning to call you."

"I'm fine. How are your flowers?"

"Thriving, despite the heat. Yours?"

"The same. It must be all that combined skill we have."

"Undoubtedly," Lilah said with a laugh, wondering why she had thought this woman had no personality.

"I called to tell you my news." There was silence for a moment. Then Lesa blurted out, "I'm going to be taking a couple of graduate classes at Georgia State. Just morning classes, when Charles is at the office," she added quickly, as if she feared disapproval.

"That's wonderful, Lesa," Lilah said with real enthusiasm. She used the corner of the robe to blot the dampness off her face. "What does Charles think of it?"

"I haven't actually told him yet." There was a moment of silence. "You don't think I'm silly to go back to school?"

"Silly? No. I think it's wonderful. But I can tell you something really silly. I'm taking piano lessons."

"You are? When did you start?"

"Today. Marabet roped me into it. She decided it would be good for Bethany if she took lessons, and for some reason, the child wouldn't agree unless I took lessons with her. Lord knows why. I could have strangled Marabet for blackmailing me into doing it, but I'm beginning to think it might be fun."

"That's wonderful," Lesa said, but her voice sounded tense.

Lilah had a sudden thought. "Lesa, are you nervous about telling Charles you're going to be taking classes?" Lesa didn't say anything for a minute, giving Lilah her answer. "Why don't you and Charles come over for dinner tomorrow night? You can tell him then. I'll back you up."

"Are you sure? He might be unpleasant about it."

Lilah heard a muffled laugh. Her brows came together. "Then we'll just have to make him pleasant. Yes, I'm sure," she said, her eyes on the door. "I'll tell Marabet to fix something special."

That's not the only thing I'll tell her, Lilah thought as she hung up the phone.

She tapped on Marabet's door and opened it, stepping inside. Marabet was sitting in her favorite chair in front of the TV, feet propped on the table in front of her, a bowl of popcorn at her side.

She looked up. "Hi, Lilah. What's up?" She picked up the popcorn bowl and rested it in her lap.

Lilah stood at the door, hands on her hips. "I want you to stop listening in on my phone conversations. It's really irritating."

Marabet didn't bother to deny it. "You sure? It saves you a lot of time telling me about them."

"Promise me."

"Lilah—"

"Promise. I will not have you listening in on the extension like some recalcitrant teenager."

Marabet sighed. "Oh, all right, but I might miss something you'd want me to know."

"If I want you to know anything that transpires during my private telephone conversations, I'll tell you myself." She looked down her nose at Marabet. "Scout's honor?"

Marabet held up two fingers in a V. "Scout's honor."

"Good." Lilah dropped down on the loveseat. "Give me some of that popcorn. What are we watching?"

Bethany sat curled on the sofa in her sitting room, her fingers drumming out songs on the cushion beside her. Nine o'clock, and it was just getting dark outside, that summer dark that seemed to want to hold off as long as possible. She had turned on the television, but there was nothing on. Boring sitcoms, news programs. The usual network junk. She didn't know if the rest of the house had cable, but her room didn't. It didn't really matter. It wasn't a night for watching TV. She felt almost giddy with happiness.

Who would have believed she and her grandmother would have spent hours playing the piano together and talking and laughing? Grandmother. The word still sounded strange. Would she get used to it in time? She pushed the question away.

She had gone over the C scale with her. Lilah already knew that, at least in parallel motion. Bethany had gone over how much easier the fingering was in contrary motion. It had felt really funny at first to be the teacher, probably because she had always been the student. After a while, though, it had gotten to be fun. Lilah was already playing the C scale in contrary motion. Tomorrow they'd work on A minor. It was almost the same. A piece of cake.

She hugged a throw pillow to her middle. Her grandmother had actually laughed when Bethany reminded her they only had twenty-three more scales to go. Laughed! She looked pretty when she laughed, happy and young.

Bethany put the pillow aside and picked up the picture of her mother. "Oh, Mama," she whispered, "I hope you don't mind if I'm nice to her. She seems so sad all the time. Or mad. Sad and mad both at the same time. But today she seemed almost happy.

I know she was horrible to you, but—well, I don't think she'd be horrible if you were here now. Do you think it's all right if I help her not be so sad?"

There was no sound in the room, but Bethany felt her answer. After a while, she went into her bedroom, taking the picture with her. She put it on the bedside table while she changed into her nightshirt. She tossed her clothes into the laundry hamper. She knew they'd disappear from there and reappear in her drawers, clean and folded. She liked that. A lot.

After she washed her face and brushed her teeth, she went back out into the sitting room and ran her hand over the books on the shelves. Lots of Jane Austen, *Heidi,* which she'd already read a dozen times, some yucky looking school type books. She could go down to the library and get some different ones tomorrow. She grinned. How cool was it to have a whole library in her own house? Well, not really *her* own house, but kind of, by association. Or it would be while she was here. The words made a knot in her stomach, so she ignored them.

After a minute, her hand came to rest on *The Great Gatsby* by Fitzgerald. She hadn't read that one, but she remembered seeing it on the school's recommended reading list. What the heck, she thought, taking the book back into the bedroom with her and climbing into bed. If it was really awful, it would only put her to sleep. She stacked the pillows up behind her and reached over, picking up her mother's picture and tucking it into bed beside her. Then she propped the book on her knees and opened it to the first page. Within half an hour, she was sound asleep.

Chapter 13

Lilah came in just as Marabet was putting the final touches on the table. The dining room had never been one of her favorites, although Gerome had liked it. It was forbidding: chairs too straight to be comfortable, table and sideboard too heavy. Still, Marabet had done her best.

"It looks nice, Marabet."

Marabet grunted.

"Is it dark in here?" Lilah asked, looking from the light switch to the window, where the drapes were open.

"Dark as a tomb, and just as welcoming."

"Maybe some candles on the table."

"They don't have enough candles in Atlanta to brighten up this room. I know, I know," she said before Lilah could speak. "I'll put half a dozen on the table, but you'll see. It won't help."

"What's for dinner?"

"It's a surprise," Marabet said over her shoulder as she left the room.

Lilah went to the window and pulled the drapes further back, then shook her head. Marabet hadn't exaggerated. There probably weren't enough candles in all of Georgia to improve this room.

She headed up the stairs to change her clothes. On a sudden impulse, she walked down the hall to Bethany's room and knocked.

Bethany opened the door and looked at Lilah in surprise.

"Um—I was just going to change for dinner. I wondered if you'd be joining us."

"Sure, if you want me to."

"I do. Lesa's going to spring a surprise on Charles. She's going back to school."

"Wow. She is?" She hesitated, then swung the door wide. "Do you want to come in?" she asked.

Lilah hesitated. "All right."

She stepped into the room, taking it all in at a glance. So little had changed since Elizabeth was here. The chair and sofa covers and the drapes were the same warm plaid that Elizabeth picked out in her senior year in high school. Lilah had thought the room would look busy with all the plaid, but instead it looked friendly and comfortable. She recognized a number of the books Marabet had put on the shelves, especially the early ones. She and Elizabeth had read a lot of them together.

Her eyes came to rest on the end table, on the picture of Elizabeth. She felt her heart wrench, and for a minute it was hard to catch her breath. She realized Bethany was watching her.

"Do you want to sit down?"

Lilah perched on the edge of a chair, and Bethany flopped on the sofa, crossing her legs yoga fashion. Another wrench. Elizabeth had often sat in the same loose-limbed manner.

"You said she's going back to school?" Bethany prompted.

Lilah forced her attention back to Bethany. "Uh—yes. She called last night. She's going to be working toward her master's degree. She hasn't told Charles yet."

"I don't think he'll like that much. He doesn't think much of education."

"Not for Lesa, at least," Lilah agreed. "I thought we'd give her some moral support. Are you willing?"

Bethany grinned. "Sure. I think it'd be fun."

"He doesn't intimidate you, does he?"

"You mean scare me?" When Lilah nodded, she shook her head. "No. I don't understand a lot of what he talks about, but I don't think he wants me to."

Out of the mouth of babes, Lilah thought, smiling inwardly.

Her eyes were drawn back to the picture of Elizabeth. "She was so special," she whispered, then realized she had spoken aloud.

Bethany's reaction was immediate. Tears filled her eyes. "I know," she said through trembling lips.

Lilah rose to her feet. "Bethany, I'm sorry—"

"No." Bethany shook her head. "I'm sorry." She wiped her eyes with her index finger, a gesture Lilah could see was reflex. Bethany swallowed hard. "What time's dinner?" Then, with a watery smile, "I promise not to cry."

Lilah felt another wrench at her heart, but this time it was for the girl in front of her who was trying so hard to be brave. "Seven."

"Should I dress up?"

Lilah looked at her jeans and shirt. "I think you look fine just the way you are."

"I'll get it," Lilah called out when the doorbell chimed. Charles stood on the porch, with Lesa a step behind. He was dressed in his inevitable three-piece suit, expertly tailored but snug across the belly. In his hand was a leather portfolio.

"Mother," he said, kissing her on the cheek.

Lilah allowed the kiss, then reached behind him and took Lesa's hand, squeezing it. "Come in," she said, pulling Lesa in front of Charles. She was dressed in her usual dark colors, navy this time, but she was wearing a red scarf around her neck. A little flag of rebellion?

She led them to the living room, where Marabet had set out

cheese and crackers on the coffee table. Charles dropped the portfolio on the sofa and crossed immediately to the bar, taking out a glass.

"Charles?" When he glanced over his shoulder, Lilah said, "Since you're acting as bartender, maybe someone else would like something." She looked at Lesa. "What can he get you?"

Lesa looked uncomfortable. "Oh, nothing. Really."

Charles started to turn back, but stopped when Lilah said, "I'll have a glass of white wine, Charles. I believe there's a bottle in the refrigerator there, and why don't you fix Bethany a Coke. She should be here any minute."

Charles stared at her for a moment. Then he turned and put down his glass, picking up the wine opener. "Certainly, Mother."

Just as he finished pouring Coke into a glass, Bethany came rushing into the room. "Sorry I'm late," she said. "I was helping Marabet."

"It's no problem," Lilah said, sitting down on the sofa with her glass of wine. She noticed that Bethany had changed her shirt and tied a matching ribbon in her hair. "Charles fixed you a Coke."

Bethany looked at him in surprise. "Uh—thank you." She walked over and took the glass from him. Then she perched on one of the chairs near the sofa.

Charles ignored her. He poured scotch over ice cubes in his glass. Then he came and sat beside Lilah. "To what do we owe the honor of this invitation?" he asked, crossing his legs and pulling down his vest.

Lilah smiled. "No special reason. I just thought it would be nice to get together and chat," she said. Then she turned to Lesa. "Are your flowers surviving the heat, Lesa?"

Lesa was sitting on the edge of her chair, her knees pressed together. "Yes. They're—fine."

"Mine were looking a little limp this afternoon," Lilah went on, trying to will some courage into the younger woman. "I think this heat will kill everything before it breaks."

"I have some afternoon shade where mine . . . are," Lesa finished weakly, glancing at Charles.

"Is this the gardening hour?" Charles asked, looking from one to the other.

"Gardening is one of the things I enjoy doing, Charles," Lilah said evenly. "It's an interest of mine. Lesa's, too." She turned back to Lesa. "Have you ever thought of growing vegetables?"

Charles answered for her. "Our vegetables come from Kroger, dirt free and wrapped in clear plastic." He reached over and picked up the portfolio. "I brought some information about those investments," he said, reaching in and pulling out several colored fliers.

"Not now, Charles," Lilah said, taking the papers from him and placing them face down on the coffee table. "I'll look at those some other time. In your office." she added.

"Mother, I don't think—".

"Dinner is ready," Marabet said coming into the room.

Lilah could have kissed her.

The dining room was dreary, even with the six white candles Marabet had placed in the center of the table. "I apologize for the gloom," she said as everyone was taking their seats. "I think I'll redo this room next. Maybe you can help me, Lesa."

"You don't want Lesa's help," Charles said, draining his ice cubes. "She wanted to do ours up like a breakfast room."

Lilah saw the spots of color on Lesa's cheeks and felt her own face grow warm. "That's exactly the look I want," she told Lesa. "Something bright and cheery. I'll definitely get your help when I start picking things out." She looked up at the hunting print over the sideboard. "Who wants to look at a dead animal strapped across a saddle while they're eating?" she asked, picking up her salad fork.

Bethany giggled.

Charles scowled at her. "That painting was one of father's favorites," he said coldly. "Mine, too."

Lilah smiled. "Wonderful. I'll give it to you, Charles. You can hang it in your study." She looked around her, nodding. "A little fresh paint, some lighter furniture—"

"More new furniture?" Charles demanded.

Lilah looked at him and raised one eyebrow. "Yes, Charles. More new furniture, and a rug and drapes."

He held her gaze for a minute, then looked down and picked up his salad fork. "Do you intend redoing the whole house?"

"I'm not sure yet. I'll let you know when I decide."

They ate in silence for a few minutes. Lesa kept stealing glances at Lilah. At Bethany. Bethany looked at Lilah, at Lesa. Charles kept his eyes on his lettuce.

Just as the silence reached unbearable, Marabet came in pushing a cart. In the center was a platter of plump salmon steaks, garnished with lemon and parsley.

"Salmon?" Lilah asked, her eyes widening.

"It's your favorite," she answered, placing it on the table. "I'm having steak," she whispered in Lilah's ear as she bent to take more dishes off the cart.

"Who cares?" Lilah whispered back.

After Marabet had removed their salads, Lilah picked up the salmon platter, handing it to Lesa. "Will you pass the asparagus, Charles?"

About halfway through dinner, Lilah could stand it no longer. "Any special plans for the fall, Lesa?" she asked, breaking off a bite of her fish.

Lesa's fork clattered to her plate. "Oh. Yes." She looked down at the table. "I'm thinking about going back to school."

Charles turned to stare at her. "Since when?"

"I talked to the dean of admissions—"

"Without discussing it with me?"

"I didn't know—I wasn't sure—"

"What a ridiculous idea."

"I think it's a wonderful idea," Lilah said.

"Me, too," from Bethany.

"You would," Charles said, turning on her. "What would one expect with your background?"

"You're right," Bethany said, setting her jaw. "My father was a professor. He thought education was important."

"For kids, maybe. Not for grown women with husbands and homes."

Bethany squared her shoulders. "A lot of his students were grown with husbands and wives. He said some people weren't ready to finish their education until later in life."

Charles ignored her and looked at Lilah. "Surely you don't support this absurd notion, Mother."

"Surely I do, Charles. I think it's an excellent idea."

"Right," he said, dropping his fork on his plate. "A middle-aged woman making a complete spectacle of herself trying to pretend she's half her age." He turned to Lesa. "Will you be trying out for cheerleading, dear?"

Lesa flushed. "No, I—"

"Or maybe you'll play in the school band."

"No—" She appeared close to tears.

Lilah jumped into the pause. "Speaking of the school band, Charles, you'll never guess what I'm doing these days."

With his cold stare still fixed on Lesa, he said, "What?"

"Taking piano lessons."

His head swiveled to her. "You're joking."

"I'm quite serious, and from the nicest young man. Bethany and I are taking lessons together."

Charles sat back in his chair, his attention fully on Lilah. "I don't believe you."

Lilah put down her fork. "Of course, Bethany is a lot better than I am. In fact, why don't we have coffee in the living room? Bethany can play for us," she said, winking at Bethany.

"I will if you'll play that Latour piece of yours."

Lilah hesitated only a moment. "Why not? Marabet?" she said, not raising her voice.

"Yes."

"Coffee in the living room after dinner?"

"Certainly."

Lilah and Bethany sat together on the piano bench. Lesa stood just inside the living room door, Marabet beside her. Charles was across the room on the sofa, flipping through the papers he'd brought. Lilah had played her song, laughing when she stumbled over notes. Then Bethany had played three pieces, finishing with Bach's Prelude in C. Now Lilah and Bethany were playing the C scale together. When they finished, Lesa and Marabet applauded.

Charles looked up from his papers. "Is the little recital over? Some of us do work for a living, you know, and I have an early morning tomorrow." He got up and headed for the door, brushing past Lesa and ignoring Marabet. "Good night, Mother," he said without turning, "I'll be in the car, Lesa."

Lilah rose from the piano bench and went over to Lesa. "You stick to your guns, Lesa. He'll come around." Impulsively, she put her arm around Lesa's shoulders and gave her a hug. "Call me any time. Seriously. And thanks for coming."

"I—you're welcome," Lesa said. With a tumultuous smile at Marabet and Bethany, she grabbed her purse off the hall table and hurried out the door.

Total silence reigned for a full minute before Lilah said, "Thank heavens that's over."

Marabet looked ready for a battle. "He could have been nicer."

Lilah looked at her in surprise. "That's an understatement. His behavior was deplorable. I thought I'd taught him better than that."

"It wasn't your teaching that was the problem," Marabet said, scowling.

If she was expecting an argument, she was disappointed, because Lilah was beginning to think the same thing.

Charles reinforced that belief when he came to visit a week later. Marabet had run up to the store and Bethany was at the piano. Lilah answered the door. She had been helping Marabet strip the dining room and she looked like it, complete with jeans and a ratty shirt, with a sweat band wrapped around her head. Charles took in her appearance, his eyes traveling from her damp forehead to her untied sneakers. "What in God's name are you made up as?"

Lilah had a sharp retort on the end of her tongue, but she bit it back. Actually, she was glad Charles had come by, even if only because she would rather tell him what she thought of his behavior when they were standing face to face. She opened the door wider. "Come in, Charles. I'm glad you stopped by."

When he started into the living room, she stopped him. "Come into the kitchen. I don't want to interrupt Bethany's practicing," she said, and could feel his eyes bore into her back as she led the way.

He stopped at the door to the dining room, glancing inside. "What in the world is going on in here," he said, walking into the room and looking around.

Lilah almost felt like giggling. "I told you the other night. I'm redoing the dining room." She followed him into the dismantled room and almost felt sorry for him when he saw the hunting print, now relegated to an empty spot on the floor. Almost.

His eyes went to hers, and for just a second, he looked hurt, which was nonsense. Lilah couldn't imagine that he had a huge emotional commitment to the room. After a long, silent minute, he turned and walked back into the hallway.

Lilah followed him into the kitchen. "Can I get you something?" she asked out of pure habit.

Charles sat down on one of the tall stools at the island, ignoring her question. "I assumed by what you said the other night that you would be calling my office within a few days." He snapped open his briefcase and took out a sheaf of papers. "Opportunities like this don't come along often, and you certainly can't expect them to wait around because of some investor's whim."

Lilah walked past him and opened the refrigerator, taking out a pitcher of iced tea. She didn't sit down until she had poured herself a glass and added ice. "Sure you don't . . ." She motioned at the tea pitcher. This was beginning to feel a little like fun.

Charles' color spiked up a notch. "Will you please come and sit down?"

His invitation sounded all too much like an order, but Lilah sat down anyway. "All right. It was some kind of building, wasn't it?"

Charles spread a handful of colored brochures in front of her. "The Warren Harding Building. It's in midtown, in an area that is seeing a huge redevelopment spike. Once the buildings are completed and fully tenanted, you could probably see a return of . . ."

Lilah barely listened to what he was saying. Instead, she studied this man who had become almost a stranger to her. When had buildings and investments and dollars become his world? Before the question was fully formed in her mind, so was her answer. Charles hadn't really changed. He had only become more of what he was. His father had worshipped finance with the same single-minded devotion. Gerome and Charles had worked together as partners until Gerome's death. After that, Charles had taken over the CPA firm. Looking at it now, Lilah could see that Charles was only carrying on where his father left off. In more ways than one. Lilah looked up when Charles stopped speaking.

"Have you heard a single word I've said?" he asked, exasperation clear in his voice.

This was not how she had wanted this meeting to go. "Not many, I'm afraid." She pushed the brochures aside. "I have something else on my mind."

"And what would that be?"

Lilah took a sip of her tea before answering. She hated confrontation above all else. "I was concerned by your behavior the other night."

Charles sat back. "My *behavior?* What are you talking about?"

"The way you treated Bethany and Lesa. I thought you were—unnecessarily harsh with Lesa, and you were abrupt with Bethany."

His mouth fell open. "I was—I can't believe you're saying this. How do you expect me to react when my wife announces to a room full of people that she's gone behind my back—"

"Not behind—"

"Behind my back and signed up for college courses, for god's sake."

"What's wrong with Lesa taking classes?"

"That isn't the issue and you know it. She deceived me."

"Deceived you how?"

"By not telling me—"

"That's not deceit," Lilah said, beginning to get angry. "It may have been an omission—"

"And deceit of omission is still deceit, just like a lie of omission is still a lie."

"It's not the same thing at all, Charles."

"What's this sudden interest in Lesa?" Charles demanded. "You've practically ignored her for six years, and now you want to start butting into our marriage."

"I'm not butting in. I just think it's a good idea for Lesa to go back to school. She has so little else in her life."

"She has a husband and a home, but what she has or does not have is not your concern. Lesa and I will resolve this between us without outside influence."

"But Charles—"

"You can bandy words all you want, but interference is what it is, and I don't appreciate it."

Lilah sat back. Was she butting into Charles' marriage? Her mother had done that to her, and Lilah had hated it. "Well, Bethany then."

"What about the brat?"

Lilah felt her face go hot. "Bethany is not a brat. She's a lovely young woman who—"

Charles jumped up from his stool. "You see? You see?" His face was red, distorted with fury, and for just a moment, Lilah felt afraid. "I warned you. This is exactly what those people do. They convince you to take the child with emotional blackmail, and then they leave her there until you can't imagine life without her." He began pacing, running his hands through his thin hair. "Why do you think they want you to take her? Do you think they don't know you have money? They certainly should, the way you've been throwing it around lately. I'll bet that brat—" He spat out the word "—is already lobbying for a new wardrobe. You're already redoing the whole house because of her and taking piano lessons, for god's sake. Piano lessons, at your age. It's ridiculous. And you've got my wife doing it too. Well, I'll tell you, I'm not going to allow it. I thought you had more sense than this, but obviously I was wrong."

Of Words & Music

He stormed out of the kitchen. Lilah followed, afraid he was headed for the living room. Bethany would be terrified if she saw him like this. At the dining room door, he detoured inside, snatching the hunting print off the floor. "I'm not going to let you destroy this along with everything else that means anything."

"Charles, please . . ."

Her words rolled off him. He stomped to the front door, flinging it open. "Don't think you've heard the last of this," he said, walking out and slamming the door behind him.

Bethany was sitting at the piano, looking out into the hall. Lilah was relieved she'd seen and heard only the end of the diatribe. Bethany started to stand, then sank back on the bench. "Are you all right?" she asked.

Lilah bit her lip and nodded, unwilling to put the lie into words. Baiting Charles didn't seem like much fun anymore.

Chapter 14

Two days later, Lilah walked into the kitchen and found Bethany crying.

She hadn't heard any more from Charles, which was a blessing, but she also hadn't heard a word from Lesa, which concerned her a bit. She was afraid to call, afraid that there might have been a germ of truth in his accusation that she was meddling in his marriage. She certainly didn't want to cause more trouble between the two of them. Charles had been completely wrong about Bethany, though, and Lilah was still furious with him about that.

Bethany was hunched over a bowl at the island cleaning carrots, but from the looks of it, there wouldn't be much left of them if she continued. She quickly averted her face when she saw Lilah.

"Bethany? What's the matter?" Lilah asked, coming around to face her.

"Nothing," Bethany said, blinking back more tears before they could escape.

"Where's Marabet?"

"At the store. She forgot to get potatoes for the stew."

"Oh." Lilah watched her for a minute. "Are you sure nothing's wrong? You were looking very serious." She didn't want to say sad. If the girl didn't want to confide in her, she certainly wasn't going to try to force her.

"I was just thinking." She glanced at Lilah, then back down

at the carrot she was scraping. "About my father," she added, her voice tentative and defensive at the same time.

"Ah . . ." Lilah didn't want to know. She didn't want to know anything about the man who had married her daughter. She didn't want him to become a person. And yet it seemed unkind to turn and walk away without saying anything at all. "Did he—play the piano, too?"

"No," Bethany said with a sniff. "He said mama and I had all the musical brains in our family. He loved to listen to us, though. He didn't even mind when we made mistakes."

Lilah wrapped her arms across her middle, curiosity winning out over caution. "Was he a good man to live with?"

"The best," Bethany said, her voice wobbling a little. She cleared her throat. "He was—kind. Mama said he was the kindest man she ever knew. I was just thinking about his students how they loved him and—" She glanced up at Lilah, then back down into the sink. "And how he never got mad at me or yelled at me, you know? I knew kids whose parents even hit them. My parents would never have hit me. Sometimes if I did something really crummy, they'd tell me I'd disappointed them. That was worse than getting hit a hundred times."

"Because you respected them and wanted them to be proud of you."

"Yeah." She dropped the carrot she was peeling in a colander and picked up another one. "I guess they were. Proud of me, I mean. Usually."

"I'm sure they were."

Neither spoke for a minute. Bethany glanced over at Lilah, "What was my grandfather like?"

So this was to be an information exchange. Lilah tried to think of a way to phrase her answer. "He was—strong-willed, I suppose you'd say. Rigid, perhaps."

Bethany stole another glance out of the corner of her eye.

"Marabet said he was butt-headed."

"Marabet sometimes expresses her opinion with more enthusiasm than sense."

"I like her."

Lilah smiled. "I like her, too, but I'd like her better if she were a little less quick to call the kettle black."

After a minute, Bethany asked, "Are you rich?"

"What kind of question is that?"

Bethany blushed. "A rude one, I guess. I'm sorry. I just asked because when you were talking about re-doing the dining room, I kept thinking about how much it would cost, but it didn't seem to bother you."

Lilah nodded. "Well, that's fair enough. Rich is relative, I think. By some people's standards, I'd probably seem very rich. By *Who's Who In America*, no." She reached over and picked up a carrot, nibbling on it. "I'm not rich, but I'm certainly not poor. In fact, I've been thinking that you're going to wear out those few clothes you have here with you. Would you like to go buy some new ones?" Her face burned as she remembered Charles' words. The girl hadn't asked for so much as a nickel or a stick of gum since she arrived.

Bethany looked down at her shorts and shirt. "Nah. I have plenty in Athens."

"Should we go get you some from there?" The instant the words were out of her mouth, Lilah wondered where they came from.

"To Athens? Would you want to?"

No, her mind cried out. "I think we'd better before those fall to rags. How about next week? I can call Miss Greenlea and get a key."

"I have a key."

"Still, I think we should let her know we're going."

They both looked up as the doorbell rang. Bethany hopped

off the stool. "That's got to be Elliott." She wiped her hands on her shorts. "I'll go let him in."

An hour later, Bethany was in the kitchen getting Elliott a soda. Lilah was glad she wasn't there to hear what Elliott was proposing.

"That'll give you almost six weeks to practice your piece," Elliott said, gesturing at the sheet music on the piano.

"No. Absolutely not," Lilah said. "I will not perform in a recital. I'd be ridiculous. All the six year olds and me."

"Bethany's twelve, and there are five other adult students on the program."

"I'd certainly be the oldest."

Elliott sat down on the piano bench beside her. "So what if you're the oldest?" he asked quietly. "That should be a point of pride, Lilah, not a point of embarrassment."

"I don't care what it should be, I'd feel ridiculous."

"Recitals are a part of the whole piano experience," Elliott said, trying another track.

"Then that's a part of the experience I'd rather miss. Besides, I could never learn the song that fast."

"Sure you could. That's one of the good points of performing. It really puts the pressure on you to—"

"What puts pressure on you?" Bethany asked, coming back into the room and handing Elliott his drink.

"Performing," Elliott said. "I want you and your grandmother to take part in a recital in August."

"Cool," Bethany said, coming over and looking at the sheet music.

"Not cool," Lilah said, flipping it closed and handing it to Elliott. "I have no intention of getting up on a stage in front of people and making a fool of myself."

Bethany took a step back. "Oh."

Elliott glanced at Bethany, then back at Lilah. "Look," he

said, putting the sheet music back on the piano, "don't make a final decision right now. You and Bethany were going to work on a piece together anyway, so you might as well work on this one. Bethany, I'll get you started on a couple of songs you can play solo at the recital."

He stood and shoved his hands in his pockets, looking miserable. "I didn't plan this. The opportunity just came up. Southern Keyboards has recitals scheduled all the time. This one seemed perfect because it was right before most of my students and I go back to school, and there was room for all of you to take part. I jumped at the chance. My other students have all agreed to perform. I think Bethany would like it," he said, looking at her.

Lilah saw Bethany give an almost imperceptible nod.

"Just give the song a shot, Lilah. If you decide a few weeks down the road that you don't want to do it, no harm will be done. They won't print the programs until a couple of days before the recital. What do you say?"

Lilah couldn't help but take pity on him, standing there looking like a whipped puppy. Not that she had any intention of taking part in a recital, but there was no reason to tell him that now. "All right. I'll agree to work on the piece with Bethany, but if I decide not to play in the recital, I don't want any arguments—from either of you."

"It's a deal," Elliott agreed, grinning broadly. "Okay," he said, motioning for Bethany to sit beside Lilah. "Let's take a look at this music and see what you think."

Half an hour later, they were listening to Elliott play each part. "It's a really pretty piece," he said when he finished.

"It is when you play it," Lilah said with a grimace.

Elliott smiled. "Faure actually wrote it for four hands, so it's an excellent study piece." He turned to Lilah. "Do you have a music dictionary in the house?"

"I'm not sure."

Of Words & Music

"There's one in the library," Bethany chimed in, then blushed.

"Good. I want you both to read about Gabriel Faure. Maybe you could even get a CD of his music at the library."

"Why?" Lilah asked.

"It will help you get a feel for the composer and for how this should sound."

"Do you do that with every piece you study?" Lilah asked.

He nodded. "I'm afraid so. It makes for lots of reading and listening, but I think it's worth it. Some pianists don't want to hear someone else perform the music they're working on. They say it influences how they play it. I don't know if that's true or not, but in your case, it's exactly what I want to happen. Their influence will show you how to approach the music."

"I'll approach it with trepidation," Lilah said, looking at the sheet music doubtfully. "This looks a lot harder than anything I've played so far."

"That's the whole point. Onward and upward."

"Well, onward anyway," she said.

After he was gone, Bethany sat at the piano picking out the notes of her part of the piece. "It really would be neat to play a duet," she said with a quick glance at Lilah.

Again, Lilah couldn't bring herself to argue. The child seemed excited about getting up on a stage in front of a bunch of strangers. She remembered Elizabeth had felt the same way. Did they both have a streak of exhibitionism in them? "We'll see," she said, sitting down beside Bethany, feeling a little like a traitor. "Let's try that first part and see what we can do."

They had been at it for over an hour when Marabet stuck her head in. "Miss Greenlea's on her way over."

Bethany looked up. "To see me?"

Marabet frowned. "No. She wants to talk to Lilah."

"Did she say what she wanted?" Lilah asked as she followed Marabet into the hall.

"No, but she didn't sound very happy."

Lilah waited alone in the living room. Marabet had immediately headed into the kitchen to bake something. Her form of meditation, Lilah supposed. Bethany had grabbed a handful of books off the shelf in the library and headed up to the attic. Lilah worried about her always up there in the heat. Surely she'd be more comfortable in her sitting room, at least temperature-wise. Maybe she could look into having air conditioning vents installed up there. Or she would if Bethany were staying.

She walked over to the front window and looked out. When she realized what she was doing, she came back to the sofa and sat down. A dozen scenarios had played through her mind during the last hour. The likeliest was that Social Services had located some remote relative of Bethany's father who had agreed to take the child. But maybe Felicity's visit was about foster home placement. Had they moved ahead with that? Surely they hadn't had time to find a permanent spot for her. She hadn't even been introduced to any prospective parents. Unless that's what this was about. Setting up appointments with couples.

Lilah realized her hands were clenched, and she relaxed them. Maybe she could be involved in the process, interview the parents herself. Bethany was a special child. She deserved people who would appreciate her finer points and her sensitivity. And her music. Bethany definitely had to continue her music education. If the parents were local, perhaps Elliott could be persuaded to continue her lessons. Money needn't be an issue. Lilah could help, and Elliott could let her know how Bethany was doing from time to time.

She caught her breath at the sound of the doorbell. A moment later, Marabet brought Felicity into the room. Lilah stood. It took all her self-control not to blurt out her questions. "Felicity, please sit down. Would you like some coffee?"

Felicity sat on the sofa, her posture so stiff she looked starched, her face a mask of control. "No, thank you. Nothing."

"Should I call Bethany down? I think she's up in the attic."

Felicity crossed her legs. "No. I don't think we'll need her. I appreciate you seeing me, Mrs. Kimball. This really concerns a visitor I had—" She broke off, glancing over at Marabet.

"Thank you, Marabet," Lilah said.

With good grace, Marabet walked out of the room.

"A visitor, you said?"

"Yes. This morning. Your son."

Lilah drew in a sharp breath. "Charles came to see you?"

Felicity nodded.

"What did he want?" Lilah could feel tension coming off the young woman. It was all she could do not to reach over and pat her hand.

"Then you didn't know he was coming?" When Lilah shook her head, some of the starch seemed to go out of Felicity. She put her purse on the chair beside her and sat back. "He said he felt we were moving too slowly on making permanent arrangements for Bethany. He indicated that she is a burden on you, and that we are increasing that burden by allowing her to remain here."

Lilah's lips compressed tightly. "Bethany is no burden."

"I wondered if you might be having problems with her behavior."

"Her behavior is exemplary—" She stopped, sensing that Felicity had more to say. "Go on."

Felicity looked uncomfortable. "I thought that might have prompted your son's visit. As I told you before, we are combing her records for paternal relatives, although I do admit our progress has been nonexistent as yet."

Lilah opened her mouth to speak. Then she shut it. After a minute, without raising her voice, she said, "Marabet, will you bring us some coffee?" She looked at Felicity. "I need some even if you don't."

Felicity looked relieved. "I think I'd like a cup after all."

Their silence was tense as they waited for Marabet. Felicity gestured toward the piano. "How are the lessons going?"

Lilah couldn't help but smile, even if the smile felt forced. "I'm having a wonderful time with them. Bethany tells me Elliott is a friend of yours." When Felicity nodded, she said, "He's a very nice young man."

"I think so, too, and a wonderful pianist."

"He certainly is," Lilah agreed. "Do you take lessons with him, too?"

"Me? Oh, no. I'm afraid I'm not musical," Felicity said, relaxing back in her chair. "I met Elliott through a project at his school. We—my department and the Board of Education—are trying to develop a music therapy program for disadvantaged children. I was trying to enlist Elliott's aid as a volunteer."

"Successfully?"

"Not at first," Felicity said, smiling. "I remember him saying something about a band aid on a severed artery, but he seems to be reconsidering his decision now."

"I'm glad." Lilah looked thoughtful. "I never thought about music therapy for the disadvantaged, but it makes sense. Music is a language all its own, don't you think? It seems to cut through barriers." Her words startled her, and she looked away uncomfortably. "Or that's how it seems to me."

"I couldn't agree more." Felicity broke off as Marabet came in with the coffee.

When she was gone, Lilah rested her head against the chair back. "We were talking about Bethany and your efforts to place her." She took a sip of her coffee. "I have been thinking lately—well, that maybe we could hold off on that. At least for the rest of the summer."

Lila heard a strangled sound from the hallway. She could see Felicity trying not to smile.

"Of course. If that's what you want."

"As you told me, Bethany has been through a lot of very difficult transitions over the last few years. She seems to be—comfortable here now," Lilah continued, "and she has her piano lessons. I'd hate to interrupt those so soon after they began. She loves music so much, and she seems to have taken a strong liking to your friend. As have I."

"Hard not to," Felicity agreed, grinning now.

"Bethany truly loves the piano. It would be almost criminal to take her away from her music, don't you think?"

"I agree completely. Bethany should certainly be allowed to pursue her music."

"Good, then." Lilah sat forward and picked up her coffee cup. "That's settled. Don't worry about Charles. I'll speak to him. He won't bother you again."

"Before you do, Mrs. Kimball, you should know that he said a few things that—concerned me."

Lilah raised her eyebrows. "Oh? Like what?"

"He assured me that he was acting as your agent."

"My agent? In what capacity?"

"He said a personal capacity. He told me that he's your financial advisor—and your personal advisor since your husband's death. He assured me that he had a power of attorney to act in your behalf."

"In financial matters only," Lilah said sharply.

Felicity bit her lip, then continued. "That's what I suggested to him. He said that you tended to be swayed by—by erratic emotions at times in your decision making and weren't in complete control of your faculties—"

"Why that rotten little twerp!" Marabet burst into the room. "How *dare* he!"

"Sit down and be quiet, Marabet," Lilah said without looking away from Felicity. "Was that all he said?" she asked, her voice dead calm.

Felicity let out a long breath. "That's pretty much it. He said I hadn't heard the end of it."

Lilah remembered him saying the exact same words to her.

"Mrs. Kimball, maybe your son really thought he was acting in your best interests. It's possible he said those things just to intimidate me into believing he might take legal action. It's possible that he really doesn't believe the things he said."

Lilah held herself straight with effort. "I appreciate you trying to put a better face on my son's actions, but I think Charles meant every word of it. He was a difficult child and he's becoming an insufferable adult." She suddenly seemed to realize what she was saying. "But I won't burden you with my failed attempt at child rearing. I appreciate you coming here and telling me this. I know it can't have been easy for you."

Felicity hesitated for a moment, but then she picked up her purse and stood.

Lilah stood, too, and offered her hand. Felicity shook it, and then held onto it. "Please. If you're right, well—just protect yourself."

Lilah patted her hand. "I will, dear," she said, walking Felicity toward the door, "and thank you again for coming." They stopped just inside the door. "We'll leave things as they are with Bethany for the next month or so. Are we agreed?"

"We are," Felicity said. "What will you tell her?"

"Nothing for the present," Lilah said with a bitter laugh. "I wouldn't want to get her hopes up in case I'm swayed the other way by my erratic emotions."

She was surprised when Felicity leaned forward and gave her a brief hug. "You take care of yourself."

Lilah nodded. "Thank you, dear. I certainly will."

When she walked back into the living room, Marabet was standing in the middle of the room, her face contorted with rage. "Well?" she demanded.

"Sit down, Marabet." Lilah took a seat on the sofa.

Reluctantly, Marabet came to sit beside her.

"You're too good a friend to gloat," Lilah said mildly.

"And too good a friend not to worry."

"We'll handle it."

"How?"

Lilah poured herself another cup of coffee. "Want some?" she asked Marabet. When she shook her head, she picked up her own cup and took a sip. "First I'll call Tom." When Marabet looked blank, she said, "My attorney. Thomas Mulligan. I'll find out what steps I need to take to revoke Charles' power of attorney. I will not have a privilege I bestowed—and pay for—thrown back in my face this way. I'll find out from him if I need to do anything to establish my mental competency."

"You shouldn't have to—"

"I probably won't have to do a thing. Surely it can't be all that easy to declare a parent incompetent, or half the children in the world would have done it already. I just want all the legalities out of the way before I talk to Charles. Now," she said, draining her cup and putting it back on the table, "not a word of any of this to Bethany. There's no reason she should bear this burden on top of all the others."

"Of course not." Marabet leaned forward. "Did you mean it? Is she staying?"

Lilah nodded. She still looked deeply disturbed, but there was a trace of a smile on her face. "Until the end of the summer. She does love her piano lessons, and that will give Social Services more time to locate other relatives. I don't like the thought of the girl having to be uprooted more than necessary."

Marabet didn't look completely happy at her answer, but at least she was silent.

They rode most of the way to Athens without talking. Lilah was glad they had Faure in the CD player. The drive was only an hour, but she felt more and more tense as they neared the place where her daughter had lived for the last fourteen years. What had her life been like? Had she been happy? Surely she had been. After all, she had her daughter and her husband. And her job. Lilah remembered Marabet telling her Elizabeth had worked as a librarian. It wasn't what she would have pictured for her, but it certainly wasn't a job to be ashamed of. At least she had been surrounded by books—Elizabeth had loved books—and at home she'd had her music and her family. Her new family, she amended.

When they reached the city, Bethany gave Lilah directions. A few minutes later, they pulled into the driveway of a small house on a dead-end street. Lilah made no move to get out of the car. Finally, she took a shaky breath and let it out slowly. "All right," she said, giving Bethany a bleak smile. "Let's do this."

Bethany followed her to the door and opened it with her key. She led the way into the living room and stood, looking around. "It looks so small now."

Lilah nodded, but her eyes were taking in the room: the pictures on the mantel, on the bookcases, everywhere she looked. The room was warm and cluttered and it felt exactly like Elizabeth. Books and sheet music were stacked everywhere. Floor pillows competed with furniture that was clearly secondhand. "What a wonderful room," she said softly.

"Do you think so?" Bethany asked, relief evident in her voice. "I thought you'd think it was—I don't know. Shabby, maybe. Not big and beautiful like your house."

Lilah squared her shoulders and looked at Bethany. "It looks beautiful to me." She walked over to the mantel and picked up a framed photograph. "Is this your father?" she asked, holding it out for Bethany to see.

It was a picture of a tall, lanky man with lots of dark hair. His arm was slung carelessly around Elizabeth's neck. Elizabeth was staring up at him with an expression Lilah had never seen before. It was totally correct, and yet there was something about it that was almost too intimate to bear.

Bethany nodded.

"He was a handsome man," Lilah said. "Would you want to take it with you?"

Bethany searched her face. "Can I?"

"Of course you can. You can take whatever you want."

Bethany stood looking up the stairs for a long time before she climbed them and disappeared. Lilah could almost imagine what she was feeling, since she was feeling a bit of it herself. She wandered around the room, touching photos, mementos. She moved through the dining area and peeked into the tiny kitchen. This was where Elizabeth had cooked. It was messy—Bethany's doing, no doubt. There was no more to see down here, and she couldn't make herself go upstairs to her daughter's bedroom. That was too personal somehow.

Back in the living room, she brought the pictures to the coffee table, grouping them in what appeared to be chronological order, reconstructing her daughter's life. She sat on the couch with her head bowed. "And I missed it. Dear God, I missed it all."

She heard Bethany coming back down the stairs and straightened, giving herself a quick shake. Bethany put the bag down on the floor. "Did you find some you want to take with us?"

Lilah nodded, not looking at her. "Let's take them all. Did you get your things together?"

"Enough. Most of them." Then, "Uh—there's some photo albums in the coat closet. We could take those if you want."

"Marabet would never forgive me if I said no."

Lilah was already in the car when Bethany came out of the house with the last of the albums.

"Ready?" she asked, turning the key in the ignition.

Bethany bit her lip, looking troubled. "Yes."

"Is there somewhere else you'd like to go?"

"There is one place—if you don't mind."

Lilah had spent much of the evening looking through the albums Bethany had brought back from Athens. Now it was late, but Lilah couldn't sleep. She padded quietly downstairs. The ache inside her was like a tumor, so big she felt like it had pushed all her organs out of place. Her restless feet drew her to the living room. The grandfather clock in the corner ticked like an extra heartbeat. Dim light fell from the lamps across the room, casting the piano in shadow. She sat down, pressing random keys one by one. She wasn't surprised when she felt Marabet's presence behind her. She didn't look up or otherwise acknowledge her presence. Gently, she closed the cover on the piano. "What have I done?" she whispered.

Marabet sat down beside her on the piano bench.

"What in God's name have I done? How could I have let this happen?"

"It wasn't you—"

"Don't whitewash me, Marabet," Lilah said sharply. "Of course it was me." Then, "Believe me, if I could paint Gerome the ogre in all this, I would." She traced the hinges of the keyboard cover with her index finger. "No gun was held to my head. No threat of physical harm hung over me."

"You did what you thought was best."

The finger stopped before it resumed its blind tracing. "Yes, I did what I thought best, and what I thought best showed really poor judgment on my part."

"That's not fair. You lived the only way you knew how."

"The product of my generation?" Lilah turned on the bench and faced Marabet. "Don't you think I tried that rationale? I've tried them all—made every excuse. My whole life is one long excuse for weak-willed behavior," she said bitterly. "I took the easy way out. Always the easy way out. My parents wanted me to marry Gerome, so I did. He wanted our bedroom brown, so we had a brown bedroom. My son wanted to play little Hitler, and I turned a blind eye rather than take action. I slid by, always the easy way." She closed her eyes. "And I'll pay for that for the rest of my life."

"Lilah—"

She held up her hand as if to ward off Marabet's words. "There are some really ugly truths here, Marabet, and I don't seem to be able to hide from them anymore. I don't like my son at all right now. He's not a nice person. And I don't like his father, either. I can't even remember if I ever did. But worst of all, at the very heart of it is the fact that I stupidly, *stupidly* threw away my daughter. She's gone—and I can't get her back."

Marabet let out a long slow breath. She reached out and touched Lilah's arm. "That's true. You can't get her back."

Lilah's head fell forward. "I want her back, Marabet," she whispered. "I want my baby back."

"I know you do, honey," Marabet said, putting her arms around Lilah.

As Lilah's head dropped to Marabet's shoulder, she thought she heard something in the hallway, but when she looked up, the doorway was empty.

Chapter 15

Marabet walked into Lilah's bedroom without knocking. "I got phone numbers for some schools this morning. I didn't know for sure if you'd want her in public or private school, so I looked up the numbers for both."

Lilah was seated at her dressing table putting the last touches on her makeup. She blotted her lipstick and turned around. "What are you talking about, Marabet?"

"About Bethany's school for this fall. We need to make some arrangements."

"Bethany? This fall?" Lilah bit her lip, shaking her head. "Oh, Marabet."

Marabet took a step backwards. "What? But—but last night . . ."

Lilah's shoulders straightened. "Last night I said I wanted my daughter back, Marabet. Bethany is not my daughter."

"But she's her child."

"I know she is, but it's not the same thing," Lilah answered gently. "When I said I wanted Elizabeth, I meant just that. Bethany is a lovely child, but she's not Elizabeth."

Marabet's face turned crimson. For a minute, Lilah feared she was going to have a stroke. "What in God's name is the matter with you Lilah?"

"Marabet—"

"I can't believe you're so hard and cold and—"

"Marabet, stop this," Lilah said, her voice sharp. "I told you not to get your hopes set on—"

"On you being a person? Stupid me, when what you are is a—"

"*Enough!*" Lilah jumped to her feet. "That's enough. We can fight about this later. I don't have time now." She took a deep breath and let it out slowly. "We'll talk when I get home. I'm late now." She started from the room. Then she stopped, turning back. "Marabet," she pleaded, "please try to see it through my eyes. Please."

"I can't," Marabet said, turning away. "I'm not blind."

Thomas Mulligan's office was exactly what Lilah needed after her latest confrontation with Marabet. Soothing. The walls were a soft blue, the carpet the deepest forest green. The overstuffed furniture was upholstered in muted greens and blues, giving one the impression of having stepped into a Monet canvas. In fact, a couple of beautifully framed Monet prints graced the walls, glowing under recessed lighting. Soft music came from hidden speakers. Tom's attractive assistant typed soundlessly at a computer, stopping occasionally to smile at her. Her skin glowed in the soft light like polished ebony.

Lilah was grateful for the wait. It gave her time to shift gears, to compose her thoughts.

A door off to the left opened, and Tom came out, leading a woman by the elbow. Tall and broad, he had a full head of waving hair which had been white ever since Lilah had known him, almost thirty years. She remembered hearing once that he had played football in college, but unlike so many athletes, Tom had never gone to fat. His face was square and lined with sixty years of solving other people's problems, but the lines looked good on him. Dark suit, white shirt, striped silk tie. His clothes, his entire demeanor, suggested competence.

He winked at Lilah. "Don't you worry about a thing, Mrs.

Samuelson," he said, as he walked his client to the door. "The papers are filed. I don't foresee any problems down the road."

"Thank you, Mr. Mulligan," the woman said, taking his offered hand.

When she was gone, Tom turned to Lilah.

"Lilah," he said, crossing to her and taking her hands. "You get more beautiful every year." He pulled her to her feet and kissed her cheek.

"And you more full of nonsense," she said, smiling.

"Not a bit of it," he said. "Why don't you divorce your husband and we'll run off together."

Lilah was taken aback for an instant. Then she realized he was teasing her. "Too late. He's dead."

"If he were alive, would you divorce him?"

She hesitated, about to come back with some light rejoinder. Then her face grew serious and she said, "Yes, Tom, I believe I would."

"Glory hallelujah," he said. "The woman finally got the words right."

"Tom," Lilah hissed, nodding her head toward his assistant, who was watching the exchange with amusement. "Can we go into your office?"

"Of course," he said, taking her elbow. "You didn't hear a word," he said to his assistant as they passed her desk.

"Never do," she said, turning back to her computer.

Lilah sat down on his office sofa and looked around. "Your office looks nice."

"My office looks exactly like it did two years ago when you were here last. Okay, Lilah," he said, sitting down in a chair at right angles to the sofa and leaning forward, "you've managed to avoid beating down my door for the last two years, and you would barely speak to me on the phone the few times I called, so if you're here, I assume it's a legal problem. Tell me what's happening."

Lilah smiled at him. "I can't begin to tell you all that's been happening, Tom." Her smile faded. "Elizabeth was killed in an accident a few months ago," she said, clutching her purse in her lap.

"Oh, Lilah. I'm so sorry. You didn't say a word about it when I called. At least tell me you had reconciled with her when it happened."

She steeled herself against the pain that waylaid her. "No. I'm afraid I can't tell you that, but she had a daughter, Bethany, who's with me now—temporarily—and Charles is apparently trying to stir things up." She stopped, looking at him helplessly. "It's all such a muddle."

His eyes searched her face. Finally, he sat back. "Well, it's my job to unmuddle it," he said, crossing one leg over the other, "but I think you'd better tell me everything that's happened in the last two years. Start with the day after we read Gerome's will."

Lilah took a sip of her now-cold coffee. Sometime during her monologue, the assistant had slipped in with two cups of coffee. Lilah had been too caught up in her story to do more than nod her thanks. She had given Tom a carefully edited version of events, but she told him everything she knew about Charles' visit to Felicity Greenlea.

"Why, that little shit!" Tom exploded when she quit speaking.

Lilah almost choked on her coffee. Laughing, she said, "I thought attorneys were supposed to be objective."

"I am objective," he countered. "About you. About him I'm highly prejudiced. He's just like his father."

"He is acting more like him every day," Lilah said, nodding.

"Did you mean what you said?"

"What?"

"About divorcing Gerome."

"Oh." She squirmed uncomfortably. "I—yes, I think so."

"I was afraid you'd grieve for him. In fact, I was pretty sure I saw signs of it."

"I thought I was grieving. I seem to be very good at deluding myself about things like that." She lifted her chin. "Yes, I think I would want to divorce him. He was highhanded and unkind. Whether I would have had the courage to do so if he hadn't died?" She shrugged, shaking her head. "I can't answer that."

"Well, fortunately he died and saved us the trouble of finding out."

Lilah laughed again. "Did you really dislike him that much?"

"I loathed him," he said, nodding.

"Then why did you represent him?"

Tom shrugged. "You know how it is, Lilah," he said with a grin. "Or maybe you don't. Fresh out of law school. At first I did it for the money, plain and simple. You have to remember that I was a struggling young attorney, and Gerome paid big bucks. At least, it seemed like big bucks back then. Later, well, it's pretty hard to fire a client without just cause, and Gerome didn't actually give me a hard time."

"He didn't dare," Lilah interjected.

"You flatter me," he said, smiling. "Thank you, but I think it was more a case of him not caring enough to spar with me. The closest we ever came to terminating our legal relationship was over that will-changing business about Elizabeth. I couldn't believe he could be that stupid." He shook his head. "I finally went along with it because I was sure he'd come to his senses eventually. Wrong again. Maybe you should look for an attorney who's a better judge of character."

"I think I'll stick with the devil I know," Lilah said with a smile.

"I'm wounded."

"I'm certain," she shot back. She took another sip of the cold coffee, barely concealing a grimace. "Well, that's my story. So what do you think I should do about it?"

"Eat lunch."

"What?"

He looked at his watch. "I don't know about you, but I'm starving. How about it? Vini Vidi Vici's right down the street, and they serve a mean lasagna."

"I didn't come here for you to buy me lunch," Lilah protested.

"Oh, be a sport. Let me buy you lunch," Tom said, standing and grinning as he reached down to her. "Besides, I'll bill you for it later."

The restaurant was packed, one large, elegant room, with lots of gleaming wood and terrazzo tile and windows on two sides over-looking the midtown lunch crowds. There were outside tables, but few diners were hardy enough to brave the heat and traffic fumes.

While they had their salads, Tom caught her up on what had been happening in his life during the past two years. He'd been offered a judgeship and turned it down. "I don't play politics. There are much better games around." He was working out three times a week. He'd bought a sailboat. "It's up at Lake Lanier. I wish you'd go sailing with me." He was taking hang-gliding lessons.

"Hang-gliding lessons? You have to be joking."

"Why? Think I'm too old?"

"Well, no, but it's so dangerous."

"So is crossing Peachtree Street, and I do it every day."

"Tom."

"It's true," he insisted. "More people are killed annually crossing that road up there than are killed in five years hang-gliding."

"You're making that up."

"Of course I am," he grinned. "No one has those statistics, but I'll bet I'm right." He pushed his salad plate away. "So, what are you doing these days?"

Lilah shook her head, looking over at him. "Well, nothing as exciting as what you're doing. I'm redecorating several rooms in the house."

"Which ones?"

Lilah looked at him questioningly. "What does it matter which ones?"

"Which ones?" he insisted.

"The dining room. My bedroom."

"Ah . . ."

"Ah what?" she asked laughing.

"Getting rid of all the traces of that old fart, I'll bet. Lilah, you restore my faith in the inherent good sense of womanhood." He grinned at her. "So, what else?"

"Oh." She felt a bit flustered. "Well, I'm getting to know my daughter-in-law after neglecting her for six years. She's much too good for Charles."

"Anyone is," he said dismissively. "What else?"

Suddenly shy, she said, "I'm . . . um . . . taking piano lessons. With Bethany. She's very good."

He sat back, smiling. "No kidding? Piano?"

"You probably think that's silly."

"I think that's magnificent." He looked over at her, a smug smile on his face. "I do believe my little Lilah is finally coming of age."

"Age being the operative word."

"Now that is silly. Don't you realize these are the best years of our lives, woman? We're finally doing what we want in life. We're financially independent. We can decide what we care about and pursue it. We don't give a damn about impressing anyone, and we don't answer to anyone. It just doesn't get any better than that."

Lilah gave him a bemused smile. "When you put it that way, it does sound rather appealing."

"Damn right. So blow your own horn. Seize the day, or whatever they're saying these days. We old folks have trouble keeping up with the latest expressions."

"You'll never be old, Tom," Lilah said sincerely.

"Neither will you, my dear. We're perfect together. Tell me you'll marry me."

Lilah opened her mouth, and then closed it as she realized the waiter was standing behind Tom, beaming at them both. "Your lunch, madam," he said, putting it on the table with a flourish. "Sir." He served Tom, and then vanished.

Lilah could feel her cheeks burning. "He heard you," she hissed.

"Good. Shall I announce it to the world? Lilah Kimball has finally seen the light. She no longer pines for that jerk she married. She's ready for a real man now."

The waiter materialized at Tom's elbow, carrying a split of champagne and two glasses. "On the house, sir," he said softly to Tom. "Just in case you need it," he added with a wink.

"You idiot," Lilah sputtered. "He'll probably be humming the wedding march when he serves dessert."

"Fine young man," Tom said, tackling his lasagna. "We'll have to come here for lunch on our first anniversary."

"Tom, be serious."

He looked over at her consideringly, but then he shook his head. "I can't. You're not ready for it, but at least we're moving in the right direction." He sat back in his chair. "Okay, back to business. Charles is a windbag. He won't have a legal leg to stand on if he tries to declare you mentally incompetent."

With some reluctance, Lilah turned her mind back to her situation. "He's been making noises about my recent expenditures. Could that be a problem?"

"What kind of expenditures?"

"The renovations. New carpet and furniture."

"Household improvements? God, I would hope not. Now, if you'd gone out and bought three orange Porsches in a week, that might give a judge pause. It's your money to dispose of as you wish, Lilah," he said seriously. "That was clearly stated in the will. Charles got his own money—and Elizabeth's, for that matter. More than the little shit deserves, if you ask me."

"Still, he keeps making remarks about it."

Tom nodded. "He's his father's son. Lives to intimidate." He gestured at her plate. "Eat. If you were going to lose your girlish figure, you'd have done it by now. The food is great."

Dutifully, Lilah picked up her fork and took a bite. "You don't think this will go to court?"

"I doubt it, more's the pity. I'd love to humiliate him publicly for the way he's treated you, but it'll never get that far. I have too many friends, and we have strong legal grounds. You do need to get your money out of his hands, though."

Lilah thought for a moment. "Is there any way to do that without—oh, I guess making him angry?"

"Nope."

She blinked. Then she nodded. "All right. Then let's make him angry."

"That's my girl," he said, raising his glass of water to her.

"What do I need to do?"

"Nothing. I'll draft a letter. Make a phone call."

"That's all?"

Tom nodded. "The minute he's notified that it's revoked, it's revoked. If he pulls anything after that, we sue his ass off. We'll follow it up with a document, just to keep it tidy." He reached over and squeezed her hand. "I'll give him a call as soon as I get back to the office."

"No," Lilah said quickly, then, "No. I think I want to wait. I'll tell him once you have the document drawn up."

"Are you sure, Lilah? I'll be glad to handle it for you."

She frowned, undecided. "No, I'm not sure. Let me think about it, will you?"

"Of course. Okay then. I'll probably have the revocation ready for your signature . . ." He looked at his watch. ". . . oh, in time for dinner Friday night." He put down his fork. "What do you say?"

She looked down at her plate. "Don't be silly."

"What's silly?"

"You don't want to take me to dinner."

Tom looked to either side. "Then who did I just ask?"

"Tom, you don't have to do that."

"No. You're right. I don't *have* to do that. I *want* to do that. Free agents, remember? Doing what we want? The best time of our lives? Did I give that lecture to someone else? I would have sworn it was you sitting here at this table."

She glanced away.

"Lilah," he said seriously, "I've been attracted to you for years, and I've spent several more waiting for you to get over the loss of your husband, bastard that he was. Don't get me wrong," he said, holding up his hand as she turned back to him. "I haven't been pining away during that time, but you were always somewhere out there on the edge of my consciousness. I'm not asking you to marry me. Well, I did, but I think we should have a few dates first," he said, grinning. "It's just dinner, not a lifelong commitment. So, what do you say?"

She looked at the ceiling, at the bar in the corner. She bit her lip to keep from laughing. "I say—okay." She spread her hands. "Why not?"

Tom raised an eyebrow. "Well, I've been accepted with more enthusiasm than that, but what the hell. I'll take what I can get.

Let's seal it with a glass of champagne."

As he reached for the bottle, the waiter materialized at his elbow, smiling broadly. "I take it the lady said yes?"

Tom grinned at her. "The lady indeed said yes."

"Oh, congratulations, sir," he said, shaking Tom's hand, "and you, too, madam." He bowed in her direction before making a show of opening the champagne and pouring them each a glass. Then he backed away.

"To us," Tom said, holding up his glass.

"I'll kill you!" Lilah hissed, choking with laughter.

As they sipped from their glasses, the waiter led the other servers in a round of applause. After a moment, several diners looked their way and joined in. Tom stood and bowed to the room. He held his glass up toward Lilah in a toast, and the applause grew louder.

"I really *will* kill you, Thomas Mulligan," Lilah said when he sat down again.

"Not, I hope, before our first date," he said, reaching for the check.

Bethany was in the living room practicing her scales the next morning when Lilah came down, and she slipped past without interrupting her. Marabet was standing at the sink peeling potatoes when Lilah entered the kitchen. She had hoped the intervening hours would have softened Marabet, but her rigid posture said it all.

"Things went well with Tom," Lilah said, reaching into a cabinet for a glass. "He's drawing up papers to revoke the power of attorney."

Nothing.

"They'll be ready to sign Friday night."

Silence.

Lilah sighed and put the empty glass on the counter. "Okay,

Marabet. Let's talk."

"There's nothing to talk about," she said without turning.

"I think there is. Bethany—and the misunderstanding about her."

"There was no misunderstanding about Bethany," Marabet said, still facing the sink. "The misunderstanding was about you."

"Marabet, will you come over here and talk to me?"

Marabet glanced at her, her face impassive. Then she turned back to the sink. "No."

"All right." Lilah walked over and leaned against the counter next to her. "Why are you so angry with me? I told you Bethany was only here for the summer."

"And then what? She gets dumped in a foster home?"

"I was thinking more of other relatives."

"What if there aren't any?"

"Well—I guess we'll have to face that when it happens, won't we?"

Marabet threw the potato peeler in the sink in disgust. "*We?* We'll face it? Who are you trying to kid, Lilah? You'll face nothing. You never have. Bethany's the one who will have to face the fact that her grandmother not only threw her own daughter away, she tossed her granddaughter out, too."

Marabet's voice, though soft, was no less intense. Lilah knew that was for Bethany's benefit, not her own. She tried to keep her own voice low. "That's uncalled for, Marabet, and it's not fair. You're using my own words against me."

"Not fair? I'll tell you what's not fair, Lilah," Marabet said, spinning around to face her, hands on her hips. "What's not fair is what's happened to that little girl in there. She's a darling child. She's sweet and bright and giving and—and one of the nicest girls I've ever met, but she's lost so much that there's a hole in her heart. And she's got this grandmother with a bigger hole in her, a big emptiness where her love used to be. There's no love there. There's no nothing."

Lilah's mouth was a thin line. "You're condemning me because I can't feel for Bethany the way you do, but—"

"No, Lilah, I'm condemning you because you refuse to let anything touch you, because you're too damned scared to feel. I thought it was because you'd gotten cold and hard, that living with Gerome Kimball had sapped all the love right out of you, but that's not it at all."

"I don't know what you're talking about."

"Yes you do, but I'll say it anyway. I've watched you. You love that little girl in there; love her like the beautiful granddaughter she is. But you're afraid she's going to grow up one day and fall in love, and then where will you be? You'll be alone, just like you were when Elizabeth went off and got married. But it didn't have to be that way. Can't you see that? And it doesn't have to be that way with Bethany."

Lilah could barely catch her breath. "I refuse to listen to any more—"

"Don't worry, because there isn't much more. You don't want to love because love can hurt. It hurt with the Germ because he was a bastard, and it hurt with Charles because he liked his father better than you. But you had Elizabeth, and then she hurt you most of all by going away, by being driven away, if you'll ever admit it, by her own parents. You said it yourself. You've been stupid and weak. And how are you going to fix that? By being stupider and weaker?"

"This is absolute nonsense," Lilah said.

She spun away, but Marabet grabbed her arm and spun her back. "I'll tell you what's *nonsense*. Nonsense is letting that girl go. Nonsense is being so afraid to love her and lose her that you'd rather pretend you don't care. Yes, you might lose her if she goes off and marries someone you don't like and you turn your back on her the way you did Elizabeth, but you know what? At least you'll have had her and maybe, maybe you won't lose her after all. If you send her away, you'll lose her for sure. Just think about that when you're up in that cold empty bedroom across the hall from Elizabeth's room." Marabet sagged. She suddenly looked older—and tired. Her voice was soft when she said, "If you can send her away, you're not the woman I thought you were."

Lilah closed her eyes and rubbed her forehead. "Marabet . . ."

Marabet turned back to the sink. "That's all I have to say, Lilah. It's your house and your granddaughter. You'll be the one making the stupid mistake, but I needed to speak my mind. And I meant it. You'd better start taking a good look at yourself."

"Or what?" Lilah asked bitterly. "Or you'll leave?"

Without turning, Marabet said, "This isn't about ultimatums. I loved you back when you were kind, and I've loved you when you've been unkind. I guess I just love you. I only wish you loved yourself more."

Lilah started to speak, but she realized there was nothing she could say. She turned and left the kitchen. She started to go upstairs, but then she turned and walked down the hallway. At the door of the living room, she stopped, watching Bethany as she played. The child was wholly immersed in the music and unaware that Lilah was standing behind her. Marabet was right, Lilah realized. Bethany was a darling. She was open and loving and giving. She was intelligent and feisty and strong-willed. She was so many wonderful things, and yet all Lilah felt when she saw the girl was pain, a pain so intense it sliced through her, and she couldn't live with it. Feeling like she had lost a major skirmish, she turned to leave.

Bethany must have realized she was there, because she said, "Oh. Hi. I didn't know you were back."

"I just got home."

"Did Marabet tell you your son called?"

Oh sure, Lilah thought. *You're cold and unfeeling and by the way your son called.* "No, she didn't mention it."

"He said for you to call him back." She gestured across the room to the phone. "Do you want me to go so you can call him from here?"

So many of her gestures were Elizabeth's; so many of the things she said.

When she didn't answer, Bethany asked, "Are you okay?"

"Yes," Lilah said, defeat coursing through her. "Yes. I'm all right. Just a little tired. Maybe I'll go upstairs for a while."

"I'll play softly so it won't bother you."

"Thank you," Lilah whispered as she walked down the hall.

Chapter 16

The house simmered with temper and frustration, as it had for days. The temper was all Marabet's. Bethany was feeling the tension, too. She tiptoed around the two women as if they represented a minefield, which they more or less did. Charles had telephoned again, and once more Lilah had dodged his call. A minor victory.

Lilah had tried to put Marabet's accusations out of her mind and had been, for the most part, successful. Putting the actual person out of her mind had been more difficult, even though Lilah had spent as little time in the house as possible. When she was there, she was either practicing the piano with Bethany or hiding in her room. She had given up trying to pretend it was anything other than hiding. On the positive side, she had gone a long way toward catching up on her reading.

Who was she kidding? There was no positive side, and the reading was a sham. Words on a page. Nothing more. Nothing she read touched her, which only brought Marabet's accusations closer to home. Could she be right? Was Lilah beyond feeling?

She shook her head, rising from her dressing table. No. Marabet simply didn't understand Lilah's position. She refused to understand, and there was no way Lilah could make her. She turned at the knock on her bedroom door. "Yes?"

Bethany peeked in. "Marabet wanted me to ask what time you'd be leaving on your date."

"Soon," she answered, "and it's not a date." At least Marabet was speaking to her again, even if through an intermediary. She held up a suit for Bethany's inspection. "What about this?"

"For dinner? It's all right, I guess."

Which meant it wasn't. Putting it back, she pulled out another, charcoal gray trimmed with yellow. Bethany shrugged.

Lilah stepped to the back of the closet. She came out holding a dress encased in a garment bag. She struggled to unzip the bag, and pulled the dress out. It was black matte jersey with chiffon sleeves. The neckline draped softly. She held it up for Bethany to see. "What do you think?"

Bethany smiled. "It's beautiful."

Lilah considered the dress. "Why not?" she said, pulling it off the hanger. "Tell Marabet I'll be leaving about seven."

When Bethany was gone, she slipped off her robe and turned to put on the dress, catching sight of herself in the full-length closet mirror. She studied her reflection analytically, deciding she didn't look too bad for a sixty-year-old woman. She had never been one to primp in front of a mirror, but there were things about her appearance she liked. She had good legs for a woman her age, and clad in dark stockings as they were now, they looked even better. At least she wasn't fighting varicose veins like so many aging women. Her figure had remained trim, despite Marabet's cooking and Lilah's love of sweets. Genetics. Gravity, of course, had taken its toll, but decent undergarments could hide most of that. Her hair, thick and still mostly brown, was a real source of pleasure to her. Even if she wore it up most of the time, she loved to feel its weight when it was down, which was probably why she had maintained her girlhood ritual of brushing it every night and why she had never cut it short as so many older women did. If it made her look older, too bad. She was older.

Feeling unusually feminine, she slipped the dress over her

head, struggling with the zipper, and then slipped her feet into black sandal heels. She heard the doorbell ring as she was fastening on her earrings. With a last glance in the mirror, she headed out of her room.

She stopped at the living room doorway and watched as Thomas Mulligan worked his magic on Bethany. It struck her anew that he was an elegant man, almost regal. He was handsome and—solid, the kind of man with whom you could feel comfortable. Then why did she have butterflies wreaking havoc on her digestive tract?

Bethany, struck by shyness again, was sitting on the edge of her chair, looking as timid as Lilah had ever seen her. Marabet stood directly behind her, the mother hen ready to gather her chick under wing if the going got too tough.

"Your grandmother tells me you play the piano." Soft voice, modulated for the nervous witness.

A glance from under her eyelashes. "Yes, sir."

Tom sat back on the sofa, stretching his arm across the back. "I used to play when I was a boy."

"You did?" A little curiosity.

"I sure did. I remember one piece by Beethoven. Fur Elise, I think it was. I guess everyone learns to play that one."

"I did." Firmer ground now.

"I'm not sure I remember how it goes."

Lilah stepped back out of sight as Tom rose and walked over to the piano. He lifted the key cover and sat down on the bench. Then he played the first few notes. "I'm not even sure I'm starting on the right notes. It's been a long time."

Bethany was up in an instant. Her shyness returned as she neared the piano, but seemed to ease when Tom grinned and patted the bench next to him. "Why don't you get me started? Then we'll see if I can remember the rest."

She gave him a little smile and raised her hands to the keys.

As she played the first measures, the sound filled the room.

"Go on," Tom encouraged when she stopped.

It was all she needed. Lilah could see the relaxation of Bethany's muscles as she eased into the sound. The smile on her face wasn't little now, and it wasn't timid. It was a smile that began somewhere deep inside her and radiated outward. As she neared the middle of the piece and leaned into the repeated bass notes, her smile became determined, and the determination became part of the sound.

That was it, Lilah realized. That was the difference. Lilah played the notes on the page, but Bethany turned sound into emotion, or emotion into sound. Lilah didn't know why or how it happened, but she knew that was what she was hearing. As the last notes sounded, she let out a long breath.

"Bravo," Tom said, clapping and bowing toward Bethany. "It never sounded that way when I played it."

"I've been playing it a long time," Bethany said, at ease now. "That helps a lot. When you're trying to remember the notes, that's all you can do. Once you've learned them, you can start concentrating on how you play each one. Then on the phrasing—" She broke off, seeing Lilah in the doorway. "Wow."

Tom turned around. His eyes widened slightly. "I agree," he said, getting to his feet. "Wow. You look lovely."

"Thanks, Tom," Lilah said lightly, determined to get past the awkwardness she was feeling. After all, Tom was an old friend, an attorney helping her with a legal problem, not someone she was meeting for the first time. She turned to Bethany. "That was beautiful."

"Why don't you play for him," Bethany asked, getting up from the bench.

Lilah laughed. "I'm not quite as comfortable playing in front of others as you are."

"You will be after the recital."

"Recital?" Tom raised his eyebrows. "What's this about a recital?"

Lilah laughed again, but uncomfortably. "Elliott, our teacher, has it in his head that Bethany and I are going to play together in a recital at the end of the summer."

"Count me in. That's one performance I wouldn't want to miss."

"That's one performance that probably isn't going to happen, although Bethany will be playing her pieces anyway."

"It would be more fun if it was the two of us," Bethany said with a mulish expression that Lilah remembered well from Elizabeth.

"We'll see," Lilah said, patting Bethany's shoulder. "In the meantime, we can enjoy practicing together." She looked over at Tom. "Ready?"

He grinned at her. "What, no tour of the house? I really wanted to see those rooms you're redoing."

Lilah felt her face grow warm under her makeup. "Another time, maybe. We won't be late," she said over her shoulder to Marabet.

"We might be," Tom said behind his hand, winking.

Lilah slid into the car, pulling her skirt down as Tom went around to his side. Had the dress been this short the last time she'd worn it? She couldn't even remember when that was.

"All set?" he asked, slipping behind the wheel.

She nodded.

He sat back as he maneuvered the winding road, a relaxed driver, but steady, in control. "I like Bethany," he said, smiling over at her. "She's a nice girl."

"Yes, she is. She'll be with me for the rest of the summer."

"What then?"

"Then I imagine she'll be spirited off to another relative. I'm merely a way station for her."

"You're all right with that?"

She looked away. "Yes. It's my decision, really." When he said nothing, she added, "I think it will be for the best. There's really no place in my life for a child."

"Ah." Tom looked like he was going to say more, but changed his mind. They rode in silence for several minutes before he asked, "Does she remind you of Elizabeth?"

Lilah thought before she answered. "Not her appearance. She's as different from Elizabeth as night and day in looks, but some of her mannerisms are startlingly similar." She gave a short laugh. "Sometimes it's almost as if Elizabeth were standing in front of me."

"Does that bother you?"

Lilah shifted uneasily. When she did, the dress slid up two inches. She tugged it back down and was mortified to realize Tom had witnessed the whole thing. Her laugh was awkward now. "Not as much as this dress does."

Tom grinned. "It's bothering me, too," he said, "but in an entirely different way."

Lilah felt her face burn. "Do you have children?" she asked, changing the subject. It seemed strange to have known the man for so many years and not know the answer to that simple question.

He nodded. "Two boys. Men now, of course. One's a lawyer in Macon. That's Jim. The other, Fred, is a psychologist. He practices here in town. Analyzes the old man every time he comes over. I remember when Maud died. The boys were anchors. I don't know what I'd have done without them."

Lilah smiled. "Grandchildren?"

"Five. Hellions, all of them," he said grinning, "and two wonderful daughters-in-law."

"I'm just getting to know my daughter-in-law. Charles' wife. She's a very nice woman. Family can be . . . important. I think

Of Words & Music

that's why this situation with Charles is so difficult for me. We haven't been exactly close over the years, but at least we've seen each other, talked some. I don't know if he's going to be able to forgive me for taking this step."

"You have no choice, you know," Tom said, his voice mild.

"I know." She sighed. "But that doesn't make it any easier. You should understand that. You have sons."

"I do understand it, but that doesn't alter my opinion a whit."

After another silence, she asked, "Maud was your wife?"

He nodded. "She died six years ago."

"Do you still miss her?"

"Interesting question," he said, taking the West Peachtree Street exit off I-75 and sliding seamlessly into the oncoming traffic. "Yes and no. Not painfully. Not anymore. That faded a long time ago. What I miss are the things we did, the fun we used to have, the long conversations. Things like that." He glanced over at Lilah. "In another way, it's like I've internalized her. Like she's a part of me now that will always be there. So I guess I'd have to say no, I don't miss her." After a minute, he glanced over at her. "How about you? Do you miss Gerome?"

She was still laughing when he pulled up in front of the restaurant.

Four hours later when he delivered her to her door, she had to wonder how the time had passed so quickly. They'd had dinner, a long leisurely meal with wine and after-dinner drinks. After that, he drove to Stone Mountain. He hadn't asked if she wanted to go. He'd just pointed the car in that direction, and Lilah felt relaxed enough with him not to ask where they were going. They'd ridden the riverboat, an old antebellum knock-off that glided up and down the length of a small lake. Throughout the evening, they had talked. Tom was a wonderful talker and equally as good a listener. Maybe that wasn't so surprising for an attorney, but she wasn't used to it. The attention made her feel bright and witty, something else she wasn't used to.

As he walked her to the door, a bit of her earlier awkwardness returned. "It was a wonderful evening, Tom," she said, not quite looking at him. "Thank you for inviting me."

"My pleasure, Lilah. I can't remember when I've enjoyed myself more."

He put his hands on her shoulders and leaned toward her, kissing her lightly on the forehead. "I'll call you tomorrow."

Then he was gone.

She let herself quietly into the house. Before she'd taken three steps down the hallway, Marabet came out of the living room. "Early?"

"It's not that late," Lilah said, and winced at the defensiveness in her voice.

"Did you enjoy yourself?"

"Yes, I did."

"Did you sign the papers?"

"The papers," Lilah repeated, looking at her blankly. Then she felt herself flush.

"Business dinner," Marabet muttered as she turned and headed toward the kitchen.

She signed them at noon the next day.

She awoke feeling charged with energy. It was a moment before embarrassment overcame her. What was the matter with her? How could she have forgotten something as serious as signing those papers? How could Tom have forgotten?

When she asked him on the phone, he laughed. "I didn't forget them. They were in my briefcase in the trunk, but when you didn't ask about them, I figured they were good for at least one more date."

The word still made her wince. "I have to get them signed. Charles has called twice, and I can't avoid him forever."

So she signed them at noon in the kitchen of his condo. His argument was that it was Saturday and he didn't want to go into the office. When she suggested her house, he countered with, "What if your son drops by while we're going over them?"

They were sitting at the pass-through bar, papers spread between them. "Now what?" she asked as she put down the pen.

"Now we can go one of two ways. I can call your son as your attorney and notify him of the revocation, or you can tell him. I still recommend the former."

Lilah looked at him, clearly unhappy. "I'd love to push it off on you, but that wouldn't be fair. He is my son, Tom, no matter how miserably he's behaved. I feel I owe him an explanation."

"Let me go with you, then."

She shook her head. "That would just make it worse. For him," she amended with a little smile. "I'll go see him after I leave here. He'll be at his office."

Tom picked up the pad and pen and jotted down a number. "Cell phone number," he said, handing the paper to her. "I'm only a quick call away in case you need the cavalry."

Lilah took the piece of paper and tucked it in her pocket. "Thank you," she said, standing. She picked up her purse. "Is one of those copies mine?" she said, gesturing at the stack of papers she'd signed and initialed.

"You're not going already? I was going to make us lunch."

Lilah shifted. "I have to," she said, glancing up at the clock. "I want to get this over with, and I don't know how long Charles will be at his office."

Tom pulled two copies of the letter out of the stack and handed them to her. "His and yours. How about dinner this week? You're going to need a new financial advisor. I have someone in mind." He grinned at her. "I could introduce you to her over dinner."

Something in his face broke down the resistance she had felt moments before. She laughed. "Don't you ever do business in your office?"

"Sure," he said, "but that's with regular clients."

Charles' BMW was in the lot beside his office. With mounting dread, Lilah parked a few spaces away and took the walkway to the door. It was locked, and after a moment's hesitation, she rang the bell. Charles answered the door clutching a bunch of papers. He was in office attire, but his shirt was unbuttoned at the neck and the signature vest was missing. His face registered surprise, then worry, when he saw her standing there. "Mother. What are you doing here?"

In the space of a heartbeat, she saw Charles at two years old, dirty-faced and loving. Then at five, worshipful. At eleven, his haughtiness just beginning to appear, and at thirty-five, deciding his mother was incompetent. They were all her son. Suddenly she felt completely unequal to the task before her, which only made her more determined to see it through. "May I come in, Charles?"

He stepped aside without speaking. Lilah entered and followed him into his office. "I'm just catching up on some paperwork. I'd offer you coffee but I didn't make any."

"I don't want coffee." Lilah seated herself in a chair in front of his desk.

"I'm glad you're here. You haven't been answering my calls," he said, a note of accusation entering his voice.

"Why were you calling?"

He looked taken aback for a minute, but quickly recovered. "The investment properties I've been trying to tell you about for weeks. If we don't move on it soon, we'll miss out completely."

"Is that the only reason you were calling?"

"What do you mean?"

"You weren't going to tell me you'd been to see Miss Greenlea?"

Lilah couldn't tell if it was with anger or embarrassment that colored his face. "So she came running to you."

"I would rather you had told me about it."

"I'm sorry, Mother," Charles said, walking around behind his desk and sitting down. He rested his folded hands on his stomach. "I felt it was something that had to be done."

Lilah felt the first stirrings of anger begin to displace her sorrow, but she tried to keep it out of her voice. "What do you mean?"

"It was clear that you were in over your head with the situation. Those welfare people badgered you into taking the girl, and I could see that you'd just go along with whatever they decided. I felt I had to step in before you made a serious mistake."

"What kind of mistake?"

"Keeping her, for god's sake," he said impatiently.

"What if I want to keep her?" Lilah felt an inappropriate bubble of laughter well up inside of her. It sounded like they were discussing a stray puppy.

"That's just exactly the kind of emotional decision I was trying to prevent. You aren't rational when it comes to anything having to do with Elizabeth, even her offspring."

Lilah chose her words carefully. "I appreciate your concern for my well-being, however misguided. What I don't appreciate is you going to see these people and passing yourself off as my agent—"

"I am your agent."

"My financial agent. Only."

Charles scowled. "I didn't do anything Father wouldn't have done if he'd been alive."

"That's true. It was exactly the sort of thing Gerome would have done. However, I am not married to you."

"Well, you obviously need someone to keep you on track," he said, his exasperation overcoming his caution. "Just look at the kind of decisions you've been making lately. First taking in that child."

"What's wrong with me taking Bethany into my home? She's my granddaughter, my—*our* own flesh and blood."

"At your age? You have no business raising a child—"

"I must admit, I didn't do very well with you."

"That's not what I mean," he said, his voice vibrating with anger. "And this is not only about her. It's you, spending God knows how much money redoing the house. Taking piano lessons. Good God! Piano lessons at your age."

Lilah felt her cheeks flame, but Charles either didn't see the warning sign or he chose to ignore it.

"You'll go along with anything. Your housekeeper, incompetent as she is, pushes you around like you're the servant. Good God, Mother, you need someone to take control of your life. I'm glad I went to see that social worker, and I'd do it again."

Lilah felt defeat press her down in the chair. "Not as my agent, you won't. I won't have my son telling people I'm incompetent."

He took a step back. "I never said that."

"What you said to Ms. Greenlea was close enough."

If anything, his color rose higher. "If she said that, she was lying."

Lilah continued to look at him.

"This is asinine, that you'd take her word over mine. She's really conned you. Her and that—that snippet. Next you'll be changing your will to make that child your beneficiary."

"I don't have to change it. She's already my beneficiary."

Charles looked at her through narrowed eyes. "Since when?"

"Since your father changed his will." Lilah was incredulous. "Is that what this is all about? Money?"

Charles brushed her question aside. "Of course it's not about money. What do you mean, since father changed his will?"

Lilah fought to bring herself under control. "When your father cut Elizabeth out of his will, I changed mine to make Elizabeth my sole beneficiary. I thought at least she'd get something that way. Not as much as you, of course. Not then, anyway."

For a moment, Lilah could have sworn Charles looked hurt, but the expression came and went so quickly, she wasn't sure. "That's irrelevant. Elizabeth is dead."

Lilah gritted her teeth. "And should she predecease me, the bequest would pass to her children. Child. Bethany."

"You simply can't be serious. Are you saying you care more about that—that girl you don't even know than about your own son?"

"Why, Charles? Didn't you inherit enough from your father? Did you think you were going to get it all?" Lilah felt sick and exhausted.

"I told you this isn't about money. It's about irrational decisions. You're totally out of control."

That brought Lilah up straight. "Whose control? Gerome's? Yours?"

"That was merely a figure of speech. You might remember that I'm your financial advisor, and as such—"

"Were," Lilah interrupted, her voice flat. "Under the circumstances, considering your opinion of my mental capacity and your disapproval of the way I live my life, I don't think it would be appropriate for us to continue that relationship."

Charles' mouth fell open. "You can't—"

"I already have."

Lilah pulled the letter out of her purse and laid it on his

desk. Charles looked at it as if it were a loaded gun. He made no move to pick it up. Finally, he looked up at her, his face stricken. "But I'm your son."

"I know," Lilah said sadly, "but you're not acting like a son. You're acting like an overbearing parody of your father. I'm humiliated that you went to Miss Greenlea behind my back and said the things you did, but even more than that, I'm sickened that you think them." She snapped her purse shut and stood. "Whatever you might think, I'm not a weak woman. That was a serious misjudgment on your part. I'm strong, and I'm determined, although I can see why you might have thought otherwise. You're completely mistaken about Marabet pushing me around. Marabet is my friend. My best friend. I know she would always act in my best interests no matter what she might think of my decisions, but I have no faith that you would do the same."

Charles was looking at her steadily, his expression unreadable.

She almost turned and left, but she hadn't quite finished what she wanted to say. "If you're contemplating having me declared incompetent, my attorney has already indicated that he will take you to court. You remember him, don't you? Thomas Mulligan? Your father's attorney?"

Still he said nothing. Lilah knew she should leave. There was really nothing more to say. And yet—"I didn't want to take this step, but your behavior . . ." But she was talking to his back as he stormed out of the office.

Lilah bowed her head. After a moment, she turned and walked out the door.

Lilah sat in the darkened living room staring at the mantel. She didn't need light to see the pictures lined up there now. At first Bethany had kept them all in her room, but since she spent most of her time in this room with her beloved piano, Lilah had asked her if she wanted to put a few of them on the mantel. You'd have thought she'd given the girl the moon.

Lilah had studied each one at such length that she could call to mind each detail. While it still hurt to look at those reminders of the years she had missed with her daughter, they were also a salve. They told her Elizabeth had been happy. You couldn't look at her face in those pictures and question it. At least she hadn't felt the hollowness of the years as Lilah had. She'd had her child, her husband, her life in Athens.

As if summoned by her thoughts, Bethany entered the room. She didn't see Lilah sitting in the dark. She switched on the small light on the music rack and sat down at the piano. Before Lilah could call out to her, she raised her hands and brought them down on the piano keys. Softly, with very nearly the skill Elliott had displayed that first day, she began playing the first notes of Moonlight Sonata.

Lilah breathed out slowly. It was her favorite. More than any other piece of music, this one reached deeply inside and touched her. She had heard it played hundreds of times, but that hadn't diminished its ability to move her. It was one of the pieces she hoped to learn in the future. Bethany could help her. If she was here, that is. She remembered her words to Charles, *What's wrong with me taking Bethany into my home? She's my granddaughter, my—our own flesh and blood,* words born more of frustration than any forethought or conviction. They were a weapon, a means to punish her son. A way to force him to expose himself, and she hadn't liked what she'd seen. She hadn't heard a word from Charles since her visit to his office. Maybe she should be worried about him, or at least about Lesa, but her thoughts had been completely taken up with what was happening here, this situation with Marabet and Bethany. She closed her eyes.

Bethany. If Lilah didn't take her, God knows where she would end up. With some relatives she'd never met? In a foster home, living with strangers who were paid to take her in? The thought of it made Lilah feel slightly ill. She watched the child's face as she lived the music she was playing. Not a child, really. A young woman. Soon she would be grown and gone. A tear trickled down Lilah's cheek.

Even if Lilah agreed to let her stay, it would only be a few years before she left and made a life of her own, and then Lilah would have lost her as surely as she had lost Elizabeth. Another tear fell. Then another. Lilah laid her head back against the sofa, letting the tears stream down her face.

Bethany, Bethany, she cried silently, *why did I ever let you into my life? Now I'll lose you, too, no matter what.*

Send her away? As she had allowed Gerome to send Elizabeth away? Had she learned nothing from all the years of pain? Did it matter that Bethany would grow up and leave? They'd have—what? Four or five years? Nine, with college? What she wouldn't give to go back and have nine more years of Elizabeth's life. Or five. Or one. It wasn't as if she'd be leaving, never to return, as Elizabeth had. She might go to a local college. She might marry someone local. Have children.

The thought brought a watery smile to her face. She closed her eyes again. No, she might not be around to see all that. She wasn't going to live forever, even though lately she had felt as though she might. What was it Tom had said? Seize the moment? Could she? Did she have the courage to try?

"Uh—is everything all right?"

Lilah's eyes flew open. She sat bolt upright, brushing the tears off her face.

"Did the song make you sad? I'm sorry. I didn't know you were here."

The child looked so worried, so tentative. Had there ever

been a child as considerate as this one? As kind? How well her parents had raised her. How lucky they had been to have her. Lilah smiled, blinking back fresh tears. "No." She patted the sofa cushion. "Sit down. No, the music was beautiful, so beautiful it made me cry."

Bethany sat down gingerly. "I know. Sometimes it makes me cry, too."

"Did your mother teach it to you?"

Bethany nodded. Her eyes, too, went to the mantel.

"Tell me what she was like."

Bethany looked at her in surprise. "You know what she was like. She was your daughter."

"I know what she was like when she lived here. I don't know what she was like later, after she left. What was she like as a mother? What's the first thing you remember about her? What was your life like in Athens?"

Bethany looked wary. "You really want to hear about that?"

Lilah sat back against the arm of the sofa and faced her granddaughter. Her granddaughter, she spoke the phrase in her mind. "Yes, I really want to hear about that."

Lilah wasn't sure what woke her that night. Some—sound. There it was again. She climbed out of bed and pulled on her robe, letting herself out of her bedroom. Once in the hallway, she heard it again. It was coming from Bethany's room. It sounded like moaning. Was the child sick?

She made her way around the hall stopping just outside Bethany's door. More sounds. She must be having a nightmare. Lilah remembered having a few nightmares of her own after she got the call about Elizabeth. The kindest thing she could do was to go wake the child. She slipped across the sitting room and into the bedroom.

There was enough light coming from the bathroom that she

could make out Bethany's twisted features, the tears streaming down her face. The child was sound asleep, but she was thrashing about and wrestling with the sheets as if they threatened her life. "No," she moaned. "Please no." Her voice rose to a near scream. "No, *Mama! Help me!*"

Lilah hurried to the side of the bed, shaking Bethany's shoulder. "Wake up, Bethany. It's a dream." The girl twisted away, still in the throes of whatever horror she was living. "Bethany." Lilah reached out and captured her flailing arm. "Bethany, *wake up!*"

As Bethany frantically moved to the other side of the bed, Lilah grabbed her to keep her from falling. She pulled Bethany close, wrapping her arms around her. "Shhh. It was a dream. It's all right. It was only a dream."

Still half asleep, Bethany clung to Lilah as if to a life raft. "Mama, oh Mama," she sobbed. "You were dead. I dreamed you were—"

Lilah heard her suck in her breath, and suddenly she grew completely still. Bethany's body was shaking like a palsy victim. She didn't try to pull away, so Lilah held her. After a while, Bethany began to sob softly. The sound tore at Lilah's heart. God, what the child must be enduring.

When Bethany spoke, her voice barely above a whisper, Lilah had to strain to make out the words. "I dreamed—I dreamed that this was a dream, being here, and that-that Mama was still alive but I couldn't get to her. I th-thought she was still alive. Oh, *God,* why did she have to die?"

Lilah could feel Bethany's body go limp as the finality of it all soaked into her. There was nothing she could say. She had asked herself the same question a hundred times, a thousand times, and there simply was no answer. Why did a wonderful, loving young woman with so much ahead of her, with so much life in her and so much future before her have to die? Lilah had never given much thought to the deeper meaning of life and death until Elizabeth's life was snatched away so suddenly. Even pondering her own eventual death didn't move her. But losing Elizabeth, losing her beautiful, perfect Elizabeth was profane, an abomination, a slap in the face to life.

And if it seemed profane to Lilah, how much worse did it seem to this child in her arms who had lost not only her mother, but her father as well? What kind of God could allow such a thing to happen?

"I don't know, Bethany," she said, her voice barely louder than the child's whisper. "I wish I had an answer for you. For me. But I just don't know. I guess a preacher would say it was her time to go, but I don't believe that. I don't know what I do believe, but it isn't that. It was just a stupid accident, and I can't imagine a world without her in it any more than you can."

"She was so brave," Bethany said against her chest. "When Daddy was sick, she was so brave. She fixed his meals and gave him baths, and she even gave him shots when he had to have them. And after—after he died." Lilah could feel her shaking her head. "She did everything. She cried a lot, but she was so strong. So I tried to be strong, too. But I wasn't. Not like her. Mine was an act."

"I imagine some of hers was an act, too," Lilah said quietly, "for you, to help you get through it. That's what mothers do. Sometimes it's all they can do, just be there and be strong. She loved you, Bethany. I can tell by the way you are, the person you've become, that both your parents loved you very much. I won't tell you that you were lucky to have that even if you lost it, but I do know that some children never have it. Not even for one day. What you had, that love, made you a better person, a stronger person, and you'll have that love for the rest of your life. It was their gift to you."

They sat like that, Lilah perched on the edge of the bed with

Bethany in her arms, for a long time. The house was perfectly quiet. Outside, a leafy branch swayed in the breeze, barely brushing against the bricks. Lilah could hear the rhythmic tick of Bethany's bedside clock, or maybe it was her heart beating. She rested her chin on top of the girl's head, breathing in the clean scent of shampoo and child. She ached in the deepest recesses of her soul, but just for this moment, there was also contentment, a sense that she was doing something right. Meaningful.

And just for a moment, it was enough.

Chapter 17

Communication with Marabet was improving. They had graduated to speaking in whole sentences. There was none of the camaraderie they'd shared for so many years, but Lilah would take what she could get. She hadn't said anything, either to Marabet or to Bethany, about her changing feelings. It wouldn't be fair until she was absolutely sure, and this was a big step, perhaps the biggest she'd ever been called on to take on her own.

The results of her earlier decisions didn't give her much confidence in her ability to think things through. Her marriage to Gerome had been her decision, as much as she would like to blame it on parental pressure. She had also decided at some early point in Charles' life to leave the lion's share of his discipline—or lack of it—to Gerome, and look what that had wrought.

Then there was the ultimatum they'd given to Elizabeth. She might not have made the decision, but she'd certainly, if not willingly, gone along with it. No, she wouldn't make a final decision until the end of the summer. That would give her some time, some breathing room, and if it meant that she would be at odds with Marabet for a few more weeks, then so be it.

At least she had Tom, and he was turning out to be a wonderful friend. Tom might want more—at least Lilah got the feeling he wouldn't mind if their relationship moved to the next step—but that was another decision Lilah would take her time with.

Tom was a wonderful man, the most wonderful of her limited experience, but Lilah wasn't ready to commit to any kind of relationship other than what they already had. They'd been out to dinner again twice, and Tom had convinced her to go sailing with him. What a lark that had been! Lilah couldn't remember ever laughing so much. She only regretted that she couldn't talk to Marabet about how things were going, both with Charles and Tom. She'd tried, but Marabet wasn't ready to talk. She could have told Bethany about the sailing trip, at least. The girl seemed completely smitten with Tom, but she wasn't ready to share personal confidences with Bethany. So she just kept her own council, as she had for most of her life. If it was lonely, at least it was familiar.

She and Bethany could talk about piano, and they did. Only a few nights before, Lilah had decided to go ahead with the recital. She was probably mad to even consider it, but it seemed to mean so much to Bethany and to Elliott. Now, on the eve of the big day, she and Bethany were going shopping for their recital dresses.

She heard the telephone ring. A minute later, the intercom buzzed. "It's Felicity Greenlea."

Lilah froze in the act of clipping on her earring. She hadn't heard a word from Felicity since Lilah and Bethany went to Athens. What if this was about some long lost relative turning up? Lilah gave herself a shake. What were the chances of that after all these weeks? No, it was probably a routine call to see how Bethany was doing. Or maybe Elliott had told her about the recital.

"Thank you, Marabet," she said into the intercom. Then she picked up the phone. "Felicity?"

"I'm glad I caught you, Mrs. Kimball. Marabet said you were about to head out shopping."

Lilah could hear traffic noises in the background and a hum

on the line. Felicity must be calling from her car. "Is something wrong?" she couldn't help asking.

"I wondered if there's any way you could come by my office this morning. There are some—oh for Pete's sake."

"Felicity?"

"Sorry. Someone just cut in front of me. Anyway, do you think you could? I'd come there, but I have an appointment at eleven. I'd never make it back to the office in this mess."

"Is this something that can wait? Maybe you could come by here tomorrow. No, that's the recital."

"I really don't think this can wait," Felicity said.

Lilah's stomach clenched. She could hear the distress in Felicity's voice, but didn't know whether it was about their visit or the traffic. What she didn't like was Felicity's statement that it couldn't wait. "Well, I suppose I could. What time do you want us there?"

"As soon as possible. I'm on my way downtown now. I should be there in, say, twenty minutes." Lilah heard a horn blow. Then "Geesh," from Felicity. "Forty-five tops."

"I'll see you then." Lilah's hand was shaking when she hung up the receiver.

She and Bethany walked out into the hallway at the same time, and Lilah was reminded of that first morning. How different things were now. Bethany skipped over to Lilah, smiling up at her. "I'm ready. Are we going to get shoes, too, or just dresses? I have dressy shoes, but they're in Athens. I don't think we have time to go there, but if you don't want to spend the money, I could wear sandals. Those would probably look okay."

Lilah put her arm around the girl's shoulders. "We'll definitely get shoes, too. Something to match our dresses."

Bethany let out a whoop and raced down the stairs. As Lilah followed, she saw Marabet standing halfway up the stairs. When she saw Lilah, she turned and followed Bethany down the stairs without a word.

The drive into downtown Atlanta was harrowing for Lilah. She hated the place. Once she left the interstate and entered the city, the roads were narrow and usually under construction. Half of them were one-way streets; all were confusing. Most drivers hadn't a clue where they were going, so they were forcing their way across lanes to make turns, looking everywhere but at the roads. Even Bethany was intimidated into silence.

Following Felicity's directions, Lilah found public parking in a lot just off Peachtree Street. It was a short but unnerving walk to the government building. Next door was a mission house, or whatever they called those places, where they furnished beds and food to the homeless. Only a few people lounged on its steps, probably because the weather wasn't cold. At least the sidewalk here was clean and in good repair. Half a block over, the street was littered with trash, food wrappers, and other things that didn't bear closer scrutiny. A transitional neighborhood at best.

The streets were crowded with people—lunch shoppers, conventioneers, vendors, some in business attire, but more in rags. The city reminded Lilah more of New York every day, not a favorable comparison in her opinion.

"I guess this is it," Lilah said, looking from the piece of paper in her hand to the red brick building looming in front of them. Bethany stood beside her looking like a wild rose in a sorely neglected garden.

Lilah suddenly realized this was the world she had intended to send the child into. Bethany didn't belong here, not in a place like this where people who passed you only looked at you to see how securely you held your purse. She realized Bethany was studying her and cleared her throat. "The address is right.

Let's go inside."

They pushed through the double glass doors and into the lobby, abruptly silencing the sounds of traffic and humanity.

The inside of the building was tidy and unadorned. Green-gray walls, some kind of textured paint meant to look like wallpaper, fake marble tile floor. The elevators had fake brass and wood trim. The only thing real Lilah could see was the glass on the directory, and she wasn't certain it wasn't Plexiglas.

Felicity was listed in office number 6-04.

"Did she say what she wants?" Bethany asked.

"Only that she wanted to talk to me."

"Not both of us?"

"I don't know," Lilah answered absently. "She didn't say."

She and Bethany crossed to the elevator and pushed the up button.

"We need to practice for tomorrow."

"This shouldn't take long."

Lilah ushered Bethany inside and pushed the button for the sixth floor. During their brief ride, Bethany stared at the elevator doors without speaking, her posture rigid.

The elevator stopped, and they stepped out into a hallway, even barer than the ground floor had been. The walls were the same drab green and completely unadorned except for little black plastic signs with room numbers on them. They finally found 6-04. The door was open. They entered, only to find a deserted office—more a cubicle, Lilah thought, looking around. Whatever portion of taxes the government was allotting to this agency, it clearly wasn't being spent on amenities.

The desk was government-issue gray metal, as was the bank of file cabinets across the room. Plastic chairs lined one wall, and a battered table was stacked with magazines that had been read too many times. Only the plastic nameplate on the desk looked new, and it identified the office as Felicity's.

"She's not here," Bethany said, her voice faint, and Lilah realized she wasn't the only one who was nervous.

She patted Bethany's arm. "She's probably caught in traffic. We'll wait a few minutes."

They perched on the edge of the plastic chairs. No more than a minute passed before the silence began to weigh on Lilah. She stood. "I'm going to run to the ladies' room. I saw one at the end of the hall."

Bethany jumped up. "I'll go with you."

Lilah knew the child was just nervous. "Why don't you wait here for Felicity? I'll only be a moment. Then you can go if you'd like."

Bethany's lower lip poked out a bit, but she said, "Okay."

Bethany watched Lilah's back disappear out the door. She felt frightened and alone. Well, she was alone, but it was a worse kind of alone. And she knew it was silly to feel afraid. This was an office building. There were people all around.

She sat down and hopped up again when she spotted a framed photo of Elliott on Felicity's desk. He was a nice man, Bethany thought, walking over and picking up the picture, and he could play the piano even better than her mother had. Of course, he did it for a living. Had her mother ever wanted to do that for a living? Bethany remembered that she had taken lots of music classes in college, but there was nothing in her diary about wanting to be a professional piano player.

As she put the picture back on the desk, she saw a folder in the center of Felicity's desk. *Freemont, Bethany,* the tab on the edge read, and there were some colored bands down the side. She knew she shouldn't. She knew it was wrong, but she flipped it open anyway. It was about her, wasn't it? So it couldn't be too wrong if she knew what it said.

The first page was a handwritten letter. A glance told Bethany it had been written to her father. Then the world tilted as she read on.

Dear Professor Freemont,

I don't have enough words to thank you and Mrs. Freemont for taking my baby to raise, and for paying the hospital people and everything. The people I talked to at the clinic said they'd have to contact my parents if I decided to give the baby up. I know it would kill my mom and pop, and that would kill me. I know I did the right thing, giving the baby to you and Mrs. Freemont and I know it will be easier if I'm not around all the time. My parents don't know anything. I'm going to ask them to let me transfer to Valdosta State. They'll probably say yes, since they never wanted me to go to school so far away from home in the first place. I know you said you don't think I'm a terrible person and I hope you really don't. I would raise her if I could. Really I would, but I just can't have a baby right now. Please take care of her. Love, Sallie Jo.

Bethany felt all the blood drain out of her head, and the room grew dark for just a minute. She put her hand on the desk to steady herself. Maybe the lady was talking about another baby, maybe one that died before Bethany was born or something. There was no date on the letter, but there was an envelope under it. She turned it over and looked at the postmark and had to grip the edge of the desk with both hands to keep from falling. A bunch of other stuff was in the file. She started to pick up another piece of paper, but then she heard a sound out in the hall. Barely knowing what she was doing, she snatched up the folder and stuffed it in the front of her jeans, pulling her shirt over it. A moment later, Lilah walked into the room.

She seemed surprised to see Bethany standing by Felicity's desk, but then she saw the picture of Elliott and smiled. "He's a very handsome young man, isn't he?"

"Uh—I guess." She edged toward the door. "I'll be right back."

Once in the hall, she didn't know what to do. She was afraid she was going to throw up. She had to read the rest of the file. She *had* to, but she didn't want to go to the bathroom. Someone was sure to come in there and hear the paper rustling. She couldn't take it home with her. Felicity would be here in a minute and would know it was missing. She looked up and down the hallway. More doors.

It was the dinging of the elevator that galvanized her into action. Without a backward glance, she bolted for the stairwell.

Felicity hurried into the office. "I'm so sorry. There was an accident at the Grady curve. I didn't think I'd ever get past it. Did you get my message?"

Lilah stood. "I didn't get any message."

"I called Connie and left a message asking her to check to see if you were here and let you know." Her brow furrowed. She snatched up her phone and dialed a number. "Connie, didn't you . . . oh, well never mind. I'm here now." She hung up the phone, looking at Lilah helplessly. "Connie was stuck in the same mess. She just got in." She pulled off her jacket and threw it on the back of her chair. "I'm sorry I made you wait."

"It was no problem. Let me just get Bethany."

Felicity was putting her purse in the file cabinet just inside the door. "Bethany is with you?"

Lilah nodded. "We were on our way shopping. She went to the little girl's room." She glanced at her watch and her brow creased. "She's been gone quite some time. Maybe I'd better check on her."

"It might be better if I talked to you alone."

"Of course," Lilah said, frowning. "Just let me check . . ."

She walked out into the hallway and looked both ways. No

Bethany. The child was probably playing with the hand dryer. Shoving her worry aside, she walked down the bare hallway and into the ladies' room. No one. She looked in each stall to make certain she wasn't playing some kind of trick. No Bethany. Worried now, she hurried back to Felicity's office. "Did she . . ." Her voice trailed off as she saw Felicity alone in the office. "She wasn't there."

Felicity seemed distracted as she searched through her desk drawers. "Maybe she's hiding in one of the stalls. You know girls."

"No. I checked. She isn't there."

Finally she had Felicity's attention. "You didn't see her in the hall?"

"No. Where could she have gone?"

Felicity pushed her drawer closed. "Let me check some of the other offices. They all look alike. Maybe she wandered into the wrong one."

But Lilah knew better.

She was back in less than five minutes. She went directly to her desk and picked up the phone. "I'm calling building security," she told Lilah.

Lilah only half-listened to her as she gave them a description of Bethany. "She's wearing blue jeans and a red t-shirt. And red sneakers," she said when Felicity asked. How could the child have just vanished? She was too old to wander off or Lilah never would have let her go to the bathroom on her own. She wouldn't have left knowing Lilah was waiting for her. They were going shopping. Bethany was excited about it. She wasn't angry or anything.

Unless—she closed her eyes—unless someone had taken her. Such things weren't unheard of, and certainly not in this area of town. Oh, God, why had she brought her here? Why had she put her at risk this way? She couldn't bear to think about anything happening to the girl. What if—She felt Felicity's hand on her arm, and she opened her eyes.

Felicity was frowning down at her. "I'm sure she's okay. We're going to find her. Don't worry. It's a big building. Easy to get lost in, but we have five security guards searching. They'll find her in no time. Really. She probably just wandered off looking for a vending machine or something. We'll find her." But Lilah could see the panic in her eyes.

Chapter 18

Two hours had passed. Lilah felt like she was holding onto her sanity by a thread. Every footstep in the hall caused her heart to race unnaturally. She had been fighting hysteria since the call came from security. There was no sign of her. They had pretty much scoured the building. All the restrooms. The stairwells. They were conducting an office-by-office search now, and several were outside the building asking people if they'd seen her.

"Did she have any money?" Felicity asked.

Lilah looked up. "Money? Why?"

"Bus fare home. Or cab fare."

Lilah shook her head. "I don't think so. A few dollars maybe." She studied Felicity for a minute, her face rigid. "I should call Marabet."

Felicity nodded, turning the phone around to her. Lilah's hand shook as she dialed the number. "Marabet, this is Lilah. There's—a problem." As briefly as she could, she told Marabet about Bethany vanishing. "The security guards are checking outside now, just in case someone saw her out there. I can't imagine that she would have left."

Marabet was as nearly speechless as Lilah had ever known her. Promising to call as soon as she heard anything, she replaced the receiver in its cradle.

Felicity snatched it up, dialing a number from memory. "Barbara, it's Felicity. Bethany is missing. She's been gone over two hours . . . She was here in my office . . . She might. It was her home. I don't know where else she'd go . . . All right. Thank you. And call me immediately." She turned to Lilah. "Barbara is the social worker in Athens. She's going to keep an eye on the house."

"She has a key," Lilah said weakly, "but how would she get there?"

The phone rang again, and Felicity snatched it up. "She's right here," she said and handed the phone to Lilah.

"Tom?" Lilah said when she heard his voice. "How did you know I was here?"

"Marabet called me. I'm on my way there."

"There's no need for you to come."

"I'm pulling into the parking lot. I'll be there in a minute."

"Oh." She hung up the phone, looking at Felicity. "That was my attorney. He's—" She shook her head. "He's here. Marabet called him."

"Oh," Felicity said in a small voice. "Well, I can't blame you."

"You can't blame . . ." Comprehension dawned. "No, Miss Greenlea. Tom is a friend, too. He's coming here as a friend."

When Lilah heard the elevator bell, she jumped to her feet. In the next second, Tom was in the room.

He stopped inches away from Lilah. "Are you all right?"

"I'm fine," she said, looking both embarrassed and relieved. She turned to Felicity. "Tom Mulligan, Felicity Greenlea."

The phone rang, and they all jumped. Felicity grabbed the receiver. "Yes?" She listened for a minute. Her posture sagged. "Thank you," she said. "No, I understand."

She hung up the phone, turning to Lilah. "They've completed the search of the building. Nothing. A couple of people outside think they might have seen her come out. They weren't sure."

Lilah felt lightheaded. She looked from Tom to Felicity. "What should we do? Can we call the police?"

Felicity rubbed her forehead. "She seems to have left of her own volition. It's too early to notify the police officially that she's missing, but I have a few friends at the Atlanta PD. I'll have them ask the others to keep an eye out for her. They're really good about things like this." She glanced at her watch. "I'll stay around here in case she comes back."

Lilah looked at Tom helplessly.

"I think we should go to your house," Tom told her. "That's the most likely place for her to show up." When she seemed reluctant, he added, "There's nothing we can do here, Lilah. We can stay in phone contact with everyone." He pulled a business card out of his breast pocket and handed it to Felicity. "My mobile number is on there. Will you give it to the police and call us if you hear anything?"

"Of course," she said, taking the card. She picked up one of her own cards from the desk and handed it to Tom.

"I'm—I'm so sorry," she said to Lilah.

Lilah nodded, looking at Tom. He took her hand and tucked it into the crook of his arm. "Let's take my car," he said, leading her from the office.

Lilah looked up into his face. She bit her lip, nodding.

When she looked back, Felicity was rummaging through her desk drawers again.

Marabet met them at the front door, her face lined with worry. Lilah opened her arms, and Marabet stumbled into them. "Where could she be?" she mumbled.

Lilah guided her to the living room. She heard Tom say, "I'll make some coffee," but she only nodded. She sat Marabet on the couch, keeping an arm around her shoulders. Who would have guessed that she, almost paralyzed with worry such a short time ago, would be the one to offer comfort?

"Bethany's a smart girl," she said, as much to herself as to

Marabet. "She's not a small child, so she wouldn't have gone with someone without a struggle, and there was no sign of that. Felicity thinks she may have gone back to Athens. She has someone watching her house there. But—" Her voice broke off. "But I don't think Bethany would do that. She didn't have enough money to take a bus there, and I think she's too intelligent to hitch a ride. And she'd know we'd be worried. Bethany is too considerate to do that to us."

Marabet pulled away. "If she's too smart to get snatched and too considerate to worry us on purpose, what does that leave?"

Lilah looked at Marabet, her face bleak. "I don't know."

The doorbell rang. Marabet jumped to her feet and headed to the front with Lilah a step behind.

Lesa stood on the porch. She started to speak, but she stopped when she saw Marabet's face. "What's wrong?"

Marabet stepped back, clutching her chest as Lilah stepped forward. "Come in, Lesa. Please. Bethany's missing. It's a long story. Come in." She took Lesa's hand, putting her arm around Marabet's shoulder and leading them both down the hallway. They met Tom in the hallway carrying a tray of coffee. Without a word, he turned and led them back to the kitchen. When they were all sitting at the kitchen table, Lilah told Lesa what had happened at Felicity's office. "They searched the building. She wasn't there. Felicity has the police looking for her."

"What are you going to do?"

"Wait, I guess. I don't know what else we can do."

No one said anything for a minute, then Lesa cleared her throat. "Can I talk to you for a minute, Lilah?" She looked around at the others apologetically. "I mean, alone. It won't—"

She broke off at the sound of the doorbell. Marabet beat Lilah to the front door by only a step, flinging it open. Lilah had been so sure that it would be Bethany that it took her a moment to adjust.

"Charles?"

Charles thrust a stack of files at her. "The last of your papers. I wanted to personally deliver them. I'm glad I did. I see Lesa's car in the driveway. I suppose she's here, too."

"In the kitchen," Lilah said, surprised at the venom in his words.

"Well, you can tell her to go to hell for me. I suppose she came to cry on your shoulder. Well, it's a lot of bull. She left me—"

"*What?*" The word echoed down the hallway. Lilah looked toward the kitchen just as Lesa came down the hallway. "Lesa, is it true?"

She nodded, her face pale. "I'm sorry, Lilah. I wanted to tell you myself, but . . ."

"I don't understand." But she did. Clearly.

Charles pulled his suit coat together and buttoned it. "I don't suppose she mentioned that she wiped out the checking account."

"That's not true. I took less than half—"

"And God knows what else she might have told you," he said as if she hadn't spoken.

Tom walked up behind them. Charles nodded toward him. "Who's he?"

"Tom Mulligan, your mother's attorney," he said, looking Charles up and down.

"You're the bastard who handled the revocation."

When Lilah started to speak, Tom held up his hand. "I am," he said, taking a step forward, "and I begin to see why she felt it was necessary. You burst in here raising hell in the middle of a family crisis—"

"What family crisis? You mean her?" He pointed at Lesa.

Now Lilah spoke. "It's Bethany. She's missing."

"Missing? You mean she ran away?"

"No." She shook her head. "I don't know."

Charles looked incredulous for a moment. Then he smiled. "You seem to have a talent for running off young women," he said.

Tom started toward him. "Why, you little—"

Lilah put her hand on Tom's chest, stopping him. "Charles, I want to see you in the library." When he looked like he would turn away, she said, *"Now."*

After a moment, Charles turned and followed her down the hall and into the library.

Halfway across the room, she spun around to face him. Her cheeks and neck were splotched with red. "What in God's name is the matter with you? Are you really so callous, so completely unfeeling that you think this is funny?"

"What? That first Elizabeth ran off, and how her daughter's done the same thing? Yes, I think it's funny."

She stared at him, speechless.

"What? You think I should be upset? Why should I? Here you were thinking you got Elizabeth back so you dumped me. Now you don't have anyone."

"You are despicable," Lilah hissed out. "You're a carbon copy of your father."

"My father was a wonderful man."

"Your father was an unhappy, cruel man who hurt others as some kind of sport."

"You married him."

"Yes, I did, and it was one of the worst mistakes I ever made."

"There are plenty of people who thought he was great."

"Who?"

Charles crossed his arms. "All those people who came to his funeral, to name just a few."

"Hangers on, that's who attended his funeral, and people who thought they should be seen there. They were not there because they admired him."

"Including his loving wife?"

"Especially his wife."

"You're a hypocrite," Charles said, dropping his arms to his side. "You took his money for thirty-five years, and now that he's dead, you can't say a good word about him."

"There is nothing good to say, and I earned every dime of that money, believe me."

"How? By sitting around the house while he was out busting his ass to make a living?"

"By making him a home, raising his children. By putting up with his tyranny—"

"Oh, for god's sake! You did nothing, and in exchange you got this." He waved his hand to indicate the house.

"Do you think this house means anything to me?" Lilah demanded. "Because if you do, you're even a bigger fool than you seem." The words tumbled out of her mouth. "I'd give all this and more to know where Bethany is at this moment. Do you know how that feels?" she asked, her voice growing quieter. "To care about someone?"

"What do you mean, you'd give it all to find her?"

"I mean exactly that. Good God, Charles. Where are your human emotions? A child is missing. And that's your wife out there." She gestured toward the hallway. "Your marriage has ended, and all you can hear are the words about money."

"I asked you a question."

"And I gave you an answer," she said, furious now.

"I won't let you do it."

He sounded so much like his father that Lilah flinched, and that made her even angrier. "Oh?" She raised her eyebrows. "Just how do you intend to stop me?"

"It's obvious that you're incapable of making decisions rationally. Throwing away a fortune on some little—"

"Are you planning to file suit?" Tom asked, standing in the doorway, his face grim. "Please tell me you are."

Charles spun around. "What were you doing? Eavesdropping?"

"The door was open," Tom said, gesturing toward it. "I'd have to be deaf not to hear your yelling."

"A gentleman would have walked away."

"How would you know?" Tom asked, coming to stand beside Lilah.

Charles stared at the two of them and took a step back. "Oh, I get it now," he said with a sneer. "He's the one calling the shots here. I should have known."

Lilah started to speak, but Tom said, "You're wrong, Charles. The person calling the shots here is your mother, who is quite capable of making her own decisions. She doesn't need you or me to do it for her, and the sooner you realize that, the better."

Charles glared at the two of them. Then he turned on his heel and slammed out of the room.

Lilah stared after him. Then she turned and looked up at Tom, her eyes wide with pain. "I think the whole world's gone crazy."

Tom put his arms around her and pulled her to him. "Your corner of it sure has. Are you okay?"

"No," Lilah whispered against his chest. "I don't think I am."

She had called the number Felicity had given her for her contact at the police station a half-dozen times, and a half-dozen times the officer who answered told her they'd had no word. If nothing else, she had to admire his patience. Lesa had left to go to a hotel. No matter how hard Lilah argued, she couldn't convince her to stay. She felt sorry for the young woman.

When everyone was finally gone, Lilah climbed the stairs to her room. She could sit by the phone holding her breath there as well as downstairs, and she wouldn't have Marabet watching her every facial expression. She started to change into a nightgown but decided to stay dressed in case . . .

She refused to carry the thought further. Instead, she went to the closet and pulled out the photo album she'd hidden there. Well, maybe hidden was too strong a word. She had kept that one photo album in her room because it was filled with pictures of Elizabeth as she'd looked when she walked out the door, never to return. But this time she was looking at the pictures of Bethany.

Lilah flipped back to the first picture of Elizabeth holding a tiny baby. Bethany couldn't have been more than a few weeks old. Her hair was only a shadow across her scalp, and her face still had that wizened look that all new babies have. Elizabeth looked beatific as she gazed down on the face of the infant, a look Lilah remembered having herself when she first looked on her own babies. It was the Madonna look, or close enough. On the next page was a professional portrait of Elizabeth with her husband and daughter. Again, happiness radiated from her face. Lilah reached out and touched the plastic covering the photo, and she felt—something, something rectangular behind it.

She felt only curiosity as the pulled the envelope out from between the two pictures, imagining it was maybe some documents about the baby. But it was addressed to her. Across the front of the still-sealed envelope were the words, "Return to Sender," and Lilah immediately recognized both handwritings, the one who addressed the envelope and the one who returned it. She had seen them enough times over the years.

Her fingers trembled as she tore the envelope open. Two small snapshots fell out into her lap, but she barely noticed them. She read the first words, and her heart stuttered.

Dear Mama,
First let me say that this isn't the first letter I wrote you. I've

written dozens, but I couldn't bring myself to mail them. I know you're really mad at me, and Daddy is furious. I thought maybe I could get around you because I always knew how to do that, but Daddy's such an old sourpuss. Besides, I figured he'd just give you grief about it. So I waited, hoping I'd hear from you first, knowing you would forgive me eventually. You're not the kind of person to stay mad for long, but I can't wait any longer.

I love you, Mama, and I've missed you so much it almost killed me. I always knew one of us would break down. I don't mind that it's me, especially since I have such a gift to give you. Your very own granddaughter.

She's beautiful, Mama! She's a miracle, and I love her so much. Now I'm beginning to know how you must have felt about me, and, well WOW! It's the most incredible feeling, and it's something I just have to share with you. Please say that you forgive me, Mama, and please forgive Julian, even though all the poor man did was fall in love with me. When you get to know him, you're going to love him as much as I do. He's so good and kind and loving. He's got to be the best father in the world. He changes diapers and gets up in the middle of the night to feed Bethany when she cries, just so I can get some sleep, even when he has classes the next day. I can't wait for you to meet him.

I know we can't come there to the house without starting some kind of war, but you have to meet Julian and your beautiful new granddaughter. You know you want to. Don't you? I thought maybe you could come here to Athens, or maybe you and Marabet. Don't feel bad because I know Daddy won't come, but you don't have to say anything to him. Anyway, it's only fifty miles, and it's highway all the way. I could send you directions, and I could cook lunch for you and Marabet in my very own kitchen. If you don't want to do that, we can come to Atlanta, and we could meet you someplace. Daddy would never have to know.

Please say you will. I'm going to hold my breath until you say yes, so don't wait too long or I'll be dead. Just joking. I know you'll give in, so I'll go ahead and plan a lunch menu. Something easy, so we can spend all our time talking instead of cooking.

I love you, Mama. I just can't say that enough times. I've thought it and thought it, and it's wonderful to be able to say it again. Write me! I love you love you love you!!!

Lilah felt a scream well up in her center and grow and expand as it fought for escape. She stuffed her fist in her mouth and bit down, drawing blood.

It wasn't enough. She wanted to smash something, everything. She wanted to rip at her hair. She wanted to kill. She jumped to her feet, scattering the letter and the snapshots that had fallen out of the envelope. She looked down at them without picking them up. Three-by-five copies of the pictures in the album. Pictures Elizabeth was sending to her.

She sank to the floor and picked up the letter and the pictures, hugging them to her as tears streamed down her face. "Oh God, she loved me," she whispered. "She really did love me."

She cried until there were no more tears left to shed, and then she cried even more. After a long time, she got to her feet and went over to her closet. She reached up pulled down an old handbag, one she hadn't used in over a decade, taking it over to the bed and pulling out its contents. Letters. Letters she had written to Elizabeth and never mailed. She looked over the first one and almost smiled at its formality. It was a "you've done wrong so admit it" letter. The next was more in the form of a plea. There were half a dozen of them. The last one, the one in which she poured out her feelings for Elizabeth and begged her to come back home on any terms, had been wadded into a tight ball before being smoothed out again. Lilah remembered how angry she had been at herself for writing it, but something in her, some perverse need to punish herself, had prevented her from throwing it away. She had taken the letters out a few times over the years and re-read them to torture herself, but she had never mailed them.

So many mistakes, both with Elizabeth and Bethany. And now they were both gone. Again, Lilah looked at the "Return to Sender" scrawled across the envelope. She wanted to summon up anger, or *something*, but all she could muster was sorrow.

She picked up the letter from Elizabeth and put it in the handbag with the ones she'd written, putting the purse on her bedside table. Then she made herself change and, picking up the photo album, she climbed into bed.

Chapter 19

Bethany inched her way out onto the limb of the huge old oak, praying it wouldn't snap under her weight. The tree was taller than the house, but the limbs near the top weren't thick like the ones down lower. Still, she had to try.

Just a little further. One more heave. She heard a crack and froze, but the limb held, at least for now. If it gave, she would fall three stories to the stone terrace below. Maybe one of the lower branches would break her fall. Maybe it wouldn't. She tried not to think about it. Sweat rolled down her forehead and into her eyes, but she didn't have a hand free to brush it away. She reached out and curled her fingers over the window ledge. First one hand, then the other. Another inch. Another. She pushed up on the window. It stuck for a minute, then opened. She was able to hitch one elbow over the windowsill. She felt the metal on the ledge scrape painfully across the underside of her arm, but she ignored it. She was so close. So close.

She had thought she'd never find her way home. She'd wandered around downtown for a long time with the stolen file still hidden under her shirt, its words burning into her. Not her mother. Elizabeth Freemont wasn't her mother. It was like after the accident. She heard the words and a part of her even registered what they meant, but they couldn't get past her ears and into her brain.

She realized she'd gone around one block twice when she saw the same policeman give her a strange look. She started to turn away when he approached, but she was afraid that might make him suspicious. Instead, she held her ground.

He was big, with lots of muscles and a gun strapped onto his belt. Other than that, he looked nice enough. "Lost, miss?"

"Yes," Bethany answered with a nervous laugh she didn't have to fake. "I'm from Athens. I'm looking for the bus stop for Riverside Drive."

His eyes took in her clothes, and he nodded. "Five Points. Two blocks that way," he said pointing. "All the busses go through Five Points. Just ask any driver."

"Thanks," Bethany said, already walking in the direction he pointed. "I will."

She had intended to keep walking when she got to Five Points, but then she realized she desperately wanted to go home. Home. She almost wept with the need. It took two busses and a long walk, but she finally made it. Then she saw all the cars in the driveway, and her courage evaporated. She had climbed the tree to get out of sight, but then she had looked up and . . .

She heard another crack and felt the branch begin to droop. She managed to throw her other arm over the windowsill and held on for dear life. The branch didn't fall, but it dropped two feet. She hit the house hard, the bricks tearing at her.

Bricks. Toe holds. She got the toe of her sneaker wedged in one of the crevices and pushed up. Again. It took all her strength, but she was finally able to pull herself over the windowsill.

She lay on the floor of the attic for a minute, gasping for breath. Her arms ached. Her knees were scraped. She could feel them burning, and the skin on the underside of both her arms was burning, but she had made it.

She could see little bits of silver dust floating in the afternoon light filtering in through the tree limbs. It looked so . . . normal . . . in a world where nothing was normal anymore. She reached up to brush the sweat out of her eyes, only to realize it wasn't sweat at all, but tears. Her breath hitched, and she folded in on herself and gave way to silent sobs.

It was dark when she woke. As she eased back into consciousness, she had that terrible sense that something was wrong. Something horrible. It was pitch black. For a minute, she couldn't remember where she was. Everything hurt. Her arms. Her knees. Then she remembered, and she curled in on herself, wishing she could disappear. Or die.

After a few minutes, she became more aware of how miserable she was. She was burning up. Sweat slicked her face and filled the bends at the back of her knees. She tried to straighten her limbs and sit up. Terrified that any movement would alert the house to her presence, she slipped off her sneakers and got gingerly to her feet. For just a minute, the room seemed to tilt, and she caught a box to balance herself. She took a step, and her bare foot connected with her shoe. It sounded loud to her ears. She stayed perfectly still for a minute, listening for sounds in the house below, but it was silent. She lowered herself back to her burning knees and felt around for the flashlight she'd hidden back when she was still afraid they'd quit letting her come up here. She had to read the rest of the stuff in the file. She had to *know*.

When her hand touched the flashlight, she blew out a breath of relief. She was afraid to turn on the overhead light, afraid that someone would see it from the outside or under the door. Instead, she switched on the flashlight, shielding it with her body. Then she pulled the file folder out of the front of her jeans and spread the papers across the floor. She focused the flashlight on the first one, the one she'd read in Felicity's office. It was signed Sallie Jo.

She laid it aside and reached for another. Purple splotches covered a good quarter of the page . . . *thank you and Mrs. Free-*

mont for taking my baby to raise.

Bethany blinked and read the words again. They still said the same thing.

There were other things in the folder. A tiny bracelet was stapled to a birth certificate. *Freemont Girl*, it read. Sex, female. Date of Birth, September 17, 1992. Mother, Sallie Jo Mitchell, father, Julian Freemont. Name, Bethany Melissa Freemont. A cancelled check made out to St. Joseph's hospital in Athens, dated March 20, 1992, was attached to a hospital bill. Elizabeth Kimball Freemont. Total abdominal hysterectomy. Bethany knew what that was because one of her friend's mothers had one. It meant she couldn't have a baby. Ever. She had the operation six months before Bethany was born.

Blinking away tears that fell unheeded, she read the next piece of paper.

Dear Dr. Freemont,

Please don't hate me for writing to you. I don't know where else to turn. You've been more than my advisor this last year. You've been a real friend.

I am pregnant, and if my parents find out, they'll kill me. When I told Eddie about the baby, he said I should have done something to prevent it, but I never thought it could happen to me. You've always been so kind to me that I knew I had to ask you what I should do.

Please, please don't call my parents. I went to one of those clinics to get tested, and they said I should tell my parents right away, only they don't know them. I'm the only one in our family to ever go to college, and if I have to drop out now because I did one stupid thing, they'd never forgive me. You know I'm Catholic, so I can't fix it that way. Anyway, one of the other girls did it, and she said she wanted to die afterward. I swear, I want to die now.

I know Mrs. Freemont has been sick. The lady at the library said she just got out of the hospital, so I didn't want to come over to see you unless you wanted me to. I know I have no right to bother you with all this, but I don't know what else to do. Please call me and just maybe talk to me.

Sallie Jo

Bethany felt her hands begin to shake as it all began to sink in. It was a lie. It was all a lie. She wasn't their baby at all. They had lied to her all those years. And that meant—she choked on a sob—that meant that Lilah Kimball wasn't really her grandmother. She'd never want her now.

Lilah lay awake staring at the ceiling. Where could the child be? Felicity Greenlea had called Lilah to see if Bethany was home, and Lilah could tell from caller ID that she was still at her office. She'd asked if Lilah had noticed some kind of file folder on her desk, but Lilah clearly remembered thinking how tidy the desk looked, with nothing but that framed photo of Elliott on the corner. Lilah knew Felicity somehow felt responsible for what had happened, but there was no way it was her fault.

And then there was Marabet. Lilah had never seen the tiny woman so subdued. She could barely form a word, let alone string words together into a sentence. Lilah knew Marabet was probably doing the same thing she was doing right now, lying in bed, staring up at the ceiling.

She heard a sound, a scuffle coming from somewhere above her. Then silence. Lilah sat up in bed, switching on her bedside lamp. Had she really heard a sound, or was it her overactive imagination? She held herself perfectly still. Silence. After a minute, she lay back on her pillow. Wishing wouldn't make Bethany appear or she would have been back long ago. She was just starting to turn over on her side when she heard it again. This time she was sure. There was something moving up there. Of course, that didn't make it Bethany. It could be a tree branch scraping the house. Or a mouse—she refused to consider anything larger. Except maybe a squirrel. Squirrels sometimes got into the attic. She slipped out of bed and pulled on her robe, tying it around her. She was almost to her sitting room door when she realized it could be something much larger. Like a prowler. She hurried into the bathroom, returning with a can of spray deodorant, thinking that might do more harm than hairspray.

She let herself into the hall as soundlessly as possible, and tiptoed up the attic stairs. There was no light coming from under the door. Nor could she hear anything as she stood holding her breath. She could go back to bed and forget it. Or she could go get Marabet. Or she could make a total fool of herself and call the police.

She reached out and slowly turned the knob, swinging the door open while she stayed out in the hall. After a moment, she peeked around the door. Nothing. She flipped on the light and blinked in surprise. Marabet was right. The attic was immaculate. Just some piles of books and boxes stacked head high. No cobwebs. No speck of dust on everything. She was about to turn around and leave when she spied the toe of a single red sneaker sticking out from behind a box. Her breath caught in her throat. "Bethany."

She didn't realize she'd said it aloud until the girl inched out from behind a stack of boxes in the corner. Lilah didn't even realize she was moving toward her until she had the girl clutched in her arms. "Oh, my God. You're all right. Thank God," she said into Bethany's hair. She could feel the girl trembling in her arms. "We were terrified that something had happened to you."

Bethany started to speak, and then stopped, swallowing hard. "I'm sorry."

Lilah held her away. "Where have you been? We've been frantic with worry. How in the world did you get in the house?

Are you all right?" She began running her hands over Bethany's arms and saw her wince. "Oh, God, what's happened to you? Let me see." She turned Bethany's arms over. The scrapes weren't life threatening, but they looked inflamed. She noticed that Bethany's jeans were ripped at the knee. "What happened? How did you hurt yourself?"

Bethany didn't answer, but when her eyes cut over toward the open window, Lilah gasped. "You didn't . . . you . . . *climbed* in the window?" Her voice was nearly a screech. Bethany flinched.

Before Lilah could say another word, Marabet ran into the room. "I heard . . ." When she saw Bethany, she thrust her fist in her mouth as a low moan escaped her. "Oh, my God. You're all right."

Then Marabet was crying and Bethany was crying, and Lilah still couldn't get past the image of Bethany climbing into the attic window. She must have climbed that old oak. She could have been killed. She closed her eyes and swayed.

Marabet was beside her in an instant. "Are you all right?"

Lilah's voice was taut with strain. "I'm fine." She reached over and grabbed Bethany's hand. "Let's get you cleaned up. Marabet, make her a tray and bring it up. The child hasn't eaten since breakfast." She knew she sounded like a drill sergeant, but she couldn't help it.

What if Bethany had fallen? What if someone had grabbed her before she could get back home? Oh God, the things that could have happened. She glanced back as she herded Bethany down the stairs. Marabet was still standing like a statue at the attic door. No matter. Lilah would fix the damned tray herself after she got Bethany settled.

She supervised her bath. Too bad if it embarrassed the girl. She wanted to see with her own eyes that there weren't any more injuries. She spread Neosporin on Bethany's arms and knees and bandaged them loosely. There was nothing she could do about the bruises across the child's abdomen. Bethany said it didn't hurt to breathe, so she hoped time would take care of those. She stood over her like a prison matron until Bethany was propped up in bed with the comforter pulled up to her waist. Then she ordered her to stay put.

As she came out of Bethany's room, Lilah glanced up the attic stairs. The door was still open. No sign of Marabet. Feeling every day of her sixty years, Lilah trudged up the stairs. She ought to leave the damned door open, but if a squirrel did get into the attic, it could get into the house, and how in the world would they get it out again? Marabet could have closed it. It wasn't too much to ask, was it?

Down in the kitchen, Marabet was standing with her back to the door when Lilah came into the room. "I closed the attic door. I think just some soup and toast," Lilah said. "Something easy on her stomach. After the day she's had . . ."

Lilah's voice trailed off as Marabet turned, her expression bleak. In the space of a heartbeat, it turned to fury. She clutched a handful of papers, shaking them at Lilah. "This was in the attic. This was why she ran away. It's all here, Lilah. Your ticket. Your excuse to send the child away. That should make you happy. It's what you wanted, isn't it?" Her face crumbled on the last word, and tears streamed down her face as the papers she'd been holding cascaded to the floor. She brushed past Lilah and hurried to her room, slamming the door behind her.

"Marabet—"

But Marabet was gone. Lilah reached down and picked up the papers. She smoothed out one on the counter. Then the next.

An hour later, she climbed the stairs to the second floor, the folder in her hand. She tapped on Bethany's door. At the child's mumbled, "Come in," she turned the knob and entered. As she crossed the sitting room into the bedroom, she kept her eyes on Bethany's face. First the girl looked confused. Then she saw the folder, and her eyes widened. She looked ready to bolt when Lilah dropped the folder on the bed and said, "At least now I know why you ran away."

Then she did bolt. She leapt out of bed and ran past Lilah. Lilah took off after her, but her legs were no match for Bethany's. Bethany was almost down the stairs when Lilah cried out, "Bethany, *stop!*"

Bethany froze.

"Stop, please. I can't chase you. I would if I could, but I—just—can't."

They were a tableau: Lilah gasping for breath, hanging onto the banister for support, and Bethany, clad in only her nightshirt, staring back up at her, wide-eyed.

Suddenly the air in the house felt too thick to breathe, and for just an instant, Lilah felt her mortality, that fine thread that held her to this existence. Then fear became anger as she realized she could die without ever really having lived. On the heels of the anger came determination. She simply would not allow it, not when the future was finally before her, beckoning.

She lowered herself to a sitting position. Gradually, her breathing returned to normal. She knew the words she was about to speak must come out right if they were going to reach Bethany, and she was afraid she might not be equal to the challenge. Still, she had to try.

"I don't care, Bethany." She shook her head hard. "That's not true. I care because you care, because I know this has hurt you terribly and you've already been hurt enough, but it doesn't matter to *me*. Do you understand that? As far as I'm concerned, you're my granddaughter, the child who was raised by my daughter and her husband. You. Are. My. Granddaughter. Period. And I love you. And I want you to stay." Tears filled her eyes. "Please stay."

    Bethany searched her face for some sign of deception. After a minute, she came slowly up the stairs and sat beside Lilah. For a minute, neither of them moved. Then Bethany flung herself into Lilah's arms. Lilah stroked her hair, making shushing sounds as she rocked her back and forth. She looked over Bethany's head at Marabet, standing at the foot of the stairs. She tried to smile, but it came out more a grimace. It didn't matter. Marabet's smile could have lit up the entire eastern seaboard.

    It was late when they finally got Bethany fed and settled back in bed. Bethany didn't seem ready to talk about this latest development in her roller-coaster life, and Lilah was glad. She wasn't ready either. Too much had happened too fast. She hadn't stopped reeling from one blow before the next one hit her broadside. She told Marabet they could talk tomorrow. She'd had enough of everything tonight. Still, there was one more thing she had to take care of. She dialed the cell phone number on the card Felicity Greenlea had left with her that day so long ago, and it was answered on the first ring.

    "I'm sorry to call so late, Felicity, but I wanted you to know that Bethany is here . . . No, she's fine . . . I thought you needed to know that she found that file folder with the information about her birth mother . . . No. Please don't come over now. I've just gotten her settled . . . No, really, she's fine. We're all fine . . . We can talk tomorrow . . . Yes . . . I'll see you then."

    After she hung up the phone, she couldn't resist one more peek. She walked softly around the U-shaped hallway and let herself into Bethany's darkened room. Moonlight illuminated the bed, spreading a golden glow across the girl. She was fast asleep, with one arm hugging a pillow and the other tossed above her head, looking almost like one of the ballerina prints on her wall. Her dark hair was spread out in sharp contrast to the white pillowcase. She looked so young in sleep, so incredibly young and vulnerable.

Lilah remembered doing this same thing when Elizabeth was young, slipping in just for one more look. She had no second thoughts about wanting Bethany to live with her. Bethany was her granddaughter, just as certainly as if she had been born to—or adopted by—Elizabeth and her husband at birth. The fact that there had been no formal arrangement—or at least no papers indicating one—might pose a legal problem, but that didn't alter Lilah's feelings one whit.

She would deal with the legal problems. Somehow. She had a good attorney and plenty of money to pay him. But what if the child's mother wanted her now? Even more frightening, what if Bethany decided she wanted to live with her birth mother? Was she selfish enough to stand in their way? Her gut clenched, and her jaw tightened. She hoped to God she didn't have to find out.

Chapter 20

"I want Bethany to stay with me." Lilah's voice echoed in the vast living room. She had sent Bethany out shopping with Marabet. This was one conversation neither of them needed to hear. "Her mother had physically abandoned her at birth, or close enough to it. She'd given her away like a stray puppy. Surely she can't have any legal rights."

Felicity looked miserable. "But she does, Mrs. Kimball. Unless something comes to light to indicate that your daughter and her husband actually adopted Bethany, her mother has full legal rights. There's not a judge in the country who would deny her custody. I'm afraid there's not a thing I can do. My legal responsibility is to Bethany and her mother. I have to reunite them if I can. I need to take Bethany—"

"*No!*" Lilah clenched her hands together and tried to inject some semblance of reason into her voice. "Felicity, when you came to me three months ago and asked me to take Bethany, you said it would be best for her to stay with a family member—"

"But you're not—"

"I am, though. I'm the mother of the woman who raised her. Surely that counts for something."

"Not according to the law."

"Then the law is stupid."

Felicity sat back, blinking.

"I'm sorry, Felicity." She shook her head. "No, I'm not. The law is stupid, and you know it."

Of Words & Music

Felicity looked away.

"Felicity, I saw you up in that tree with Bethany. You care. I know you care. Just give me a little time. Let her stay with me while you search for her mother. You know it's the best thing for her, and her well-being is your top priority, right?"

The clock ticked in the corner. Lilah heard the air conditioner click on. Other than that, the room was silent.

"I don't know," Felicity said finally.

"You *do* know." Lilah sat back and tried to compose herself. It wasn't in her nature to ask for anything, especially a favor, but she had to try. "Please, Felicity. Just until you locate the mother. Bethany has a life here. She has her piano lessons. It isn't fair to disrupt her routine unless it absolutely can't be avoided. Please."

Felicity still seemed undecided, but finally she nodded. "All right. I'll need to get that file from you."

Lilah wasn't prepared for that one, but she wasn't about to let those papers go, either, until she'd gotten all the relevant information off them. "Marabet put it away somewhere. She'll be back in an hour or so. I'll bring them to you later today."

She watched the argument form on Felicity's face. If Felicity insisted on waiting until Marabet got back, Lilah would just slip out the back door and race to Kinko's. Felicity glanced at her watch, then at the grandfather clock in the corner as if for confirmation. She stood. "I have an appointment in Roswell at nine-thirty. I could swing back by here and pick them up afterward. Do you think Marabet will be home by eleven?"

Lilah had to fight to keep from grinning like an idiot. "I'm almost certain she will. Why don't you call on your way back." As Felicity turned to the door, Lilah said, "I—have to ask you one question."

Felicity turned back.

"Did you know all along? I mean, did you have the file folder

265

the whole time?"

Felicity's mouth fell open. "No. Oh! No! How could you think—"

Lilah walked over to her and touched her arm. "I'm not blaming you."

"But I didn't. Barbara—you remember Barbara? The neighbor in Athens?" When Lilah nodded, she said, "I'd asked her to search Bethany's house for anything she could find about other relatives. You seemed so sure about not wanting Bethany." Lilah winced. "She just brought it to me. That's when I called you."

Lilah nodded. "I didn't think you had it before, but I had to ask. Like I said, I wouldn't have blamed you if you had."

She walked Felicity to the front door. "I'll see you later."

Felicity started out, but then turned back. "You're sure you don't know where that file is?"

"Marabet will know."

Felicity studied her for a moment. "You're not going to do anything foolish, are you?"

"Of course not," Lilah said with complete honesty. "I never do foolish things."

An hour later, she was sitting in Tom's office. Thank heavens he was here and not in court. She hadn't thought to call ahead. She'd probably have to get one of those cell phones if things kept up this way.

Tom put aside the last piece of paper. "What do you want me to do?"

"I want you to find this woman. Before the social services people do. I have to talk to her, Tom. Felicity said she has to try to reunite them, and I know from personal experience just how persuasive Felicity can be," she added with a rueful smile. The smile faded. "I know that if the woman is determined to have Bethany back and Bethany wants to go live with her, there's nothing I can do about it, but that's a lot of 'ifs.' I'm not ready to throw in the towel yet. I want to meet the woman. See what she's like. I have to do that first before I can look any further than that."

Tom's eyes gleamed. "That's my girl. Fight for what you want." He flipped the file closed. "If you can leave these with me—"

"I can't. I told the social worker that Marabet had put the file somewhere. She's coming to pick it up . . ." She glanced at her watch. ". . . in less than an hour."

"You lied to her?" Tom said, sitting back in his chair, grinning. "Good move. I'm proud of you. Give me five minutes." He punched a button on his desk phone. "I have a rush copy job. Then I want you to get Dick Marist on the phone. We need his services. Now."

Lilah arrived back home fifteen minutes before Felicity showed up. She was counting heavily on the excellence of Tom's detective friend and the slow-grinding wheels of the bureaucracy. As she headed upstairs for a well-deserved rest, Bethany came racing out of her room. "The recital! It's at six, and we don't have our dresses or shoes yet. We have to hurry."

Lilah had forgotten completely about the recital. It was on the tip of her tongue to tell the girl to forget it, but the light in Bethany's eyes stilled the words. "Let me just wash my hands and I'm ready," she said instead. What the hell. She could rest after she was dead.

When they reached Southern Keyboards, Lilah discovered she was the only one who'd forgotten about the recital. When they walked into the music store, she immediately saw Tom standing off to one side. A few feet away, Felicity and Elliott were in earnest conversation. All three descended on them at once. As they turned to enter the recital hall, Lesa came hurrying in the door. "Am I late?" It was all Lilah could do not to laugh.

Minutes later, she sat in the darkened recital hall. Metal folding chairs were lined up in rows facing the stage, a wooden raised platform at the end of the room. A sheer golden curtain hanging across the back of the room glowed under the stage lights. She was in the second row, where Elliott had led them. Tom sat on one side of her, Bethany on the other, with Marabet between Lesa and Felicity.

The social worker hadn't said a word about trying to locate Bethany's birth mother, and Lilah certainly wasn't going to remind her. She felt rather than heard Tom's cell phone vibrate in his pocket. He pulled it out and looked at the display. Excusing himself, he stood and walked over to a corner. Lilah could see him whispering. Then a grim smile formed on his face as he made his way back to the group. Before Lilah could ask him about the call, Elliott bounded onto the stage to introduce the first piece.

Lilah heard none of the music. Instead, her mind swept back over the years since Elizabeth had left home, empty years she had made no effort to fill. She had been lonely, but she didn't know it. She had isolated herself from everyone, even Marabet, by treating her like a servant, by living in the house as if she lived there alone, only agreeing from time to time to share a video or a shopping trip.

She'd tolerated Charles because it was easier than standing up to him, not getting to know Lesa because it would have required effort. No. Exposure. It would have required her opening up to another person, something she hadn't done since Elizabeth left. And she had gone along with Gerome's decision not because she was a dutiful wife, but because she panicked at the thought of Elizabeth leaving. Getting married and moving out. Lilah hadn't been ready. She couldn't bear to lose her so soon, so suddenly, so she had gone along with Gerome, certain that Elizabeth loved her too much to stay away forever.

And she had, Lilah thought, blinking away tears. She had.

But Lilah hadn't known that, so she had spent—no, wasted—her days flipping through magazines that left her untouched, watching television without caring what she saw, doing things designed to kill the time that hung heavy on her hands. Then Bethany had been thrust into her life, all angles and awkwardness and belligerence, and she had shied from the contact. She had wanted nothing to do with her. When had she come to love the girl? She had thought her defenses impenetrable, but, without her even realizing it, Bethany had crept past the barriers she had erected so carefully around herself.

It had begun with the piano, with music. They could talk about music. It was neutral ground. Common ground. She still wasn't sure when it had become more. Was it that night when Charles and Lesa were coming to dinner, when she went to Bethany's room and realized the pain the child was suffering? Or that day in Athens when Lilah had seen her daughter's life frozen in photographs, a life spent with this precious child. Or maybe it was when they had stood beside Elizabeth's grave and Bethany slipped her hand into hers. Whenever it was, it had only grown from there. If she had to give Bethany up now, Lilah didn't know how she could bear it.

She felt Tom take her hand, almost as if he could read her thoughts, and she tried to muster a smile. Then Bethany was nudging her. Lilah rose and walked with her to the stage, her knees shaking. Madness. This was madness.

"Remember to smile," Elliott hissed as they passed him. Lilah wanted to slap him.

Feeling like she was facing a firing squad, Lilah took her seat beside Bethany on the piano bench. Bethany started counting softly the way they'd practiced at home, and suddenly it was time.

She would never remember actually playing the song. She didn't remember any of the notes, but her hands did, hands that shook so badly she would never know how she kept them on the keys. She stumbled over a couple of the hard parts, but Bethany kept them going. Then suddenly it was over.

She didn't remember standing, but she did, and she and Bethany took their bows to even louder applause. Lilah looked over at Bethany, her eyes brimming with tears. "We did it," she mouthed. "We really did it."

As they stepped down from the stage, they found themselves in a flurry of activity, surrounded by people.

Lilah looked around. "Is it over?"

"It's over," Elliott said, smiling down at her. "You and Bethany were last on the program. I saved the best for last." With that, he sprinted away.

"But—Bethany's other songs."

Bethany looked up at her. "I'll play them next time."

"You were great," Tom said, leaning down and kissing Lilah's cheek, then Bethany's.

"I was so proud of you both." From Lesa.

Lilah looked at Bethany and smiled. "We were pretty good, weren't we?" She looked around. "Where's Marabet?"

"She said something about going home and fixing dinner," Lesa said.

Lilah breathed out a long sigh. "I'm glad it's over." She looked around her. "Let's all go home."

Elliott was at the back of the room, shaking hands with parents. As Lilah and the others passed him, he stopped them. He put his arms around Lilah and Bethany, hugging them both. "You two were wonderful. I can't wait until next time."

"Oh, no you don't," Lilah said, laughing. "This was my one

shot. I'll never put myself through that again."

"Well, if you really don't want to," Elliott said, winking at Bethany. "We can talk about it later."

"Come over for dinner, Elliott," Lilah said suddenly. "Bring Felicity. Let's make it a party."

"I will if I can find her in this crush."

As the group moved toward the door, Lesa hung back.

"Lesa?" Lilah said, coming back to her. "Aren't you coming?"

"I—I have to go."

"You mean because of Charles?"

When Lesa nodded, Lilah said, "Lesa, I know you had plenty of justification for leaving. Come home with us. It's ridiculous for you to stay at a hotel. I have a guest room that will be perfect for you. Please." The word was getting easier to say.

Lesa looked miserable. "I can't, Lilah. I'm grateful, but Charles would hate it, and I still hope . . ." She shrugged.

People were pushing past them, trying to get out of the door. "Then at least tell me where you're staying," Lilah said, trying to hold her own against the sea of humanity.

"The Comfort Inn. The one in Marietta."

Back at the house, Lilah didn't have a chance to talk to Tom until everyone was gone. Marabet was in the kitchen washing dishes, and Lilah was grateful. She didn't want to talk to Marabet about this until she had something definitive to tell her.

"We found her," Tom said softly, following Lilah back into the living room. "She's in Valdosta. Married now. Here's her phone number and address," he said, holding out a piece of paper.

Lilah took the paper and studied it as if it would give her insight into the woman herself.

"We'll get a more complete report in a day or so, but I told him I needed this information pronto."

"I'm amazed that he was able to get this much so quickly."

"What are you going to do, call her?"

Lilah bit her lip. "I don't think calling her is the right thing to do. I mean, what would I say?" She stared at the paper for several more minutes before she looked up. "I think I'm going to have to go see her."

"Want me to come along?"

"As my attorney or my friend?" Lilah asked with a smile.

Tom put his arm around her shoulders. "As anything your little heart desires."

Bethany awoke suddenly in a panic. She had been dreaming about that woman—the one they said was her mother. She could only remember bits and pieces, but the awful feeling was still with her.

The house was silent. She looked at the clock. Midnight. She had been asleep for only about an hour. It seemed like longer. She wished she could stop the clock, stop time.

Felicity had said that she would start looking for that person today. Part of her wondered if she had found out anything, and another part didn't want to know. She almost couldn't bear to think about it. Lilah had told Marabet she would fight to keep Bethany with her. That made Bethany feel wanted, but scared at the same time. What if she lost? Then what? What if the woman said she had to come live with her? Did that mean she would just pack her suitcase again and leave and never see Lilah or Marabet or any of the others again? The thought made her chest hurt. Being twelve was awful. Everyone expected you to act grown up, but they treated you like a kid who didn't know anything. Nobody seemed to care where she wanted to be. Felicity said it was the law. Felicity always said it was the law.

She shook her head, tired of her own thoughts. She pulled

the last diary from under her pillow. She felt guilty reading it now that she knew everything, but it didn't matter. Marabet was right. Elizabeth Freemont was her mother and Julian Freemont was her father, no matter what else had happened. They were the only parents she'd ever known.

The diary lay forgotten in her lap. Why hadn't they told her? She was old enough. She had been old enough for a long time. The only reason she could think of was her father's illness. He had been sick for over three years before he died. Bethany was only seven the first time he went to the hospital. Maybe her mother couldn't bring herself to tell Bethany once he got sick. Maybe she was going to tell her later. It was just one more thing she'd never know.

She flipped the diary open. The first entry started in bold, black pen. *I GOT ACCEPTED BY UGA! I can't believe it! College is going to be so neat. I just know it. The only sad thing is that I'll have to leave Mama and Marabet. Marabet says it's high time, that I'll never grow up if I don't cut the apron strings, but what if I don't want to cut the apron strings? Oh, I know I'm weird. I could never tell my friends how I feel about them, especially Mama. They'd laugh at me. They all talk about hating their parents. Well, sometimes I do feel like I hate Daddy, so maybe I can understand it a little bit. I even get mad at Mama sometimes, but I can't even imagine hating her. I hope when I have a daughter, we'll be close like that.*

Bethany swallowed hard. She closed her eyes as she remembered her mama sitting on her bed late one night. Bethany had been sick with the flu or something. Elizabeth was wiping her face with a cool washcloth.

"You're my prize," she had told Bethany. "Ever since you were born, I've felt like I was the luckiest woman in the world, and you're my grand prize." Bethany could almost see her sitting there, washcloth in her hand. She could feel the cool of the cloth against her face, the warmth of her mother's body close beside her. Her mother. She still felt like that, even now. That meant something, didn't it?

Chapter 21

A full day passed before the detective got enough information for Lilah to feel comfortable facing Bethany's birth mother, but the day wasn't wasted. She left Bethany practicing the piano and Marabet trying to sort through the chaos that used to be their dining room.

A quick stop at Charles' office earned her the information that he hadn't been in the office for two days. Rather than worrying Lilah, it gave her hope. Maybe the separation from Lesa had affected him after all.

Lilah pulled into the driveway behind Charles' BMW. She wasn't looking forward to the encounter, but whatever else Charles might be, he was still her child. She had no idea what she could say to him that wouldn't end up in the same kind of fight that all their exchanges deteriorated into these days. She hadn't told anyone about the letter she'd found in Bethany's file, nor would she. Ever. It was in the past. The far distant past. Still, she would make Charles aware that she knew about it before she let go of it. Otherwise, it would always stand between them.

She made her way up the front walk to the door. The grass, the flowerbeds, even the bushes that lined the entranceway, looked tidy. Manicured, she amended.

She knocked on the door. After a minute, it swung open to expose Charles, drink in hand. He was still in his suit, although his tie was undone and his shirt collar open.

"Ah," he said, leaning against the doorjamb, "Mother dearest. Come to soothe my fevered brow?"

Lilah looked at the glass in his hand. "Are you drunk?"

"Not yet," he said with a smile, raising the glass, "but it's early. If you'd like to ask me about—what, nine or ten tonight?"

"May I come in?"

Charles stood without speaking for a minute, his smile fading. "I suppose so," he said, turning away and leaving her to close the front door.

He headed down the hallway without looking to see if she followed and turned into the doorway to his office.

When she entered the room, he was already seated behind his desk. "Have a seat," he said in a parody of graciousness. "What's on your mind?"

The house, too, appeared immaculate from the brief glimpse she'd had as she followed him down the hallway. Then she chided herself. What had she expected, two inches of dust? It had only been a few days since Lesa left.

It seemed longer.

"A number of things. Bethany. You," she said, crossing her legs and folding her hands on her handbag in her lap.

He took a long swallow of scotch. "My least favorite subject." He glanced at her with a smile. "Bethany, I mean. I love talking about me. I assume that means she returned."

"Yes, she's home."

He shot her a quick look at the word "home." "That's nice. Now on to happier thoughts. What about me?"

Lilah had intended to tell him Bethany was staying, but she didn't know that, did she? And she could just imagine what he'd say if her staying didn't come to pass. No, that was one subject that was best left alone for the time being. If Bethany stayed, he'd find out soon enough. She mentally regrouped. "I should have said about you and Elizabeth. I found the letter,

Charles," she said, forcing herself to look at him.

For a moment he looked disconcerted, but he covered it quickly. "What letter?"

"I was going through a photo album of Elizabeth's—"

"How did you get—"

She ignored him. "There was a letter in there from Elizabeth, addressed to me. I never received it."

"I have no idea what you're talking about." His voice was cold.

Lilah went on as if he hadn't spoken. "It had been opened, though, and rather clumsily resealed before you wrote *Return to Sender* across the front and sent it back."

"You must be mistaken. I never saw a letter."

"It was your handwriting. I have innumerable samples of it in the files you returned to me."

Charles looked down into his glass.

"Do you remember what it said, Charles? Elizabeth wanted to come home to visit. Bethany was a baby, and she wanted her to know her grandmother. I believe even Gerome might have agreed to that visit."

"Father was in full agreement with m—" His mouth slammed shut when he realized what he'd said.

Lilah's head fell limply against the back of her chair. "So the two of you were in it together." She felt some of the light go out of the day as the enormity of the betrayal sank in. "I don't know why that surprises me, but it does. Or maybe horrifies me," she said listlessly. "I knew you'd sent the letter back, but I passed that off to some kind of severe sibling jealousy."

"I was not—"

"And it was too late to do anything about it, but somehow it's worse that you and Gerome were in league behind my back." She shook herself. "But that's all in the past. I can't hate you for what you did twelve years ago. You're still my son, Charles."

"So you finally remembered that, did you? The relationship never seemed to impress you in the past. I seem to recall a marked lack of maternal concern when I was younger."

He looked surprised when Lilah nodded. "You're right, but not for the reasons you think."

His lips twisted again into that parody of a smile. "This is going to be good, I'll bet. So tell me, Mother, why didn't you feel this tender concern for me when I was a boy?"

Lilah put her handbag in the chair beside her. She had done a great deal of thinking in the past few weeks about Charles and what had shaped him. She felt she owed him honesty now. It might not help, but neither would sugar coating the truth. "Avoidance and laziness, I think, in about equal measure."

He didn't react.

She leaned forward slightly. "When you were younger, you gravitated naturally toward your father. That wasn't strange. Most young boys do. I allowed it for several reasons. You always seemed uncomfortable when you were with Elizabeth and me."

"I see. The grand justification."

Lilah ignored the interruption. "The things we did bored you. You didn't like the piano. You hated working in the garden. You didn't want to sit and read. You didn't like shopping. Going to lunch with us was a torture for you, and you weren't reticent about sharing how you felt. You seemed happiest when you were with your father. For his part, he saw in you a chance to shape another human being in his own image."

"That's unfair."

"No, it's not," Lilah said quietly, "nor is it unusual. Many parents feel that way about their children, even if they don't admit it to themselves. I probably was somewhat that way with Elizabeth, although now I shudder at the thought. No, that wasn't meant as a criticism of your father. Just as an explanation of what happened. May I go on?"

He nodded curtly. "If you must."

"I think I should. As you got older, you became even more vocal in your disapproval of everything about your sister and me. You were—encouraged—in that by your father. Whenever you went anywhere with us, you told your father anything he might find fault with as soon as we got home. It caused more problems than you might be aware of. I should have tried to correct the behavior at that point, although I'm not sure how effective anything I might have done or said would have been in the face of the carte blanche your father gave you. Still, instead of attempting to change the situation, I avoided it. I quit taking you with us. I quit sharing time and attention and, I fear, eventually myself. It never seemed to bother you. Quite the contrary. You were your father's boy, and you seemed relieved to be free of Elizabeth and me."

Charles put down his glass long enough to clap his hands slowly. "Bravo, Mother. Well done. In the name of soul-bearing, you have succeeded in absolving yourself from any blame for your many years of ignoring me."

"You're wrong, Charles. I readily accept the blame for ignoring you. I more than ignored you. I actively avoided you. I should have taken a stand years ago. About many things," she added sadly. "The point in telling you this isn't to absolve myself of blame, but to explain to you that it wasn't you, Charles the boy, who caused this, but that your behavior was shaped by your father and me."

"My father, you mean," he said, draining his glass. He hesitated a minute, then reached into a desk drawer and pulled out a bottle. He unscrewed the cap and poured two inches into his glass. "Go on," he said, settling back in his chair. "This is fascinating."

Lilah pushed down the anger surging through her. Anger had no place here. "Your father certainly was a large part of it. He had no respect for anyone, so he encouraged disrespect. He disliked all the activities that interested me, so he applauded your ridicule of them."

"He thought you spoiled my sister rotten, and I agreed with him."

"I know you did. What you don't know is that when you were a baby, he thought I spoiled you rotten, too. If you cried and I picked you up, or if you didn't feel well and I insisted on staying home with you when he had made plans for us, he felt I was coddling you. He thought you should be fed at certain predetermined times whether you were hungry or not. He felt I should spank you for wetting your diapers while you were being toilet trained. I ignored him, and I ignored him about Elizabeth. By the time she came along, I'm afraid I had lost a great deal of respect for his opinion."

She took a deep breath before continuing. "I still tried to be a good wife to him, despite what I thought of him by then. Women of my generation were conditioned to do that. In marriage, the onus of making the relationship work was clearly on us. If someone's husband strayed or left her or beat her, the world wondered what she had done to drive him to it."

"That's ridiculous."

"I agree, but it's the way it was."

"No. I mean it's ridiculous for you to say you tried to make the marriage work. He was the one doing all the work, out making a living—"

"While I made his house a home and raised his children and entertained his clients, no matter whether I wanted to or not. Wait," she said, raising her hands when he tried to continue. "This isn't a debate, Charles. I'm telling you about my life and how it affected you and how that is still affecting you today. Your father unfortunately passed on to you some ideas, some behaviors and values that are clearly causing you trouble right now."

He brushed that away. "You said I'm my father's son, and that's true. I'll have you know I'm quite proud of it. I haven't turned on him like some people."

"Not some. Most. And for good reason. Gerome had—good qualities—but nowhere among them were kindness or respect for the individual or compassion. He felt those things were weaknesses."

"They are."

"Well, if they are, then all the greatest thinkers throughout history were weaklings, and I think it more likely that one unsuccessful man was wrong than all of them."

"Unsuccessful! My father made plenty of money! You ought to know. You're spending it right now."

Lilah gritted her teeth. "Success is about a lot more than money. It's about earning the respect of others and—"

"People respected him," he shot out angrily.

"No, they did not. Some people feared him and others thought they might be able to use him, but I don't know of one person who respected him in later life. Surely you know he had no friends. Not a one. He had business acquaintances. Period. And a number of those had turned their backs on him long before he died. He was an unkind, unpleasant man who thought power and money would bring him happiness. When it didn't, he blamed power and money and me and his employees—anyone but himself. In fact, it sounds painfully like what's happening to you right now."

His face flushed. "I figured you'd get that little barb in before you quit."

"It's not a barb, Charles, it's a painful observation, and if you think it gives me pleasure to bring it up—"

"Then don't."

"I have to. Don't you see what's happening? You're methodically driving a wedge between you and everyone else in your life. You're alienating everyone you come in contact with. You drove your wife away—"

"She drove herself away. In a car I purchased for her, I might add."

"Stop it, Charles!" She took a deep breath and let it out slowly. "Stop treating this like some kind of word game. It isn't a game. It's your life."

"Exactly. My life. Not yours, and none of your damned business, I might add."

"It is, because I care about you."

"Oh, *right*." He slammed his drink down on the desk, ignoring the amber liquid that sloshed onto his blotter. "You've certainly given me ample evidence of that, firing me as your accountant, banning me from your home while taking in some stray—"

"By coming to see you and sitting through your verbal abuse while you swill scotch at eleven o'clock in the morning. Ignoring that you went behind my back and abused that power of attorney when you intimated to Social Services that I was incompetent to make my own decisions. By trying to forgive you for preventing me from seeing a letter from my daughter that might have given me a few more precious years with her."

He glared past her at some point on the wall behind her, not speaking. She tried to collect herself. It was useless. His blinders were totally effective. He saw the world and life one way. Anyone who saw it differently was wrong. He did indeed sound like his father's son.

She picked up her purse, resignation coursing through her like a cancer. "I won't take up any more of your time. I just—I hoped you might see—that I could help you see that you're doing a great deal of harm to your life the way you're going right now. I know that you're grown and that your life is your own. I guess I wanted to tell you that I love you. I detest your behavior right now, but I do love you." She walked over to where he sat, holding out a piece of paper. "Lesa is staying at the Comfort Inn in Marietta. She still loves you, Charles. I don't know if the two of you will be able to work things out between you, but I'll do anything I can to help. Either of you."

Charles stared at the paper in her hand. Just when she'd given up hope, he reached and took it from her.

She was almost to the front door when she heard his voice. "Mother."

She stopped and turned. He was standing at the door to his office.

"Yes?"

It was a moment before he spoke. When he did, his voice was barely audible. "I'm sorry. About the letter."

Lilah swallowed hard, unable to speak. It was something, after all. A beginning, maybe.

Chapter 22

Her name was Sallie Jo Hampton now, Tom had told Lilah. She worked at a library in Valdosta, a coincidence Lilah found painfully ironic. They had driven by her address on the way to the library, a tidy two-story frame house in a family neighborhood. The fact that it wasn't a hovel didn't make Lilah feel any better. Tom had offered to go into the library with Lilah, but she knew this was something she had to do alone.

The room was almost empty. Only a few people were browsing the stacks, and only one, a student from the looks of her, was on one of the library's many computers. The woman standing behind the check-out counter was wearing a name tag, but Lilah would have known her without it. This was where Bethany got her dark hair and hazel eyes. That didn't make her feel any better, either.

She walked up to the counter, having no idea what she was going to say.

The woman looked up at her and smiled. Then her expression became quizzical. "May I help you?"

Lilah felt her natural reserve slip into place, and her voice was mild when she spoke. "Sallie Jo, I'm Elizabeth Kimball Freemont's mother. I wondered if I might speak to you."

Sallie Jo's face lost all color. Lilah saw her reach out to steady herself. "I—uh—" She looked around. After a moment, she hurried into a back room. A minute later, she returned. "I asked Candy to take over. She'll—" She waved toward the back room.

Of Words & Music

When Sallie Jo led her out of the library, a light mist was falling. She didn't seem to notice. "Would you mind if we walked?" Sallie Jo asked.

"Of course not."

Sallie Jo led the way to a concrete sidewalk that meandered across the grounds. Lilah took the opportunity to study her. She was a petite woman, pretty despite the few extra pounds she carried. Her voice was soft and cultured, with none of the South Georgia twang you heard so much of once you got outside Atlanta. They walked several moments in silence before she spoke. When she did, it was as if each word was being pulled up from the very depth of her soul. "It's about—about Bethany, isn't it?"

Lilah was surprised. "You know her name?"

Sallie Jo gave a short laugh. "It was on the birth certificate. Dr. Freemont let me name her. It was kind of a gesture—you know?"

Lilah nodded. They walked under trees that dripped more heavily than the sky.

"I got to see her once. Before I left campus. She was so tiny. So beautiful. The Freemonts were very kind to me. I guess I always realized that someday . . ." She left the sentence hanging. "What happened?" she asked, shoving her hands in her pockets.

"I'm afraid they're both—dead." The word stuck in Lilah's throat.

Sallie Jo looked stricken. "Both of them? How?"

"Elizabeth's husband died of leukemia over two years ago. I understand he was ill for quite a long time. Elizabeth was killed in an automobile accident this spring."

"Oh, my God, how *horrible*." Her steps slowed. "Where is she now? Bethany. Is she in a foster home?"

"No. Bethany is staying with me. Social Services didn't realize . . . well, about the arrangement, or even that you existed, until one of their case workers came across a letter you'd written to Dr. Freemont."

Sallie Jo looked at her in surprise. "I wrote him a letter?"

"Yes, telling him that you were pregnant and asking to see him. Then another thanking him for taking Bethany."

"He kept those letters?" she stopped, incredulous.

Lilah nodded, sending a rivulet of rainwater down her forehead. "They were in an envelope with Bethany's name on it, along with the medical records from Elizabeth's hysterectomy. I guess they planned to tell her the truth eventually, but they never had the chance."

Sallie Jo's brow furrowed deeply. "She didn't know she was adopted?"

"Was she? Adopted, I mean?" Lilah asked hopefully.

"Well, not really I guess. I mean, we kind of talked about it, but . . ." She shrugged and started walking again. "They were the nicest people I ever met. Dr. Freemont was my history professor and student advisor, you know?" When Lilah nodded, she said, "It wasn't just me. All the kids felt like he was their favorite uncle, you know? He was always willing to listen. He'd read you the riot act in a heartbeat if he didn't like what you were doing, but he never held it against you later. I never knew anyone else like him."

They walked in silence for a few moments before Sallie Jo cleared her throat and continued. "It was like the birth certificate. Bethany's real father—well, he wasn't too happy to find out I was pregnant."

"Then Julian Freemont isn't Bethany's birth father?"

Sallie Jo looked horrified. "Dr. Freemont? Of course not!"

"His name was on the birth certificate. I just thought maybe . . ."

"Oh, no, Mrs. Kimball. Dr. Freemont? No. It was Ernie, but

when I told him I was pregnant, it was pretty much a 'too bad' thing. It would have killed me to put his name on the birth certificate. He didn't deserve the honor of being her father. You know what I mean?"

Lilah certainly did. "He never tried to see her or to contact you?"

"Are you kidding? From the minute I told him I was pregnant, I didn't exist as far as he was concerned. He didn't deny that she was his. He just avoided me after that. If he saw me on campus, he didn't speak. That kind of thing." Suddenly her eyes widened. "They won't try to contact him, will they? I can't bear the thought of that. He doesn't deserve to know her."

"I'm certain they won't. How could they? His name is nowhere to be found. Dr. Freemont's name is on the birth certificate. As far as the world and all posterity are concerned, he was the father."

"Thank God for that." She looked at Lilah. "I guess you think it's pretty strange that I gave her up but I feel he shouldn't be allowed to know her, but you see, I didn't want to give her up."

Lilah felt the words like a blow.

"I mean, if he'd said, let's get married and make a home for our baby, I swear, I would have. I'm glad I didn't. I don't mean it like that," she amended quickly. "I mean, then I wouldn't have met John and married him, and I wouldn't have Julie and Tom." She shook her head. "Well, anyway, we did talk a little bit about adoption. I mean, it only seemed right, since they were going to raise her, that they be her legal parents, but we never did anything about it. Mrs. Freemont was still having a time getting around. It was something about a miscarriage, I think, and something happened to her inside. Maybe cancer or something. I don't know."

Tom's detective friend had been very through. "Uterine

cancer," Lilah agreed. "They found it when they did the D and C after the miscarriage."

"That poor lady. She loved kids more than anything." Sallie Jo pulled her hand out of her pocket and brushed back her hair. She seemed surprised to find it wet. "She worked at the library at school and every once in a while they'd have those story days. You know, when the kids came in and someone would read them a story? It was always Mrs. Freemont. She was so good at it. I remember one day I was there studying when that story hour, or whatever it was called, started. I got so engrossed in the story; I forgot it was for kids. I mean, she was that good."

She kicked a pinecone off the sidewalk. "I guess that's why I thought she'd be good for Bethany. Her and Dr. Freemont. They were just the best. Was she—do you know if Bethany was happy with them?"

"Yes, I do know. Bethany adored both of them."

She nodded. "I kept expecting them to contact me, you know, about the adoption. Then after a few years, I just kind of forgot about it."

Depression settled on Lilah like one of the dark clouds above their heads.

Sallie Jo squared her shoulders. "I guess I need to get busy making some arrangements."

Lilah felt a scream well up in her. *Nooooooooooo* . . . She swallowed it down, but the emotion that had risen up with it refused to be ignored. Her whole body was trembling with it. She felt as if her knees would give out if she had to take another step. "Can we—can we sit down?" she asked, motioning toward a bench. Her voice shook as much as her knees.

Sallie Jo walked over to the bench and looked down. "But it's wet." Then she looked at Lilah's dripping hair, raising a hand up to her own, and she laughed.

Lilah wanted to shake her. How could she laugh at a time like this?

She clenched her teeth to keep them from chattering, although it was August and far from cold. She knew what she *should* do. She should make every effort to see that this woman got her child back. But she couldn't. She simply could not. This woman was a stranger to Bethany.

Lilah remembered when the child had first come to them, all adolescent bristles and defensiveness, living in a world all but destroyed by the death of everyone she loved. Then in her mind's eye she saw her standing on the stage in the recital hall, beaming up at Lilah.

She felt her reserve shatter like so much brittle glass, her carefully constructed wall crashing down around her. The hell with what was right. For once in her life, she was going to fight for what she wanted. "Sallie Jo," she said in a voice that shook with emotion, "I didn't make myself very clear about Bethany. Or about Elizabeth. Elizabeth and I had a serious falling out when Elizabeth got married. It was a stupid quarrel, but because of it, we didn't see one another again before she died. I'll never forgive myself for that, but then Felicity—she's the social worker—Felicity came to me and asked me to take Bethany. I had never met the child, and I almost said no, that I wouldn't take her. Stupid. *Stupid!*" She bit her lip, unable to continue.

The rain fell harder. The trees they were sitting under gave them some shelter, but water was still running down Lilah's face. Then she realized they were tears. The leafy canopy above them seemed to wrap around them, isolating them from the rest of the world. Maybe that was why Lilah was able to talk to this woman the way she was. Or maybe she just plain cared that much.

"Then Bethany came to live with me, and over the months, we—grew on each other. We came to love each other. I don't know if I can bear to lose her now." She choked on a sob, and it was a moment before she could continue. "I know you're Bethany's mother. You have the right to insist that she live with you, but I have to ask—no, I *beg* you to consider that she's happy. More than happy. She loves it there. She's finally gotten settled. She has her own room. She takes piano lessons. We take them together. Bethany *is* my granddaughter, as far as I'm concerned." Lilah shook her head, knowing she wasn't making much sense. She brushed the tears off her cheeks. "What I'm trying to say is that if you really want Bethany to come live with you, well—I don't know if that would be the right thing for her. She's so happy where she is, and she's been through so much. She deserves a break, a chance—" She caught her breath. "Please, *please* let her stay with me."

Sallie Jo stared at her hands. She seemed fascinated with the way the rain ran off her skin. Then she suddenly doubled forward, her shoulders shaking.

Lilah felt a weight descend on her. It was all hopeless. The woman was heartbroken. She was going to take her child away, and as much as Lilah wanted to stop her, she had no legal rights here at all. She got slowly to her feet. "I'm sorry I—"

Sallie Jo shook her head, waving a hand to stop her. After a couple of minutes, she straightened up, wiping her face. "No. No, please don't apologize. It's—it's—" She looked up at Lilah, her face a study in misery. "I have two other children now. They're just—just wonderful. And a husband I love. And none of them—none of them knows anything about Bethany. I think—I think my husband would leave me if I told him the truth now. My kids would hate me. They'd never trust me again. I—I just never said anything about it, you know? But I couldn't turn my back on her if she needed me, could I? I abandoned her once. I couldn't do it again. If I thought she was unhappy where she was—well, but she's happy, you said. She's really happy, so it would be like I'm doing the right thing by leaving her there. It's not like I'm deserting her again," she sputtered, covering her face.

Lilah sank back down on the bench, feeling joy well up in her. At the same time, she ached for Sallie Jo. She suddenly didn't seem like a thirty-something-year-old married mother of two, but like the nineteen-year-old college girl who had found herself pregnant and hadn't known what to do. Her pain was just as fresh as it had been thirteen years ago.

Taking a moment to compose her words, Lilah glanced up at the sky. The rolling black clouds that had seemed so hostile during the long, silent ride to Valdosta now seemed subdued, gray and sad, but her heart was filled with sunshine. Bethany didn't have to leave.

"I truly think this is the best thing for Bethany," she said softly. "Bethany is happy where she is. She'll get love and attention, and not just from me. My hous—my best friend loves her as much as I do. She spoils her rotten. Oh, not really spoils her. I just mean she loves her totally. Bethany will never lack for anything. I promise you that. I think you'll be doing the right thing by letting her stay with us. It's where she needs to be."

Sallie Jo wiped her face. She averted her eyes self-consciously. "You must think I'm the silliest woman you ever met," she said.

"No, I don't. I think you've been living with guilt and pain for a long time," Lilah said honestly. "You did the best thing you could by placing Bethany with Elizabeth and her husband, the right thing for all of you. You went on to have two more children, but you gave Elizabeth the only child she would ever have. You brought happiness into all your lives." *And mine,* she added silently.

Sallie Jo stared at the ground.

"Bethany truly is where she needs to be. If you could see Marabet with her—"

"Marabet?"

Lilah smiled. "My friend. She worships Bethany."

Sallie Jo looked away. "What—what does she look like? Bethany, I mean."

Chapter 23

Marabet was outside before Tom had Lilah's car door open. "Where in the world have you been? I've been worried sick. I thought you'd be back hours ago, and look at you. You look like a bedraggled rat. You'd better get changed before you catch your death. What were you thinking?"

"Bethany can stay."

Marabet fell back a step. "What?"

"I just came from talking to Bethany's mother. She can stay."

Marabet's shriek could have been heard in Chattanooga. She threw her arms around Lilah's neck and squeezed until Lilah started to gasp. "When? Where? Are you sure? You get inside and get changed. You have to tell me what happened. How did you find her? What did she say?"

Lilah looked back at Tom as Marabet dragged her into the house. With a little wave and a smile, he mouthed, "Call you later." Then he climbed back in his car, and a moment later he was gone.

Lilah waited until the house was quiet before crossing the hall to Bethany's room. She knocked softly on the door. If Bethany were sleeping, she would wait until tomorrow to talk to her.

When there was no answer, she started back toward her room. Then she heard the sound of the piano being played softly, and she turned and headed downstairs.

At the living room door, she stopped. Bethany was seated at

the piano. She was in her nightshirt, but it was obvious she hadn't been to bed. Lilah looked at her straight, trim little body, her beautiful, silken brown hair, the serious yet blissful expression on her face. Her large, almond-shaped eyes were closed now, but Lilah had seen all their moods. She had seen them sparkle with both mischief and anger, and shine with love and cry heartbroken tears. How could she ever have thought the girl was plain? She was lovely, as lovely in her own way as Elizabeth had been. It was a different beauty, quieter and more understated, but beauty none the less. And there was so much beauty on the inside. She was playing something soft and soothing that Lilah didn't recognize.

"Can't sleep?" Lilah asked when the last notes died away.

Bethany turned. "This song just kept going through my mind. I thought I might as well come downstairs and play it. Was I too loud?"

"No, you were just right. Can I talk to you for a minute?"

"Sure," she said, making room on the piano bench. "Is something wrong?"

Lilah sat beside her. "No. Nothing is wrong. I just wanted to talk to you for a few minutes. About Sallie Jo."

Bethany looked alarmed. "What about her?"

"It's nothing bad," she said quickly. "I went to talk to her today."

"Oh yeah?"

Lilah smiled at the defensiveness in her voice. "Yeah," she said. "She seems to be a very nice woman. She explained how you came to live with your—your parents." She stumbled over the word. "But you already know all about that. She also told me that she never told her husband about giving birth to you. She knew you would be happy with the Freemonts, and she didn't think he'd ever have to find out."

"Couldn't he tell?" She looked suddenly flustered. "I mean, I thought a man could tell."

Lilah finally realized what she was saying. Oh, Lord. She had forgotten all about that aspect of child rearing. How much to tell her? How much did she already know? She proceeded cautiously. "He could tell that she had been with a man before," she said carefully, "but not that she'd had a baby."

"Oh." Then, "Her husband's not my real father, is he?"

"No. Definitely not. Your birth father was a student she dated. When he found out she was pregnant, he knew he wasn't ready to be a father. No, her husband is someone she met long after she left Athens, but the thing is, she's afraid he'll hate her if she tells him the truth."

"Why would he hate her?"

"Because she deceived him."

"Did she lie to him?"

"I don't know if she lied, really, but omission—not telling him the whole truth—would probably seem just as bad to him. At least, she believes it would."

Bethany was silent for a long moment. When she looked up at Lilah, her face was troubled. "Is she ashamed of me?"

Lilah took her time answering. No pap for this child, no platitudes. "No. She isn't ashamed of you. She asked a lot of questions about you." She reached out and brushed Bethany's hair back from her face. "I think she's ashamed of herself, ashamed that she didn't tell her husband about you before they were married. Now she doesn't know how to make it better without risking her marriage."

Bethany seemed to turn that over in her mind. "Why do you think she didn't tell him?"

She turned so that she was facing Bethany and took her hands. "I don't know for sure, but I imagine she was sure you'd live with the Freemonts until you were grown. She had made a decision, one she felt was best for you. She probably thought it would just complicate matters all around if she popped up some day, or if someone else who learned the truth showed up out of the blue. I guess it seemed to her that it might be better for all of you if she stayed away forever and said nothing."

"And now she has to live with it. It must be awful to live with a lie every day."

"It must be, but I hope neither of us ever has a reason to find out."

"Is that why she let me stay here? Because he would hate her?"

"Oh, no, darling," Lilah said, stroking her hair. "She had already decided that you were more important. She was going to tell him, but when she realized that you were happy here, she decided it was better for everyone if you stayed." Lilah was almost sure what her answer would be, but she had to ask the question. "Did she do right? Do you want to stay here?"

Bethany's eyes widened. *"Yes."*

Lilah drew a deep breath. "We'll have to take some steps to make it legal, but Tom thinks it would be best if I adopt you legally. Then this situation could never happen again. What do you think?" she asked when Bethany said nothing.

"Would she let you?"

"You mean Sallie Jo? Yes, she agreed. She even signed a paper." One Tom had conveniently drawn up for her in advance.

"Can you adopt a granddaughter?"

Lilah smiled. "No. I'd have to adopt you as a daughter."

Bethany frowned. "What would I call you?"

"You could call me anything you want," she said, ruffling her hair. "Within reason, that is."

"So then we'd be legally related? Forever?"

"Forever."

A broad smile transformed the girl's face. "I think that is so way cool! I—" She stopped and stared at Lilah. "Would I be

Bethany Kimball or Bethany Freemont?"

"That's up to you, sweetheart. I'm sure we could work it out either way."

Bethany tilted her head. "Bethany Freemont. Bethany Kimball. Bethany Freemont Kimball." She looked at Lilah. "I like that one. How about you?"

"I like that one too," Marabet said, walking into the room.

Lilah looked over her shoulder, exasperated. "Don't you ever sleep?"

Marabet grinned. "I sleep when you sleep, which isn't a whole lot lately." She turned to Bethany, pulling a wrapped package out from behind her back. "Well, young lady, I was going to wait until your birthday to give you this, but now seems like the perfect time."

"What is it?" she asked, taking the package Marabet offered her.

"Open it."

Bethany fumbled with the wrapping paper, finally pulling out a small leather-bound book. She flipped it open. "It's blank inside."

"It's a diary," Marabet said, "or a journal, they called it in that fancy gift shop where I got it. I thought since you'd read so much of your mother's history and since you're starting a whole new life, you might want to start recording your very own history. Maybe some day you'll have a daughter to read them."

Bethany sat for several moments caressing the leather cover. Then she jumped off the piano bench. "Thank you, Marabet!" she said, throwing her arms around her. "I love it!"

She came back to Lilah and hugged her, kissing her on the cheek. "Good night, Grandma. I think I'll go upstairs now."

Lilah watched her go, hugging her diary to her chest in a way that was now so familiar. After a minute, she stood, stretching her back. "We're going to have our hands full with that one," she said.

"Nothing we can't handle," Marabet said happily.

Lilah put her arm around Marabet's shoulder. "Any of those cookies left?"

"And some ice cream."

"Got any good movies?" she asked as they started down the hallway toward Marabet's room.

"We could watch *Casablanca*."

Lilah groaned. "Not that again. I vote for *Sleepless in Seattle*."

"Over *Casablanca*? Are you crazy? We could invite Tom over. He'd vote for *Casablanca*."

"Next time, Marabet." Lilah smiled. "Maybe next time."

Their voices faded as they disappeared into the kitchen. Then the house was still except for the ticking of the grandfather clock in the corner and the echo of music that hung like a golden mist in the air.

ABOUT THE AUTHOR

Lynda Fitzgerald was inspired to write *Of Words & Music* when she witnessed first-hand the power music has to bridge barriers caused by age and background and, sometimes, resentment. "Music is a language all its own, a language infinitely more powerful than words. It cuts through the nuances of meaning assigned to everyday words and speaks directly to our hearts. It is a language like no other."

Lynda has lived in Georgia for the last thirty years, and that's where she's set this latest story. She studied creative writing at Emory University and Georgia Perimeter College. Her previous works include *If Truth Be Told* (June 2007), also published by Five Star. Check out her website at www.fitzgeraldwrites.com, where you can get a taste of her previous and upcoming works.